Way Down
on the
High Lonely

Also by Don Winslow

A Cool Breeze on the Underground
The Trail to Buddha's Mirror

Way Down
on the
High Lonely

Don Winslow

St. Martin's Press New York

The publisher gratefully acknowledges permission to quote from "North Dakota" (Lyle Lovett and Willis Alan Ramsey) Copyright © 1992 Wishbone Music and Lyle Lovett/Michael Goldsen (Wishbone Music Worldwide Administration Don Williams Music Group, Inc.) All rights reserved.

Design by Basha Zapatka

Library of Congress Cataloging-in-Publication Data

Winslow, Don
    Way down on the high lonely / Don Winslow.
        p. cm.
    "A Neal Carey mystery."
    "A Thomas Dunne book."
    ISBN 0-312-09934-7
    1. Missing children—United States—Fiction. I. Title.
PS3573.I5326W38   1993
813'.54—dc20   93-24381
                                    CIP

First Edition: November 1993

10 9 8 7 6 5 4 3 2 1

To my parents

So I drank myself some whiskey,
  And I dreamed I was a cowboy,
    Then I rode across the border . . .
      —LYLE LOVETT

They ain't makin' Jews like Jesus anymore.
  —KINKY FRIEDMAN

Prologue

*H*e never should have turned around.

Neal Carey was looking out over a deep canyon when he heard footsteps coming up the knoll behind him. He tried to focus on the sheer rock cliff that rose on the other side of the canyon, but the two pairs of footsteps crunching on the gravel path would not go away. They were getting closer.

He put his attention back on that most delicate and demanding movement, Obliquely Tame Tiger, and watched his left arm slowly move outward and upward, hand open in the knife position. He had been trying to master Obliquely Tame Tiger for almost three years now, and the constant training was just beginning to overcome his natural clumsiness.

Neal Carey did not want to be disturbed.

He shifted his weight to his back foot and let the canvas slipper dig into the thin dirt. He breathed in the icy morning air and felt the slight warmth of the early morning sun hit his shoulders. Then he slowly raised his front leg, pivoted on his back foot, and started the slow turn to face the footsteps that were now reaching the top of the knoll. *His* knoll, damn it, his one private spot tacitly reserved for him every morning during his few free moments before dawn. Did three years of practice mean nothing to these intruders?

He swung his foot over the gnarled root of the scraggly cedar that clung to the knoll in this harsh altitude among these spare mountains. The cedar had become his closest friend over the years. They had each learned to survive in the thin air and soil, getting little sustenance and needing less.

He planted his front foot and shifted his weight forward, his left hand raised in front of his face, his right hand open behind his head, ready to whip out and strike like a viper.

He looked down the stone steps to see the two men reach the top of the knoll and begin to approach him across the stone pavilion.

Then the world that he finally had come to accept shattered in a single moment.

The young monk spoke first. He gestured to the short, one-armed man who stood beside him, staring at Neal as he struggled to catch his breath.

"Ni renshr ta ma?" "Do you know him?" the monk asked Neal.

"Wode fuchin," "My father," Neal answered.

That's where Neal Carey made his big mistake. He should have denied knowing the man, or just turned around, or run away into the dense bamboo. If he had done any one of these things, he never would have found himself way down on The High Lonely.

Part One
Cowboys

1

*T*his is some weird kind of place," Joe Graham said.

He and Neal were sitting in a small pavilion at the edge of the knoll. The tiled roofs of the monastery below glinted in the sunshine. Monkeys perched on the curved eaves, waiting to leap down onto the courtyard to pounce on any morsel of unguarded food. Brown-robed monks crossed the courtyard with one protective hand held over the tops of their bowls, steam from the hot rice gruel rising through their fingers.

"Tell me about it," Neal answered. He'd been a prisoner in the weird kind of place for three years, long enough for the strange to have become the familiar. He filled Graham's cup with green tea, made a small bow out of habit, then filled his own.

"You have any coffee?" Graham asked.

Neal shook his head. If three years' confinement in a Buddhist monastery had done nothing else for him, it had cured his caffeine addiction.

"How about milk and sugar?" asked Graham.

"Sorry."

"A clean cup?"

"It *is* clean."

Right, Graham thought. He'd seen the rats scurrying around the dining hall down the hill.

"I've missed you, son," Graham said.

"I've missed *you,* Dad."

Neal had never met his real father, a guy who apparently hadn't figured on getting a kid for his twenty buck investment, so Joe Graham had pretty much taken over the role. Neal had thought about him every day of his imprisonment. No, not imprisonment . . . "internment" is what the Chinese had called it. An internment that was finally over. Or was it?

"Did you come to bring me back?" he asked Graham.

"No, I'm picking up my laundry." Little asshole, Graham thought. I've only been tracking you down for three years, ever since they told me you were dead.

"Let me tell you, kid," Graham said. "It cost the Bank one hell of a lot of money to spring you. Next time get yourself popped in Rhode Island. A pizza with extra cheese and you're out of there." Graham tasted his tea and grimaced. "What, they mow the lawn and then dump the grass into a pot of water?"

"How much money?" Neal asked.

"I don't want you to get a swelled head. But we're talking about a low-interest, unsecured loan for 'agricultural development in Sichuan Province.' "

"A bribe," Neal said.

"Big time bribe."

"Thanks."

"You're a 'friend of the family.' "

Friends of the Family, Neal thought. The Bank's shadow department that handled difficult problems for its larger investors. His erstwhile employer. Or was it?

"Do I still work for Friends?" Neal asked.

"Did you ever?"

Since I was twelve years old, Dad. Since you caught me picking your pocket and put my dubious skills to work for you. And now you've come to take me home.

"Besides," Graham said, "we got an errand for you."

"What?"

Graham looked at him quizzically. "Three years' vacation isn't enough for you?"

"Vacation! You call hauling wooden buckets of water up this

frigging mountain a vacation? Lugging bundles of firewood on my back? Listening to a bunch of religious fanatics chant the same god-damn note for three years—that's a vacation?''

"To each his own." Graham shrugged.

"I want to go back to New York, Graham. I want to sit in the Burger Joint, with the ink from my *New York Times* smudging the bun of a rare Swissburger as the juices run down my wrist. I want an iced coffee sweating there right beside me . . . where I can just reach out and grab it. I want to walk down the west side of Broadway and then amble back up the east side. I want—''

"I, I, I," Graham titched.

"Graham!"

"Don't get all worked up," Graham said. "I'm just talking about a little job I need your help with. We'll stop off in Los Angeles, do this thing, and you'll be back in New York slobbering your food before you know it. I worry about you, though, you know? Locked up all this time and you think about cheeseburgers.''

"What kind of job? What 'thing'?'' Neal asked. The last job had landed him in this place.

Graham peered into his teacup. "I don't suppose they have egg creams, huh?''

Neal shook his head.

"A missing kid," Graham said. "Daddy picked him up on Friday for their one weekend a month visitation. Didn't bring him back on Sunday night. No big deal.''

"What's wrong with the sheriff's department?''

"Nothing's wrong with the sheriff's department," Graham answered, "except that they don't pay much attention to custody cases, even when the mother is famous.''

"What's she famous for?'' Neal asked. Famous was bad, famous was trouble.

"Something to do with movies. What, you need a resume? Are you working for us, or what? Because the Chinese can't cash the check until you're safely back in the States, so we can still tell them that you'd rather stay here. I just need you for backup. I can get anybody.''

Actually, I can't just get anybody, Graham thought. I need you. But we got to take this one step at a time, ease you back in while I can keep an eye on you. See if you can still do the job or whether you're a burnout case. Three years of what amounts to solitary confinement can do strange things to even the best. And Neal Carey was the best . . . had been, anyway.

"Look," Graham continued as Neal sulked, "we'll pick up little Cody, drop him back on Mommy's lap, and go right back to New York. You'll have the whole summer to jerk off before you start classes.''

"What classes?''

"Weren't you in graduass school when we last saw you? Trying to con them into giving you your masturbator's degree? Which should be a lock, if you ask me.''

Columbia University . . . English department. His would-be master's thesis, "Tobias Smollett: The Outsider in Eighteenth-Century English Literature.'' It seemed like a different life. Come to think of it . . .

"Wait a minute," Neal said, "I'm supposed to be dead.''

Graham nodded. "It's an appealing fantasy, I agree. So you were dead, now you're alive. A glitch in the computer. Nothing a little WD-40 and a contribution to the library can't take care of.''

We have to get him back in school, Graham thought. If Neal's finished as a detective he's going to need a trade. Seeing as he can't do anything useful, he might as well be a college professor, which is what he wants to be anyway.

Neal poured himself another cup of the excellent green tea. He knew it had been provided only because he had a foreign guest, so he might as well take advantage of it. He listened to the sound of the morning chants rising up from the main temple, the numbing monotony that was supposed to focus the chanter on nothingness—and did.

"So," Neal began carefully, "all I have to do is help you pick up this kid, and then I can go back to New York and back to grad school?''

It sounded too good to be true—a life again.

Graham asked, ''You think you got that now, or would you like me to repeat it again? Make up your mind; I want a cold beer and a hot steak.''

Neal laughed. ''It's a long hike down the mountain, Graham.''

Graham stared at him for a long moment. ''What, you never heard of a helicopter? Honestly . . .''

Neal lifted his cup to his lips, thought it over, and then poured the tea on the ground.

''Do they serve coffee on this helicopter?'' he asked.

''For the money we're paying, they'd better.''

Neal stood up. ''Let's go.''

''About goddamn time,'' Graham said as he got to his feet.

Then Neal Carey did a very un-Chinese thing. He reached out, grabbed Joe Graham by the back of the neck, and pulled him close.

''Thanks for coming to get me, Dad,'' Neal said.

''You're welcome, son.''

So Neal Carey came back from the dead.

2

Neal woke up between the cool, crisp sheets of a king-size bed. He opened his eyes and looked through the sliding glass door where the sun sat like a fat orange in the haze of a southern California morning. The air conditioner was humming happily, a cheerful reminder of the comfort that came with wealth: it may be getting hot outside the hotel, but in here it's any temperature you want it to be.

A similarly welcoming voice lilted from the corridor, "Room service."

Neal wasn't quite sure that this was all real, but if it was a dream, he was willing to go along with it.

"Come in!" he called back.

A young waiter in a starched white uniform rolled in a stainless steel cart, flipped up a folding panel, opened the side doors, removed a white linen tablecloth, and laid it over the panel to form a little dining table. He placed a narrow vase with a single yellow rose on top, then the silverware wrapped in a linen napkin, then the silver coffee service, then a little silver container with slivers of butter in a small bowl of ice.

"I'm Richard," he said. "Are you enjoying the Beverly, sir?"

"So far," Neal answered, although he could barely remember even arriving at the Beverly. He sat up against the cushioned headboard.

"Do you want me to serve you now, sir?" Richard asked. "Or would you like to shower first?"

A shower? The closest thing Neal had come to a shower lately was a freezing waterfall.

"Shower, I think."

"But may I pour you some coffee first?" Richard asked.

You bet, Richard, if it means that much to you. "Please," Neal said.

Richard took out a heavy, cream-colored cup and saucer and carefully poured the coffee.

"Cream and sugar?" he asked.

"Neither."

"All right," Richard announced, "you have the Beverly Breakfast—coffee, grapefruit juice, scrambled eggs with bacon, and the basket with a selection of wheat toast, muffins, croissants, and Danish. I'll keep it in here over the heater, so be very careful when you take it out, okay?"

"Okay."

Richard placed two folded newspapers on the foot of the bed. *"LA Times, New York Times . . ."*

God bless you, Richard.

". . . and if there's anything else, you will please call and let me know. Now, sir, if you wouldn't mind just signing here . . ."

Richard approached his bedside and handed him the check and a pen. Neal signed, added a tip to the already substantial service charge, and handed it back.

"May I ask you a question, Richard?"

"Of course, sir."

"Where am I?"

Richard didn't even blink. He was used to serving breakfasts on many mornings after the night before.

"The Beverly Hilton, sir."

"Keep going."

"Beverly Hills . . . Los Angeles . . ."

"Yeah?"

"California."

"I just want to hear the words, Richard."

"The United States . . ."

"Of . . ."

"America, sir."

"Beautiful, Richard."

"Far out, sir."

Far out, indeed, Neal thought as he took his first sip of coffee. Black coffee, strong coffee. His caffeine addiction came back like an annoying old friend.

Richard left and Neal took his coffee into the bathroom, which was larger than his cell back in China. He looked at the telephone on the wall, within easy reach of the toilet, and decided that the people who stayed in this place must be busy people. He turned the shower on and reveled in the smell of clean, hot water. He opened the little cardboard box of designer soap, took the little bottle of designer shampoo, and stepped into the shower.

He scoured himself with the soap, scrubbed his hair with the shampoo, and then stood under the steaming jet for a good five minutes longer than necessary. In China he had been treated to a weekly bath in a shallow tub full of lukewarm water that had been used by at least three other men before him, so this shower was a treat.

He stepped out reluctantly, lured by the scent of coffee, the image of scrambled eggs and bacon, and the thought of a newspaper. He found a white terrycloth robe in the closet, slipped it on, and went back into the main room to investigate breakfast.

Joe Graham was munching on his toast.

"How did you get in?" Neal asked.

"I could get used to this," Graham mumbled. "A very clean place. I got an extra key from the front desk. Can I warm that up for you?"

Neal held his cup out and Graham filled it.

"You don't mind if I eat, do you?" Neal asked.

"Careful with the plates, they're hot. And you have a fine selection of croissants, Danish, and muffins."

Neal took the hot plate out of the tray's warmer, set it on the table, and lifted the cover. The smell alone brought him close to tears, but then again, he'd breakfasted on rice gruel for the past few years, except on holidays, when he'd been allowed to add peanuts to the gruel.

"Is your bacon nice and crisp?" Graham asked. "Mine was."

Neal slipped a slice of bacon into his mouth. It crunched between his teeth. "I've dreamed about this," he said.

"You're a sick puppy."

Neal selected a plain croissant, spread a sliver of unsalted butter on it, took a mouthful, and then dug into the rest of his breakfast. He didn't even look up until all that was left on the plate was a shiny residue of grease.

Joe Graham watched in awe.

"You eat like you're condemned," he said.

"Let me see those Danish."

Neal picked out an apricot pastry and devoured it in three bites.

"Now for the newspapers," he said. "I don't even know who's president."

"Ronald Reagan."

"No, seriously . . ."

Neal tore into the papers while Graham wandered out onto the terrace and checked out the early morning swimmers in the pool below.

"Exercise is a wonderful thing," he observed as the two young lady swimmers stretched limbs and torsos.

The doorbell rang.

"It's for you!" Neal yelled, absorbed in *The New York Times*. He was on serious sensory overload.

Graham tore himself away from the view and answered the door. Richard was standing in the hallway beside a luggage cart.

"It's your clothes!" Graham shouted to Neal.

"I don't have any clothes," Neal answered as he tried to figure out the changes in the Yankees' roster from the box score.

"You do now," Graham said. "Bring them in, kid."

Richard rolled in the cart and started to hang up the clothes bags and put the boxes of shirts, underwear, socks, and shoes into a bureau.

"I don't need any clothes," Neal said. "I'm going to stay in this robe, in this room, for the next couple of months, eating and reading newspapers."

"You got about an hour," Graham said. "We have an eleven o'clock meeting."

"Let's meet on the terrace. I'll bring the iced tea."

"I don't think so," Graham answered. "We're going to Hollywood."

"They're remaking Rumpelstiltskin and you got the part?"

"We're going to meet Mommy."

Neal looked up long enough to grab a blueberry muffin.

"What happened to Thurman Munson?" he asked, pointing at the Yankees' batting order.

"Will you hurry up and get dressed?" Graham said. "The limo will be here in less than an hour."

"The limo?"

"Short for limousine," Graham explained.

"We *are* going to Hollywood, aren't we?"

Neal felt a little stiff in his new clothes—khaki slacks, blue shirt, olive jacket, and cordovan loafers. He also felt a little stiff sitting in the backseat of the stretch limo, Joe Graham beside him and a fully stocked bar, a television, and the back of the uniformed driver in the front seat.

Neal found a club soda, filled a glass with ice, and sipped at it as he watched the scenery on Sunset Boulevard. "I'm into consumption these days," he explained.

"I can see that."

"You look good, Dad," Neal said.

Graham glared at him.

Graham did look good, though, Neal thought, although somewhat awkward in a blue blazer, white shirt, gray slacks, and those black leather shoes with the little pinholes in them. A big change from his usual plaid jacket, chartreuse trousers, and striped tie.

"Levine made me go shopping with him at Barneys," Graham explained grumpily.

"I like the look," Neal said.

"You also like English poets," Graham accused.

"True."

The limo pulled onto a side street and up to the gate of a film studio. Neal looked at the crazy quilt combination of nineteenth-century building facades, Quonset huts, and enormous movie bill-boards on the other side of the gate.

"I've seen movies about this," he said.

The security guard at the gate approached the driver's window.

"They have a meeting at Wishbone with Anne Kelley," the driver said with no discernible effort at courtesy.

The guard gave him a placard for the windshield and opened the gate.

"Building Twenty-eight," he said.

"No kidding," the driver snapped, then steered the limo through the narrow streets of the studio, edging past a group of young men dressed as 1920s gangsters and a small platoon of harried production assistants carrying clipboards. He eased the big car into a slot marked GUESTS-LIMO across from a big Quonset hut and opened the back door.

"Wishbone Studios, right through that door."

"Oh boy," Neal said.

The driver rewarded him with a wry smile. He had delivered any number of cocky screenwriters to this door and picked them up half an hour later when they weren't so cocky, when that Oscar-winning screenplay in the briefcase had turned to just another pile of paper. If they didn't hit the limo bar on the way in, they'd sure enough hit it on the way out.

Neal saw the big HOLLYWOOD sign on a hill behind the studio. It seemed less real than it did on television or in the movies, but maybe that was the idea. He followed Joe Graham into Building 28.

He'd expected the polished, plush setting of the stereotypical Hollywood mogul, but he didn't get it. Wishbone Studios was stripped for speed. A utilitarian metal desk defined the edge of a small reception area. Posters of Wishbone's latest films decorated the walls, which were colored in cheap blue industrial paint. The yellow carpet was worn with frenzied foot traffic. A small couch, a couple of chairs, and a coffee table littered with trade papers were set across from the desk to form a waiting area. On the other side of the reception room an open door revealed a small kitchen, where a Braun coffee maker struggled to meet the energy needs of the chronically undercaffeinated.

Graham went up to the desk.

"Joseph Graham and Neal Carey to see Anne Kelley."

The receptionist looked like she belonged in a suntan oil commercial but was remarkably cheerful about sitting behind her desk. She checked her log book.

"Right, you're her eleven. I'll let her know you're here."

She got on the phone. Never releasing the dazzling smile she had fixed on Graham, she said, "Jim, Anne's eleven is here."

"Please have a seat. Someone will be here in just a moment," she said to Graham. Graham sat down across from Neal, who already had plopped himself down on the sofa and was looking over a copy of *Film Weekly.*

"Joseph?"

"Shut up."

"Yes, Joseph."

A tall, thin young man came hustling down the corridor into the reception room. Open white shirt, jeans, immaculate tennis shoes. California blond hair, big smile.

"I'm Jim Collier, Anne's assistant."

He offered his hand to Graham, blinking for only a second at the sight of his artificial arm.

"I'm Joe Graham, this is Neal Carey."

"Neal, hi, welcome. Come on down the hall. Anne is ready for you."

Terrific, Neal thought. But am I ready for her?

They walked down to the end of the narrow hallway and into a room labeled simply KELLEY.

Anne Kelley sat behind a big desk that was stacked high with scripts and books. The office floor was likewise covered with piles of papers, books, magazines, and film reels. The ubiquitous coffee table was covered with papers, as were the chairs and the sofa. Ashtrays seemed to be everywhere, and they were all overflowing. Neal wasn't at all sure that a good search of this room would not turn up the missing Cody McCall.

Anne Kelley was on the phone, and she didn't look happy. Her long face was drawn further down in a frown. Her short hair was not quite blond, not quite silver, not quite brown, not quite combed or brushed. She wore a silk shirt under a denim jacket. A cigarette in the corner of her mouth puffed like a smokestack from a factory.

"I don't care," she was saying into the phone. "I don't care. . . . So let her. . . . Fine. We'll get somebody else."

She hung up the phone, took a drag on the cigarette, and then snuffed it out.

"Could you be a real lifesaver and get me a Diet Pepsi?" she said to Collier. "You guys want anything?"

An oxygen tank, thought Neal.

A vacuum cleaner, thought Graham.

They shook their heads.

Jim Collier sprang up to get the soda. Anne came around from the desk and shook hands with Neal and Graham.

"I'm Anne Kelley, head of Creative."

Nice work if you can get it, thought Neal.

Anne dropped into a chair across the coffee table from them. "You don't mind if we don't start until the Diet Pepsi comes, do you?"

Lady, I don't mind if we don't start at all, Neal thought.

"Take your time," Graham said.

Jim came back with the soda, opened it, handed it to Anne, and took a chair in the corner. He flipped open a pad and had his pencil poised, ready to take notes.

In case Anne said something creative? Neal wondered.

Anne took a long gulp out of the can, sighed with relief, then turned her attention to Neal and Graham.

"So pitch," she said.

Graham looked at Neal and shrugged.

"So give me the ball," Neal said to Anne.

Jim coughed rhetorically. "Anne, these are the detectives."

Anne Kelley blushed. "Oh, shit. Shit! I'm sorry! I'm so sorry! I thought you were writers, pitching a project!"

Something the cat dragged in.

"I'm Anne Kelley," she repeated. "Cody's mother."

"And head of Creative," Neal said.

"You're the guys that Ethan Kitteredge sent," she continued. "You're going to find Cody."

"We're going to try," Graham said.

"Ethan said that you're very, very good."

"Probably just very good," Neal said as Graham gave him a dirty look, "but maybe not very, very good."

"I'm really sorry," Anne said. "I didn't mean to mistake you for writers."

"That's all right," Graham said charitably.

"So where do we start?" Anne asked.

Jim started to write.

"Hold on, Boswell," Neal said. "No notes."

"Jim memorializes all my meetings."

Memorializes? Neal thought. "That's nice," he said, "but notes have a funny way of showing up in funny places, like newspapers."

Anne stiffened. "I trust Jim implicitly."

Neal looked over at Jim. "No offense. I'm sure you'd never deliberately betray the queen here—"

"Neal, shut up," Graham said.

"—but unless you have a shredder, or unless you take your notes on single pages on a hard surface, it's better not to take them. I can't tell you how many cases I've made—unfortunately—going through someone's trash, or sneaking into someone's office to look at the impressions left on a notepad or a desk blotter—''

''Neal . . .'' Graham warned.

''Well, you taught me all this stuff, Graham,'' Neal answered. He turned back to Jim. ''Besides, *you* don't need notes. *I* need the notes, and I keep them in my head. You want anything 'memorialized,' give me a call and I'll recite it to you, okay?''

Jim closed the notepad.

So much for burnout, thought Graham.

''You're being rather hostile,'' Anne Kelley said to Neal.

''Right, which is what your ex-husband will think about me when I find him. Now, do you want to throw a little tea party, or do you want your kid back?''

''I want my kid back.''

Neal sat back in the sofa.

''So pitch,'' he said.

Harley McCall was a cowboy. They met on a film shoot in Nevada. He was working as a wrangler—a horse handler—on the movie she was producing, one of the last of a brief resurgence of westerns.

He was tall, lanky, and bowlegged and spoke with a slow drawl that she found charming, especially contrasted with the affected inflections of the Hollywood men she'd been seeing. His dirty blond hair had natural streaks in it, his mustache was bronze, and his tan stopped at the level of his rolled-up sleeves, a tan he got from working outdoors, not frying himself in oil on a Malibu beach or poolside at the Beverly.

He ate chicken-fried steaks, eggs and bacon, and wicked hot burritos, and never—ever—queried the waiter about where the sun-dried tomatoes were grown. He liked his beer cold and his women warm, and he touched a warm spot in her all right, a warmth as soft and fine as a summer afternoon.

They'd walked out on the desert one night, away from the horrid little motel that was their location headquarters, away from the director, and the actors, the crew, and the business types, out onto the open desert under the stars and she'd seduced him there . . . or maybe he'd seduced her into seducing him . . . but she wanted him—badly—so she took him.

The sex was fantastic—that was never their problem—and she felt that he'd changed her life, turned her into the natural woman they all seem to sing about. He brought desert flowers to her trailer, took her out on long rides, called her ''ma'am'' everywhere except in bed, and one afternoon they'd jumped into his pickup and rode to Vegas, went to one of those tacky chapels, and actually got married.

She got pregnant right away, maybe that very night. They wrapped the shoot, and she headed back to LA with a film in the can, a baby in her belly, and a brand-new husband in tow. Queen Anne, happy at last.

They would have named the baby Shane, after their favorite movie, but that seemed a bit much, so they settled for something almost as good. Cody was a golden child, with his dad's rugged good looks and his mother's soft beauty, and they were both crazy in love with him.

The movie came out a little later and was a hit, and they bought the place in Malibu.

But somehow the film came to be known as the *last* great western, a nostalgic farewell to a classic genre, and in that weird Hollywood way, everyone was saying it because that's what everyone was saying. Pretty soon the only horses in the movies were the ones pulling carriages through Central Park, and Harley McCall found himself with a lot of time on his hands.

There just wasn't a lot for a cowboy to do in Malibu.

For a while they thought he could be a big help at Wishbone, a fresh eye, an honest voice, that sort of thing. But he picked the dumbest projects—unfilmable books, remakes of old flops, stories that were pitched by writers he went out for beers with . . . it didn't work out.

And she discovered, to her immense sorrow, that West Hollywood was a lot different from the West, and all the qualities that she'd found so fresh and exciting out on the desert became old and grating at the lawn parties, studio meetings, and premieres. And if

"Harley doesn't say a lot" was something she had originally said with a measure of pride, she found herself saying it as an apology more and more, especially as Harley's reticence changed from quiet confidence to sullen despair.

There just wasn't a lot for a cowboy to do in Malibu.

But what there was, he found. He started drinking his cold beers for breakfast. He found that a joint or two made the afternoon pass in a pleasant torpor, and that high-stake poker games gave him his balls back, win or lose. Mostly it was lose.

And he found the women. None of her friends, thank God, or her competitors, but the would-be starlets and country-western singers who found him witty and handsome and who were content with afternoons.

She heard about them, of course—Los Angeles is a *small* big town—and she felt surprised and a little ashamed that she was relieved. She didn't find him witty, his handsomeness didn't travel well, as they say, and she was too busy in the afternoons to try to think of things for him to do.

He was good with the baby, though, always that. Always sweet with his little cowboy. Worried about him growing up "in this atmosphere," as he always called it, to her annoyance. Worried about his values. Talked about how they should get a little ranch somewhere, go there summers, teach the boy to ride and rope, let him breathe some fresh air for a change. All while Harley was drinking more and smoking more dope.

He got disgusted with himself, finally. Woke up one morning, put the cork in the bottle, gave his stash away to a local surf bum, told the dollies adios, and asked her to leave with him. Sell this play toy house on the beach, get that ranch, do some honest work, and live a real life.

She told him that her life was quite real, thank you very much, but if he felt that's what he had to do, he had better go do it. The marriage was pretty much over by that point anyway.

What wasn't over—what's never over—was the fact that Harley McCall had a child, a son, whom he loved more than he loved anything. More than the open prairie, more than the blue sky, more than his freedom. And so the greatest joy of his life was also its tragedy—he was shackled to the hated LA by a chain of love, by the every-other-weekend and one-month-in-the-summer visitation the judge had awarded him, like it was some kind of game show, which it kind of was.

Ironically, now that they weren't married anymore, Anne could reach down the status ladder and find him some work. She got him a gig as a stunt cowboy for one of the studio's tours. So, twenty-five times a week, real-life cowboy Harley McCall put on a black hat and vest, stood behind the railings of a saloon facade, fired his blank six-shooter at the sheriff, got shot, and tumbled down onto the grain sacks of a wagon conveniently parked below. All to the delight of the tourists watching from a grandstand.

It was boring, humiliating, low-paying work, but it paid the rent on a little bungalow in Venice and put gas in the pickup for the every-other-weekend drive to Malibu to pick up his son.

He tried to stick it out, he really did, but then one day he got shot by the sheriff, grabbed his chest with one hand, teetered at the edge of the balcony, and lifted the middle finger of his right hand in a pointed gesture at the sheriff. He managed to hold it there about halfway down to the grain sacks, but the tourists in the grandstands were not impressed, and he got fired.

It was one cruddy job after another after that, each shorter lived than the last. His cowboy sweetness turned as stale and bitter as the gas fumes that hung over the Sunset Strip. He started getting edgy and then mean. He quit more jobs than he was fired from, each time taking away another resentment along with his last day's pay. He took offense at almost anything, adding more and more items to the lengthening list of things he "just wouldn't take from any man."

It was a wonder Harley could even stand up straight, he was carrying so many grudges. Film producers, film critics, studio executives, executives in general, landlords, bankers, bill collectors, cops, grocery store owners, bar owners, women, Jews, blacks, Mexicans, Koreans, whores, kikes, niggers, spics, and gooks—they had all combined to make his life hell and keep him from raising his son the way a man should raise his son.

He went back to the bottle, and it treated him the way a wife treats a philandering husband—it took him back in and punished him on a daily basis. He started to become a character on Venice Boulevard, a sidewalk cowboy with a three-day stubble on his face and an incoherent diatribe spurting out of his mouth. He got himself tattooed one bad night, got one of those nifty "Don't Tread on Me" numbers with the flag and the snake on his left forearm.

But Anne Kelley trod on him hard when he showed up drunk one Friday night. She told him that there was no way eighteen-month-old Cody was getting into that truck. Harley tried to kick the door down and then succeeded in smashing a window before the cops got there. They whaled the shit out of him, he got thirty days for disturbing the police, and Anne got a court order preventing him from taking Cody for the month that summer.

Harley disappeared. Anne didn't know where he went or what happened to him, but about six months later she got a call from him. He sounded calm and composed. Gentle, like his old self. He asked if he could come over and talk to her. She met him at the office and it was like meeting a chastened version of the man she'd first met. He was clean, neat, and almost painfully sober. He apologized for having been such a jackass, explained that he'd cleaned himself up, got himself a job maintaining center pivot irrigation systems in East Orange County, and asked if he could see little Cody.

She invited him over to the house. She had to admit that she cried when she saw Cody wrap himself around Harley's neck. Harley was as gentle and sweet with that boy as he'd ever been, and she retreated into the kitchen while father and son got to know each other again.

The visits were just at the house for a while, always with Anne within earshot. Harley stayed for supper a few times and once or twice spent the whole evening watching videos of old westerns with them. *The Searchers, Shane* . . . it was after *The Magnificent Seven* that she agreed to let him resume the weekend visits.

The first one was in May. Harley picked Cody up at seven on

Friday night and said they were just going to spend the weekend at his place down in Venice. That was three months ago, and she hadn't seen her son since.

"During these three months," Neal asked, "what have you done?"

"Harley was supposed to have brought Cody back that Sunday night around seven. About eight o'clock, I guess, I started calling his place. No answer. Around ten I went over there and leaned on the doorbell. Nobody home, no lights on, no TV, no stereo. I called the police, who told me that I needed to go to the sheriff's department. I went to the sheriff's department and they told me that they'd check his last known address, which they did, and he wasn't there. They'd put a warrant out for him but couldn't give custodial cases much priority, because it wasn't a 'real kidnapping.' I got my lawyer out of bed at around two in the morning and he told me he'd start filing papers. As far as I know, he's still filing them.

"But we can't find Harley to serve him the papers. We've gone through social service agencies, private investigators, a couple of dozen police and sheriff's departments. Then my lawyer said he'd found a new detective agency that specialized in custody cases. They were a lot better at finding creative expenses than they were at finding my son. Finally I called Ethan. I heard that he didn't feel—how shall I say this—constrained by the narrowest limits of the law."

"How do you know Mr. Kitteredge?" Neal asked.

"His bank put up money for a couple of my films," she answered.

Natch, thought Neal.

"I'd heard rumors that he offered certain services for his best customers," Anne continued. "You live by rumors in this town, so I checked it out. He told me I'd be hearing from somebody. It couldn't have been twenty minutes when your Mr. Levine called. I'm sure you know the rest."

Neal was about to tell her not to be so sure when Graham interjected, "Your attorney should keep up his efforts, though, Ms. Kelley."

"At his hourly, I'm sure he will," Anne answered. "What happens now?"

"We start looking for your son and you take your eleven-thirty," Neal answered as he got out of his chair.

"I love my little boy, Mr. Carey."

"I'm sure you do, Ms. Kelley."

"I'm not a bad mother."

"Nobody said you were."

"You were thinking it."

Neal stepped over to the window and looked out at the studio lot, where the 1920s gangsters were heading to the cafeteria to beat the early lunch crowd.

"No," he said, "I was thinking that you're used to getting the story rewritten when you don't like it the way it is. But this time it's not a movie, it's your son, and it's not a story, it's all too real. I'm thinking what a bitch these custody cases are, because while the law is on your side, it's really on the sidelines. What it basically says is that once you get your child back, you can keep him. And while you're handcuffed by the law, your husband does any goddamn thing he wants. And I was thinking about how frustrated, angry, and scared you must be."

Anne drained the rest of her soda and lit another cigarette. It was a nice try, but it didn't stop the tears from coming to her eyes. "I'm terrified," she said. "I know Harley would never intentionally hurt Cody, but now . . . with what you've found out about these people . . ."

What people, Graham?

". . . I'm afraid that I'll never see my little boy again."

"We'll get him back," Neal said. He was surprised to hear himself say it, surprised at the commitment in his voice.

"We'll call you the minute we know anything," Graham said as he stepped to the door.

"I'll leave word that you're to be put right through," Anne answered.

Jim Collier hustled to shake their hands.

"A real pleasure to meet you," he said.

"Yeah," Neal said.

"I do know the difference between movies and real life," Anne said to Neal.

"Yeah? Well, maybe you can teach it to me sometime."

On the way out they passed Anne's eleven-thirty, two nervous screenwriters clutching a couple of notebooks and a pile of dreams.

"So what have we found out about 'these people,' Graham? And what people are we talking about?" Neal asked when they got back in the limo. It was as much an accusation as a question.

"Well, we found out what accounted for Harley's cleaning up his act."

"What?"

Graham told the driver to go to the corner of Hollywood and Vine.

"What's at Hollywood and Vine?" the driver asked sullenly.

"What's it to you?" answered Graham.

Neal perused the bar, found a little bottle of Johnny Walker Red, and poured it into a glass as the limo eased out of the lot onto the street.

"What's going on, Graham?" he asked.

Neal tossed back the whiskey. It was like sitting by a fire on a winter's day. He noticed that Joe Graham was rubbing his artificial hand into the palm of his real one. It was something he did when he was nervous, when he had something on his mind that he wanted to get off. Neal finished his drink and waited.

"So," Graham asked, "are you on?"

Neal didn't want to be on. God, he didn't want to be on. He wanted to be off in the world of old books, sitting in a quiet room taking orderly notes. But if this was just a simple custody case, they wouldn't need him. Graham would track Harley down, call in muscle if he needed it, and take the kid home. So there was something else.

"What aren't you telling me, Dad?"

Graham shook his head. "No. You first. Are you on?"

You owe, Neal told himself. And not just money. You were a lost kid yourself once, and the only person in the world who gave a good goddamn was Joe Graham, who's sitting here now, wearing out his one good hand.

"Yeah, I'm on."

The rubbing stopped. Graham palmed one of the little whiskey bottles and opened it with his thumb and forefinger. He took a sip straight from the bottle.

"I didn't want to tell you too much until I saw you in action again. I had to make sure you were . . ."

" 'Okay'?"

"Three years is a long time, son."

"So did I pass?"

"Yeah."

"So tell me the whole story."

"Not now."

"When?"

"After church."

The driver looked back in the mirror and sneered. "What the hell kind of church is at Hollywood and Vine?"

A placard board read THE TRUE CHRISTIAN IDENTITY CHURCH, REVEREND C. WESLEY CARTER, MINISTER. Its big white plastic cross loomed above a sidewalk festooned with broken wine bottles, free-floating newspaper pages, crumpled cans, and greasy sandwich wrappers. Pimps in all their sartorial splendor leaned on their Caddies and Lincoln Town Cars watching their little girls in white leather hot pants munch on doughnuts as they vamped passing cars. Pretty teenage boys dressed in tight denims and T-shirts sat on bus benches and peeked out from under their long bangs in a more subtle form of advertising, visible only to the informed.

If you took the view that a church was supposed to be a hospital for sinners, the corner of Hollywood and Vine was a great location for a church.

* * *

The church was immaculate, not in the immaculate conception sense, but in a utilitarian, Protestant way. The highly varnished wood shone with righteous energy, the modest carpeting was vacuumed to within an inch of its life. Pamphlets had been laid out in precise order on a table in the foyer.

The congregation was even cleaner. They were mostly older people, as you would expect of a Wednesday afternoon, but there was also a significant minority of younger men. They had the deeply tanned, lined features of outdoor workers. Their jeans were pressed and they wore collared shirts with unfashionable ties. There were a few young mothers there as well, some with toddlers in tow. The kids were all neat, clean, nicely dressed, and well behaved.

From the back of the church Neal felt as if he were looking through one of those old stereoscopes, because in back of the gaggles of kids, behind the altar, was a mural of Jesus himself talking to a bunch of clean, neat, well-dressed, well-behaved little kids, and the inscription, SUFFER THE LITTLE CHILDREN TO COME UNTO ME.

The contrast between the scrubbed interior of the church and the variegated hell on the outside was, to say the least, stark. Neal had the image of one of those old western movies where the settlers had circled the wagons against the band of marauding Indians outside. The place was just so . . . white.

Everyone was white. The older folks, the working men, the young mothers, the kids. Jesus was certainly white, with blue eyes and long brown hair that was a day at the beach away from being blond. The kids who had come unto him were white, looking as if they'd be more at home in Sweden than Judea. Neal hadn't seen so many blonds since the last time he'd gotten drunk enough to watch the Miss America Pageant.

"There's a marked lack of melanin in here," he whispered to Graham as they slid into a pew in the back.

"Whatever that is," Graham answered.

Neal was about to answer when a tall, silver-haired man in a blue suit came out from behind the altar and mounted the pulpit. The silver hair stood up in a high brush cut, his tanned face looked like it had been fashioned with an adz, and his eyes were bluer than his suit, if not quite as shiny.

The congregation scurried into their seats and sat in silent anticipation.

"C. Wesley Carter," Graham whispered.

"See Spot run," answered Neal.

"Good afternoon, everyone," C. Wesley Carter said. He had a voice like a good trumpet, clear and sharp without being brassy or harsh. It was a good voice, and he knew it.

"Good afternoon, Reverend Carter!" the congregation answered.

"Welcome to our Wednesday afternoon study session, I'm glad you all fought your way safely to our little clearing in the jungle."

Jungle? Neal thought. Well . . .

"I'm very excited today," Carter said, "because we are back to the beginning of the whole cycle in our lectures on true Christian identity, and new beginnings always fire me up. Of course, when you've given this lecture as many times as I have . . . well, let's face it, when you've heard this lecture as many times as some of you have . . . well, I won't be offended if some of you just want to get up and leave!"

"I want to get up and leave," Neal whispered.

"Shut up," answered Graham.

Reverend Carter paused for the audience to fill in the laugh. A few of the veteran listeners did, and one old man even yelled, "No way, Reverend!"

Carter continued, "But I think that there are certain things we can never hear often enough, don't you? I guess that's one reason they wrote the Bible down, so we can read those sacred words as often as we need to. And in these troubled times—and if you don't think they're troubled, you just take a look outside that door—we need to hear them a whole lot. We need to remind ourselves who we are. We need to reaffirm our true Christian identity! Our true Christian identity as the chosen people!"

The congregation burst into applause. Graham politely smacked his real hand into his artificial one.

"Now, who are the chosen people?" Carter asked, presumably rhetorically. "Well, the Bible tells us, so let's start right there. In fact, let's begin at the beginning in the Book of Genesis."

Carter opened an enormous old Bible on the pulpit.

"He's not going to read the whole thing, is he?" Neal asked Graham.

"Shut the hell up," hissed Graham.

"Nice talk, in church."

A bunch of people in the church flipped Bibles open to the Book of Genesis.

"It's right in the beginning," Neal whispered helpfully to Graham.

"Now, the Jews have always claimed to be the chosen people, but the Bible tells us differently, doesn't it?" Carter asked in a voice that attempted a professorial tone of neutral inquiry. "You'll notice in Genesis that Cain was jealous of his brother Abel, whom God favored. Now that is pretty interesting. Why would God favor Abel? The answer is simple. Because Cain was not the son of Adam, but the son of Satan! Cain was the offspring of Eve's mating with the serpent. And so of course God favored Abel."

Neal elbowed Graham. "So does Mia Farrow get to play Eve in the movie?"

"Now, we all know that Cain slew Abel," Carter preached, "the first example of a Jew killing a Gentile, and this is the important part: God cursed Cain. I refer to Genesis 4:11, 'And now art thou cursed from the earth,' and in 4:12, 'a fugitive and a vagabond shalt thou be in the earth.' "

"Sounds like you," Graham muttered to Neal. "What did you do to piss off God?"

"I know you."

"And now Adam had himself another son!" Carter proclaimed. "The son's name was Seth, and Seth—follow along now through all the begats in chapter five—was the ancestor of Noah, who, as you know, was the chosen of God. The Jews, you see, are the sons of Cain. Far from being the chosen people, they were the cursed people. Cursed by God himself!"

"Nothing like personal service," Neal whispered.

Joe Graham just shook his head.

"Now," Carter said, "you have to work your way through a bunch of 'begats' until Abraham begat Isaac and Isaac married Rebecca, and they prayed to God to have children and God answered—this is Genesis 25:23—'And the Lord said unto her, Two nations are in thy womb, and two manner of people shall be separated from thy bowels, and the one people shall be stronger than the other people, and the elder shall serve the latter.' Amen!"

"Amen!" responded the congregation.

"And now here we go again, friends, because Rebecca had twins. The first one to emerge was Esau, and listen here to the description: Esau 'came out red, all over like an hairy garment.' Now what does that tell you? Esau was the spiritual descendent of Cain, son of the devil, cursed by God! And it is Esau, friends, who will be the father of one of these two nations, the weaker nation.

"Now, the younger twin was Jacob, and we will come to read that Esau sold his birthright to Jacob, and that Isaac blessed Jacob, and that Esau was jealous. It's the same old story all over again, and sure enough, Esau plotted to kill Jacob. And Esau is described as 'cunning'—and we sure know that, don't we—but Jacob got away.

"And that night he laid his head down on a pillow made of stones, and he had a dream, and he dreamed that he ascended a ladder to heaven, and spoke with the Lord, and that the Lord said, 'I am with you, and I will never leave you.' Amen. And that spot where Jacob had this dream? It was called Bethel, and keep that in mind.

"Now, Jacob wandered as a fugitive for years, but he knew that God was with him, and Jacob became a cowboy, friends, the first cowboy, and his herds multiplied and became strong, and Jacob eventually returned to the place of his birth a rich and powerful man, and Esau came out, all alligator tears and everything, and hugged him and kissed him—now, we all know what the kiss of a Jew means, don't we—and Jacob took his wives, and children, and cattle and moved on, he went back to Bethel and saw God again . . . and I'm going to read this part word for word, because it's at the heart of everything we're about here . . . Genesis 35:10, 'And God said unto him, Thy name is Jacob; thy name shall not be called any more Jacob, but Israel shall be thy name: and he called his name Israel.'

"Jacob was the real Israel, friends. Not that phony baloney Israel that Washington gives our tax dollars to.

"But to continue, 'And God said unto him, I am God almighty: be fruitful and multiply; a nation and a company of nations shall be of thee, and kings shall come out of thy loins; and the land which I gave Abraham and Isaac, to thee will I give it, and to thy seed after thee will I give the land.''

Carter closed the Bible and paused dramatically.

"You see, folks, Jacob, descendent of Seth, was the father of the chosen people, chosen by God to form 'a nation and a company of nations.' Now, what is that nation? The present-day, so-called Israel? Don't you believe it. That's what they'd all like us to believe, that's the hogwash we've been asked to swallow, but it just isn't true. Can't be! Why not? Because, among other things, where is the company of nations to go along with it? All I see is that impostor Jew state and a bunch of strung-together Arab sheikdoms. The sons of Esau, the sons of Ham, not the sons of Jacob, the sons of Seth! That's not what God had in mind, no sir, not at all."

Neal leaned over to Graham and asked, "Do you think he's going to tell us what God had in mind?"

"I think so."

He did. The Reverend C. Wesley Carter, founder and pastor of the True Christian Identity Church, laid out the grand design for them. How the true descendants of Seth and Jacob migrated out of the Near East, how they took their wives, kids, and cattle and journeyed north and west, eventually coming to settle in Germany, England, Scandinavia, and the British Isles. They were the lost tribe of Israel, who finally found the promised land—America.

"But the Jew, the jealous Jew, the sons of scheming Satan, the sons of murderous Cain, the sons of cunning Esau, they crept into Eden again. We have a Jew banking system and a Jew press, a Jew government and a Jew-dicial system! We have sold our birthright to

Esau! And we will have to buy it back with tears and sacrifice and blood!

"But that's another sermon. Let us conclude with a prayer."

"Amen," Neal said.

Back out in the limo Neal said, "So Harley got religion."

"If you want to call it that. I just wanted you to see what we're dealing with here," Graham said.

"Less than a full deck, that's for sure."

"Funny kid."

The driver actually turned around in his seat and looked at Graham. The driver was pissed off at having had to sit for an hour and change in the crotch of the city.

"You ready to go back to the hotel now?" he asked.

"Why not?"

Neal sat back in the upholstered seat and looked out through the tinted window.

"Okay," he said. "Are you going to tell me the whole story now?"

"Not yet."

"When?"

"When we get back to the hotel."

So Neal looked out the smoky window and watched the palm trees through the haze of sunshine and smog and wondered what was waiting for him back at the hotel.

Ed Levine looked like a brown bear at the zoo as he climbed out of the swimming pool and shook off the water. He grabbed a towel off his chaise longue, wiped himself off, and stepped to the edge of the pool area to greet Neal Carey.

"I never thought I'd hear myself saying this," Ed said as he stuck out his hand, "but it's good to see you."

"Good to see you," Neal said, realizing with some surprise that he actually meant it. Ed Levine had been his boss, his rival, his nemesis for about a dozen years.

They stood awkwardly staring at each other for a few moments—
Ed in bikini swimming trunks, water dripping into a pool at his feet,
Neal trying to keep his new shoes from getting wet.

"So how have you been?" Neal asked.

"Divorced."

"Sorry."

"Don't be. I'm not," Levine said. "So how was China? Did you
have a good time?"

"Terrific."

Joe Graham asked, "Is this touching moment over? Can we get to
work?"

"Is he on?" Levine asked Graham.

"He's on," Neal answered.

"Let's grab a table. I've had lunch sent out."

They sat down at a round, white enamel table with a crank-up
umbrella. Levine put on a Hawaiian print shirt that was oversize even
on him. Neal draped his jacket over the back of his chair, put his
sunglasses on, and watched the beautiful people sunbathing around
the pool.

"You look good," he said to Levine. "You've lost some weight."

"I've been working out. Running, weights, squash . . . the whole
bit. I'm in the best shape since I was in the service."

"That's good."

"How about you, Neal, are you in shape?"

Neal thought about the endless trips up the steep mountain slopes,
carrying buckets of water and loads of firewood.

"I'm in shape."

"No, I mean, are you *in shape?* Operational shape?"

"Yeah, I think so."

Ed looked over at Graham. Graham nodded.

"I don't know," Ed muttered.

A waiter came over. Graham ordered a beer, Ed got an iced tea,
Neal an iced coffee. They sat quietly with their own thoughts until
the drinks came.

"We wanted you to meet Anne Kelley, hear her story, before you committed to the job."

"We?"

"Graham and I . . . and The Man."

"What's going on here, Ed?"

The waiter came back, and with a big tray of food.

"I hope no one minds, I ordered for us."

The waiter set down a pastrami on rye for Graham, a rare cheeseburger and fries for Neal, and a salad for Levine.

"A salad?" Neal asked.

"So?"

"Nothing."

Ed pointed to Neal's plate. "It isn't the Burger Joint," he said, referring to the little joint that was Neal's hangout in New York.

"But what is?" asked Neal.

"Right. But if you'd rather have some rice or something . . ."

Neal shook his head. He was too busy eating to speak. It *wasn't* the Burger Joint, but it was still pretty wonderful—food you actually had to grip in your hands.

Levine dug into his salad with an almost grim determination to enjoy it. He downed it in about ten seconds flat, wiped his mouth, and tried to convince himself he was full.

"So, Neal," he said.

"So, Ed."

"Here's the deal. McCall became a disciple of the True Christian Identity Church. C. Wesley Carter has some interesting ties with groups like the Posse Comitatus, the Klan, and the Nazi party," Levine said, eyeing the cottage fries on Neal's plate. "Our contacts in the FBI tell us that these groups are starting to get together, trying to establish a nationwide network. The idea is to maintain their aboveground public parties while creating underground terrorist groups loosely gathered under the rubric of White Aryan Resistance. What is this?"

"A radish."

"Jesus . . . to coin a phrase."

"Could you pass that vinegar over?" Neal asked Ed.

Ed handed him the bottle and Neal poured vinegar over his fries.

"Anyway," Ed continued, "in setting up these little cells these geeks get each other jobs, help their fugitive members hide out . . . a whole underground network."

"And if Harley gets into this network we could lose him for good," Graham added.

"Which is why we need to move fast," Ed said, "now that we know where he is."

That's interesting news, Neal thought. "Where is he?" he asked.

"So," Ed asked, "you want to do it?"

Neal just wanted to make him work for it a little more. Just to protest a little against this old bit—pretending to let you decide if you want to do the job but refusing to tell you what it is until you say you'll do it.

Ed leaned over and snatched a cottage fry from Neal's plate.

"Do what?" Neal asked.

Ed looked to Joe Graham.

"Go undercover, son."

Undercover. The most exciting and scariest word in the business. The flame that attracts and burns.

"Undercover where?" Neal asked.

Ed munched on one bite of the cottage fry and gestured with the other, making small, vague circles in the air.

"You know, out there."

Out there, out there. Well, boys, why not? I've been out there my whole life.

Six hundred miles out there, a shriek came up from the sagebrush flats. At first it sounded like a coyote in pain, but coyotes don't howl in the daytime. The sound was human, a scream of agony that lifted and then died in the vast stillness of The High Lonely.

3

*N*eal parked alongside the raised wooden sidewalk of the main street of Virginia City, Nevada. He had bought the car, a 1967 Chevrolet Nova, for three hundred dollars in a used car lot in Santa Monica and probably had paid too much for it. It had at one time in its hard life been silver; now it was a dull gray spotted with rust. The driver's side inside door handle had fallen off in his hands, and he now closed it by sticking two fingers into the panel holes and pulling as hard as he could. The upholstery was torn, you could keep track of the road through the little holes in the floorboard, and the air-conditioning was more like a faint memory of a fall day. The car idled uncontrollably at thirty-five miles per hour and bucked, wheezed, and snorted for a good eight seconds after the ignition was turned off. But the radio worked, the big engine would take a hill, and the old car would settle into an eighty-mile-an-hour gallop and hold it all day. It was a car meant for covering miles.

Which was exactly what Neal did right after pulling out of the used car lot. He had arranged to meet Graham and Levine in Virginia City. They had flown to Reno and were driving from there. But Neal had to drive the whole way because he was the point man, undercover at that, and it wouldn't do for any of Harley's buddies to see him coming off an airplane in Reno. Reno was a small town and Virginia City was even smaller. Harley was working in a bar called the Lucky Dollar. He'd apparently gotten cocky and given his employer his social security number, which is a real mistake if people are looking for you. Especially if one of those people is Ed Levine, who tends not to miss that kind of thing.

It was to be a simple bag job. Neal would find McCall, talk a little Identity talk with him, become friends, get invited to his home, then lure him into the waiting arms—so to speak—of Joe Graham and Ed Levine.

They'd follow the old routine: two vehicles with tinted windows would be standing by. At the right moment Ed and the thugs in one car would grab Harley, force him inside, and take him for a nice long drive in the country while Graham and Neal would take Cody into the other car and head for California.

It was illegal as hell, involving as it did assault, kidnapping—of Harley, that is—and a host of other potential felonies and misdemeanors. But everyone except Neal would be masked, the vans were untraceable, and as for Neal, well, he had a new identity, a phony car registration, and would be back in New York City within forty-eight hours of the operation.

And Anne Kelley would have her child back.

To his great surprise, Neal discovered he liked to drive. He liked the feel of the wheel, the surge of the car beneath him as he pushed it through the desert east of LA, then north alongside the Sierras, then over the mountains and across into Nevada. He liked the isolation of driving at night, with "Darkness at the Edge of Town" wailing in his ears. He liked pulling the Nova under the soft lights above the gas pumps, filling it up, then buying a dinner of beef jerky, corn chips, and a fruit pie and eating it back on the road.

He liked rolling down the road, watching the sun come up in the gray terrain of northwestern Nevada, getting a cheap breakfast of greasy eggs, stale toast, and bitter coffee in a roadside diner, and hitting the highway again, making that push across the flatlands to the mountains west of Reno. He liked the driving and was a little disappointed when he turned off the highway onto the small road that climbed up to the old mining town of Virginia City.

It was a small town. One broad, main street ran along the spine

---

of a ridge that overlooked the lower hills and the broad plain to the east.

Neal made Virginia City by midafternoon and then posted himself on a convenient bar stool where he could see the street. He nursed some beers until a van with tinted windows and tourist stickers all over it pulled up and parked. A few minutes later a small rental moving truck cruised slowly by and parked. Two very large men got out and went into a coffee shop.

Nice touch, Neal thought. He found a restaurant on a side street and had himself a rare steak with some fried potatoes and a piece of cherry pie. He lingered over coffee until it got good and dark out, then walked down to the Lucky Dollar Saloon and Casino. The street was about deserted on a Monday night and he listened to his own footsteps on the wooden sidewalk. The widely spaced streetlamps cut harsh silver wedges in the darkness, and it was cold for a summer night.

The Lucky Dollar was mostly a tourist trap. It had swinging saloon doors and old wooden tables. Slot machines lined three walls and an enormous wooden bar occupied the other. An old lady, thin as a weed, stood holding a plastic container of quarters in one hand and feeding the slot machine with the other. An old guy who might have been her husband sat at a video blackjack machine, staring at the electronic cards as if they might break down and show him what the dealer had down. Neither of them looked up when Neal walked in.

The guy behind the bar was about fifty. His red hair was going to orange and his cheeks were headed south. He had a drinker's nose and deep-set blue eyes. His shoulders were wide, his forearms were thick, and he didn't look like he needed a bouncer to work the place with him.

"We don't get many out-of-towners on a Monday," he said as Neal took a stool at the bar. "Most people go to Reno nights, anyway. Too quiet."

"I like it quiet."

"What can I get you?"

"Scotch."

"House brand?"

"Fine."

Neal took his drink, got ten bucks in quarters, and lost at video poker for a while. Then he went up to the bar, ordered another scotch, and asked, "Hey, you know, I thought I'd see Harley McCall in here."

Neal realized that he was nervous. Making the approach was always the dicey part of one of these jobs, because you didn't know who it was you were approaching. If the bartender here knew Harley's situation, or worse, if he was a member of the Identity movement, Neal could just as easily get a baseball bat across the face as any information.

"It's his night off," the bartender said. "How do you know Harley?"

Neal could feel sweat dripping down the back of his neck. I haven't done this shit in a long time, he thought. This is screwed. Maybe my backup is too far away. Maybe Ed should have put someone in here with me. Maybe this guy can see I'm scared.

Come on, now. Don't start doubting yourself. That's when you get hurt.

Neal gave the bartender a crooked smile and one of those I-don't-know-if-I-should-say-this shrugs.

"You knew him in jail, right?" the bartender chuckled. "Where?"

"LA."

"LA *is* a jail."

"You got that right."

"He owe you money or something?"

Neal laughed. "Nah. Harley said if I was ever in the area to look him up, so I was in the area and thought I'd look him up."

Should I say anything about Cody? Neal wondered. No, it's too quick, I might spook him.

"He lives in a little motel at the north edge of town," the bartender said. "The Comfort Rest. Shitty name for a motel. Shitty motel. Cabin 5, last one down."

"Hey, thanks a lot. I think I'll finish my drink and wander down there."

Neal forced himself to sit back, sip his whiskey, and let his heart rate go back down. It was tougher than he thought, getting back into the business.

Over at the slot machine the old woman cackled as coins poured out into her plastic cup. The old man looked up from the blackjack machine and cursed her good luck.

Neal finished his drink, waved so long to the bartender, and started a slow walk down the street toward the Comfort Rest. He didn't look behind him to see if the truck and van were trailing him, he didn't even try to pick out sounds. He knew that Friends would have the best drivers and the best muscle. He knew that Graham was rubbing his artificial knuckles into his real palm. He knew that Levine was whispering instructions a mile a minute.

This is too good to be true, Neal thought as he reached the motel. The place was a bag job dream. It sat recessed off the street by a good sixty feet of gravel parking space. The motel itself was actually a group of run-down cabins set in a half-moon pattern around the badly lit parking lot. Cabin 5 was the farthest down from the office and cabins 1 through 4 looked empty. There were no lights on in the office. An old Ford pickup was parked outside Cabin 5. A light inside the cabin shone through the closed curtain.

Neal felt the old adrenaline rush. Do it now or wait? he asked himself. If I wait Harley might talk to his boss, get suspicious, and bolt. We might never have a better chance than right now. At this time of night Cody's probably in bed. If I can just talk my way in the door we can do this quickly and quietly.

Do it now.

He turned around and found the tourist van in the darkness, angled out of sight of the motel. The moving truck was on the opposite side of the street, about fifty yards back. Neal crossed the street, walked back up the sidewalk, and tapped on the driver's window. The window slid down electrically.

Neal recognized the driver from a couple of old jobs in New York:

Vinnie Pond was the best get-away driver in the business. He had the reflexes of a cat burglar and the low blink rate of an Indy driver. Neal nodded hello and then looked at Graham.

"Let's do it now," Neal said.

"Is Cody in there?" a female voice whispered.

Neal leaned in and looked in the back of the van. Anne Kelley was there, shivering with nerves, a cup of coffee clutched in her hand.

Neal looked back at Graham.

"She insisted on coming along," Graham explained.

"I know this sounds nuts, Ms. Kelley," Neal said, "but we're committing a crime in getting your son back this way. You weren't supposed to have any knowledge of this, for your own protection."

"Cody would be terrified if I wasn't here, strangers grabbing him. This is going to be hard enough on him. I'm staying."

One look at her eyes convinced Neal that they weren't going to get rid of her and that there was no sense getting shirty about it. So he said, "Maybe it is good you're here. Maybe you can keep Cody quiet when we put him in the van."

"I guarantee it."

"You want to do it now, Neal?" Graham asked. "Are you sure?"

"I had to give up too much at the bar. This is as good a time as any. I love the setup."

Graham nodded. "It's pretty," he said.

"You're not going to hurt Harley, are you?" Anne asked. "I don't want him hurt."

Neal turned away and the window slid back up.

We don't want him hurt, either, Neal thought, but if that's what it takes . . .

He took three deep breaths and walked back toward Cabin 5. He could hear the van pull forward, within range. The truck wouldn't be far behind.

Neal knocked on the door.

A man's voice answered, "Who is it?"

Is that aggravation or anxiety I'm hearing in the voice? Neal asked himself.

"My name is Kellow," Neal said. "Reverend Carter asked me to pay you a visit, see how you were doing."

"Who the hell is Reverend Carter?"

The voice came from right behind the door.

Shit, shit, shit, Neal thought. He's hinky already. I don't think this is going to be a finesse job. This is going to be size and speed.

There was no peephole, so Harley couldn't see out. Neal stuck out his right arm and made a fast circular motion forward with his hand.

Hurry, hurry, he thought. He didn't look back to see if they were coming. He knew they were.

"Reverend Carter was getting a little worried. Seems there were some people coming around asking about you," Neal said into the door.

There was a long silence. Neal could almost hear him thinking.

"Worried about me?"

Just open the door, Harley. Just open the door and all our worries will be over. "Yeah. I guess you have some sort of situation? With your wife? Reverend Carter thought maybe we could be of help."

Graham was crouched at his feet now. Two of the muscle guys were flat on the ground under the window and by the door. Levine was squatting a few feet behind Neal.

"How could he help me?" the voice asked.

The tone was a little belligerent. Is he stalling for time? Neal wondered. Getting Cody up, getting him dressed, getting ready to go out the back window?

"Ohhh . . ." Neal answered, "a little money, maybe."

The door opened a crack. Joe Graham stuck his artificial arm in the gap as the man tried to slam the door shut again. Neal jumped out of the way as Levine slammed into the door, ripping the security chain from the wall.

The two hitters burst in. One tackled the man around the waist as the other slipped a black hood over his head. The first hitter clasped him around the neck, put one huge hand over his mouth, and lifted him up onto his toes in a lock that would break his neck if he tried to fight. The second hitter closed the door as the van pulled up alongside. This all took about three seconds.

Levine went over to the bed to pick up Cody.

Cody wasn't in the bed.

Graham came out of the bathroom shaking his head.

"Where's the boy?" Levine hissed.

"What boy?" asked the voice muffled under the hood. The voice was shaking.

Levine grabbed the hood just under the chin and pulled hard. "You can tell me now or tell me later, but you'll be feeling a hell of a lot worse later, so tell me now."

"I don't know what you're talking about."

It wasn't a voice of defiance. It was a voice of terror.

"It isn't him," Graham said.

"What?" Levine asked.

"It isn't him." Graham lifted the man's left arm and pointed to a spot beneath his white T-shirt. "No tattoo."

"What's your name?" Levine asked him.

"Harley McCall!"

There couldn't be two of them, Levine thought.

"What's your real name?"

"Paul Wallace." He was crying.

"Why are you using Harley McCall's social security number, Paul?"

"I found his wallet. I needed a new name. Are you going to kill me?"

"I haven't decided yet. Where did you 'find' it?"

"In Las Vegas."

"When?"

"Month or so."

Ed signaled for Graham, Neal, and the other hitter to get out, then said, "Paul, I have to leave now. There'll be someone watching from across the street. You stay in here for ten minutes with this hood on. If you don't—"

"I will."

Graham cracked the door open, looked outside, and then moved quickly into the van. Neal followed him in. The hitter strode to the phone booth outside and ripped the receiver cord from the phone. Then he headed for the truck.

Levine came out the door, lifted his hands, and made a gesture like a stick breaking. The hitter got into the van just as it slid off down the street. Then Levine climbed into the van.

Anne Kelley was crying. She was beating her fists on the seat cushion, crying and saying, "Cody, Cody, Cody."

Levine said to Neal, "Get in that car and drive like hell. Don't go to Reno airport. Just get across the state line, dump the car, and meet us back in New York. We'll start all over again."

"I'm sorry," Neal said to Anne.

She nodded but kept crying.

"Move!" Ed yelled to him. "The bartender can ID you!"

Neal was looking at Anne Kelley. She was a study in misery, a study in loss.

"Get going, son," Graham said quietly.

Neal opened the van door and got out. Vinnie threw the van in reverse and rolled out of town in the opposite direction from the truck.

Neal stood in the parking lot for a few long moments. He tried to shake the image of Anne Kelley's tortured face from his mind, but it wouldn't go. He opened Paul Wallace's door and stepped in.

Wallace looked small and skinny in his underwear, a white T-shirt and boxer shorts. He was an older guy, now that Neal took a closer look at him. He was in his late forties, with a lot of hard miles behind him. He had a full head of black hair, streaked with silver, greased straight back. He had heavy bags under his eyes and deep lines on his face. His skin was pale. He was trying to pour some Old Crow from a pint bottle into a motel glass, but his hand was shaking so badly that he spilled the booze on the floor.

Neal took the bottle from his hand, poured three fingers of whiskey into the glass, and handed it to him. Then he sat down on Wallace's bed.

"We have a problem, Paul," Neal said quietly.

"We!" Paul asked sarcastically. He took a heavy gulp of the cheap whiskey.

Neal nodded. "Well, you. You do."

"You were the guy outside my door. I recognize your voice."

"See, they're thinking about whacking you."

Paul tried to sound tough but his voice cracked as he asked, "What do they have against me?"

"They think you're lying. So do I."

"I—"

"Shut up. See, I have to wonder why you opened the door if you don't know who Reverend Carter is. So that makes me wonder if maybe you also know Harley McCall. Now you can talk."

"All right. I didn't find the wallet. I took it. Okay? Now leave me alone."

Neal shook his head. "You're not a pickpocket, Paul. You're a loser. A dues-paying member of the fraternity of losers."

"I'm going to walk out there and call the police!"

"You'll never hear the sirens, Paul."

"You said you'd help me! Give me money! I didn't know who this Carter was, but if he was going to give me money . . . well, look around you. I could use a little money."

Neal pointed his index finger at Wallace's face and pulled his thumb back like the hammer of a revolver.

"Maybe Harley and I were drinking together once," Wallace said quickly. "Maybe he gave me the wallet."

"Why would he do that?"

Paul stuck out his empty glass. Neal poured him another belt.

"I been having some problems. Alimony. They hound, they hound me. I just wanted a fresh start. McCall said maybe we could help each other out. Said maybe his ID was more useful to him in my hands than his. Said just to travel with it . . . use it. Throw people off his trail for a bit."

Which it sure did.

"Were you friends? Did you work together?"

"He worked at a place where I used to do a little business. We maybe had a few drinking nights together."

"Did he have a little boy with him?"

Paul was eager to answer by now. He sensed that salvation lay on the other side of the right answers. "Yeah, yeah. A cute little kid. And a woman. A real looker named Doreen."

"How old was the boy?"

"Three, maybe four?"

Neal got up and made a show of pulling the curtain aside and looking out the window. He turned back to Wallace.

"Now, Paul, I have a two-part question to ask you and you really need—*really* need, Paul—to give me a true and accurate answer. Tell me you understand that."

"I understand that."

"Where and when did you have this remarkable conversation with Harley McCall?"

Paul's eyes starting flipping around. He looked like one of those little dogs you win at the carnival. He was thinking up a lie.

Neal thought about Anne Kelley, crossed the room, and slapped the glass out of Wallace's hand. The whiskey splashed against the wall.

Paul looked mournfully at the booze dripping down the cheap paneling.

"Next time it's your brains," Neal said. He was furious at Wallace and himself. He'd never done anything like that before.

"He told me to say I found it! Not to say where he was!" Paul said indignantly.

Neal took Wallace by the shoulders and spoke softly into his ear. "He's not here, is he, Paul? I am, and the guys outside are, and you are. Now, I'm losing my patience with you."

"He said he had friends who would find me and . . ." Wallace said in a hoarse whisper. He started to cry again.

"But we found you, Paul," Neal said just as quietly. "And we'll put that hood back over your head, and put you down on your knees, and it will be blackness for ever and ever."

"It was about a month ago, that part was true."

"Good . . ."

"At the Filly Ranch."

"Where's that?"

"Just off Highway 50, between Sparks and Fallon."

Neal let him go and walked toward the door. He took two hundred-dollar bills—expense money—out of his wallet and let them drop to the floor.

"Sorry for all the trouble, Paul. Now, do you believe we could find you again if we wanted to?"

"Yessir."

"Is there anyplace you can go now, out of state?"

"I have a sister in Arizona."

"Go there. First thing in the morning."

"Yessir."

"Don't even think about trying to warn Harley."

"To hell with him."

Not yet, Paul. Not until I find him.

Neal left the cabin, walked as fast as he could to the old Nova, and headed for the Filly Ranch.

It being the middle of the morning, the neon sign over the purple prefabricated building was turned off, but Neal could make out the design: a caricature cowboy with a lascivious smile and his tongue hanging out of his mouth about to "mount" a buxom lady with long hair, long legs, and a bit between her teeth.

Four trailers were parked around the place, some junker cars sat on blocks, a big butane tank shone silver in the sun behind the low, flat building. Neal Carey had never been on a ranch, but this sure as hell didn't look like one, not even one he had seen in the movies.

He followed the path marked with white-painted stones up to the front door and rang the bell.

A short woman with curly red hair answered the door. She was wearing a high-collared western shirt, a studded denim jacket, and jeans. She had a matching turquoise necklace and bracelet on, pointy lizard cowboy boots, and the smile of a professional greeter.

"Hi," she said. "I'm Bobby. What's your name?"

"Is this the Filly Ranch?" Neal asked her.

She caught the tone of puzzlement in his voice.

"What were you expecting, honey? Horses?"

"Sort of."

She gave him an all-men-are-stupid-but-some-more-than-others look and said, "Listen carefully: horse, whores, horses. A female horse is a filly. We have female whores here. Get it?"

"I think so."

"Well, do you want it?"

"How much?"

"Another romantic. Fifty dollars a ride. You want them to do tricks, it's extra. We got a menu inside. Also air-conditioning. Also showers, which I would highly recommend to you."

"I've been on the road awhile," he explained.

"Ain't we all."

He followed her into a room called the corral and sat down on the orange vinyl cushion of a cheap, low sofa. The room was dark, low ceilinged, and close. A small bar ran across one side. Two nickel slot machines were shoved against the opposite wall. Various posters of horses were glued to the plaster. Lava lamps bubbled on glass coffee tables alongside an assortment of porn magazines. A potbellied cowboy with long black hair, a black hat, and sunglasses sat in a chair with his feet on a stool and a revolver in his lap. Neal made him for the bouncer.

"I'll call the roundup," Bobby said. She pushed a button on an intercom by the door.

"The what?" asked Neal.

"The roundup," she repeated, sounding every bit as bored as she was, "is when we bring all the fillies into the corral so you can pick one out."

Neal tried a hunch. "Do you have a girl named Doreen?"

"If you want one. I mean, honey, they'll answer to any name you like, except that they do get a little spooked at 'Mommy.' "

"I'm looking for a real Doreen."

"A real Doreen. Well, we do have us a real Doreen. Now, how would you like her dressed? Real Doreen does your basic pink teddy and garter thing, or a kind of Annie Oakley with just the gunbelt and boots, or she does a real prim schoolmarm and makes you talk to the tune of the hickory switch, but that's another twenty."

Neal pulled out his wallet and handed her three twenties and a ten.

"My, my," Bobby said.

Neal shrugged.

Bobby shook her head and spoke into the intercom. "Doreen, we have us a bad little cowboy out here who needs to stay after school with the teacher."

She turned back to Neal.

"She won't be but a minute," she said. "Would you like a drink while you wait? First one's on the house."

"Scotch?"

"You got it."

She poured him a drink, then reached under the bar and handed him a key, a towel, and a bar of soap.

"Trailer 3. Do yourself a favor, cowboy, shower *before,* this time. The schoolmarm don't like dirty little boys."

An unshowered Neal was sitting on the purple bedspread when Doreen opened the door and strode in. True to her billing she was carrying a switch, wore a long print dress, and had her light brown hair put up in a severe bun. She looked to be in her late twenties. She was tall and thin. She flashed her blue eyes at him in a determined, if unconvincing, display of feigned anger.

"Stand up when I come in the room!" she ordered.

"You can save the act, Doreen. I just want to talk."

She sat down on the bed beside him. "I'm not going to tell you the story of my life, if that's what you're hoping for."

At closer inspection, she was older than Neal had thought. Now he put her in her middle thirties and figured that she was developing this little specialty act to stretch out her working life by a couple of years.

"No," Neal said. "I was hoping you could tell me something about my buddy Harley McCall."

She leaned back and laughed.

"There is very little I couldn't tell you about that son of a bitch," she said. Her voice had turned hard and bitter. "But why should I?"

Neal knew right then that McCall had skipped out again.

"Why shouldn't you, if he's a son of a bitch?" he asked.

She looked him over.

"You're no friend of Harley's," she said.

"Neither are you."

"But that don't make *us* friends."

Neal got up from the bed and took his wallet from his pants pocket. He laid five hundred-dollar bills on the bed. "Maybe this does."

Doreen looked at the money and gave a little snort. "After all," she said, "I'm a whore. Is that what you're saying?"

"Pretty much."

"Well, you're pretty much right."

She scooped the bills up and stuffed them into the dress pocket.

"Harley stayed here awhile with the little boy," she said. "That's probably why you're looking for him, right?"

Neal didn't answer.

"Right," she said. "He got a job as a bouncer on the night shift. Bobby put him and the boy up in one of the trailers in back as part of the deal. Harley and me hooked up about the second day he was here, I guess. He's a good-looking son of a buck. I even switched over to day hours so I could baby-sit Cody nights. Fixed his meals, watched TV with him, tucked him in. It was kind of nice. I guess I had thoughts about becoming a real-life family, but it didn't last."

"What happened?"

"We had a black guy come in from one of the bases out around Fallon. He picked me out of the roundup. Harley got wind of it and went nuts. Got mean drunk and said things."

"What things?"

"You want a lot for your money."

"It's a lot of money," Neal answered.

"Said he just couldn't even think about putting his thing where a nigger had put his, called me a no-good whore. I imagine he's right. This is no kind of work for a white woman. Anyway, he packed up his stuff, put Cody in the pickup, and took off."

She put a pillow behind her head and leaned back against the wall.

"Do you know where he went?" Neal asked.

"Maybe. We had talked about it a lot, because we had been going to go together. There's a ranch near Austin that was looking for hands. Harley knew the owner from California and had some buddies working the place. We was just working here to put some money away to eventually buy our own place. I'm sure he headed there without me. I've even thought about trying to look him up myself, see if . . . so you think you got your five hundred's worth yet?"

"Do you remember the name of the ranch?" Neal asked, not believing he was going to be that lucky.

She shook her head. "The son of a bitch never said. Maybe he was always figuring on dumping me."

"How long ago did he leave?"

"It's been about a month now, I guess."

Well, at least we're whittling it down, Neal thought. "Okay, thanks."

She sat up and gave him a nasty, knowing smile.

"You still got seventy bucks' worth coming to you," she said. She flicked the switch against her hand. "I mean, you chose the school-marm for some reason, huh?"

"I figured it would be the one where you'd be wearing the most clothes."

She stared into his eyes. "You're a real bastard."

That about sums it up, Neal thought. "I'll take the shower, though," he said, "if you don't mind."

"I don't mind if you drown." She got up from the bed and stalked out.

Neal showered, then headed out the door. He was about halfway back down the gravel pathway when he heard footsteps behind him.

He turned around and the bouncer from the corral stuck a big revolver under his nose and cocked the hammer. He still had his shades on.

"Turn back around," he said.

"Absolutely."

The cowboy smashed the pistol right behind Neal's ear and Neal dropped to the ground. He was conscious just long enough to hear the cowboy say, "Help me get him in his car."

The cowboy grabbed him under his arms and Doreen took his feet. They shoved him into the passenger seat of the Nova and drove him about five miles east along the highway. Doreen relieved his wallet of the rest of his expense money, about twelve hundred dollars, during the ride. The cowboy pulled the Nova off onto a little wash-out, dragged Neal out of the car, and laid him alongside some rabbit brush.

Neal started to wake up when he heard shots. He cracked an eye open enough to see the cowboy put a slug into each of the Nova's tires and another in the gas tank.

"Let's get out of here," said the cowboy.

"Not quite yet," said Doreen.

She hauled back and planted a nice sharp schoolmarm shoe into Neal's groin and then into his ribs.

"That'll teach the uppity son of a bitch," she said.

Neal passed out again.

He woke up to the sound of tires crackling on the dry gravel.

I wonder if Matt and Miss Kitty are coming back to polish me off, Neal thought. Maybe I should try to crawl out of here.

He was lying on his stomach. He touched the right side of his head and felt blood caked in his hair. He traced the blood where it had run down his neck, then he tried to lift his head up out of the dirt. But even that small effort sent a bolt of pain searing across his ribs and started his head throbbing all over again.

He laid his head back down and settled for just raising his eyes to the battered car that sat between him and the road. He smelled gasoline and knew he should get up, but it just felt like too much work.

A car door shut. Footsteps came closer. Neal saw cowboy boots.

"What in the name of Sam Hill . . . ?" a man's voice asked. "Are you all right?"

Neal raised an eye to see a middle-aged man in a green gimme cap leaning over him.

"I've been better," Neal mumbled.

"I'll bet you have."

The man gently turned him over on his back.

"That's quite a knock you have on your head."

Not to mention my balls, Neal thought. Ouch.

"What the hell happened to you?"

"I'm not sure I know."

The man chuckled. "You didn't by chance enter the bareback event at the Filly Ranch, did you?"

"I guess I got thrown."

"Well, you wouldn't be the first. Come on."

The man gently held him under the arms and lifted him to his feet. Neal's feet didn't really want the responsibility.

The man picked Neal's wallet up from the ground and looked inside. "You won't have to worry about managing your money anymore."

"Shit."

"Although, judging by your vehicle, it doesn't look like it was ever a very big concern for you."

Neal steadied himself on the old Nova and looked around. He could have been on the moon except the moon wasn't this flat. There was nothing but desert around.

What the hell am I doing out here? he asked himself. Oh yeah, Cody McCall.

"I think I can drive," he said to the man, who was just sort of standing there staring at him.

The man laughed. "Where do you want to go?"

"Nowhere, really."

"Well, that's about where you'll get in this car. I've never seen a car that's been shot before. Somebody must've taken a real dislike to you."

"I can have that effect on people," Neal said.

"I hadn't noticed," said the man. He stuck his hand out. "I'm Steve Mills. I have a ranch out by Austin. Or it has me."

A ranch out by Austin, Neal thought. It has a ring to it. "My name's Neal Carey."

"Come on over to the truck. I have a first-aid kit."

Mills led Neal over to an old Chevy pickup, opened the passenger door, and sat Neal down. Then he got his kit, expertly cleaned the wound on Neal's head, swabbed some antiseptic on it, and applied a bandage.

"I'm a regular Sue Barton, student nurse," he said. "Out where we live, you have to be a little bit of everything—medic, mechanic, cook, farmer, cowboy, and sometime psychiatrist. You're from back East, aren't you?"

Neal focused his eyes and took a good look at the man for the first time. He was in the tall range, real thin, with that slight stoop at the shoulders that tall men get from having to duck under things. He wore a blue checkered shirt rolled up at the sleeves, with a pack of cigarettes peeking out of the breast pocket. He had on jeans over his cowboy boots, which were old, tan, and worn.

He had a handsome face that had weathered more than its share of cold, harsh winds, and baking sun. It was deeply tanned up to the telltale line on the forehead that betrayed a habitual ball cap. His brown hair was still thick at about forty-five years of age, and his dark brown eyes shone with life. It was a face you liked right away, a face with nothing to hide.

"I'm from New York," Neal said.

"City or state?"

"City."

Steve Mills scratched his cheek. "I'd have thought you could have gotten yourself mugged *there*. What brings you out this way?"

I'm looking for a man who works on a ranch out by Austin. "I like to travel," Neal said.

"Well, you don't *have* to tell me," Steve said.

Good.

"Well, Neal Carey, mystery man, why don't I throw what's left of your personal possessions in the back of the truck and take you to Austin with me? If your destination is nowhere, Austin is at least close. There's a bus that comes through every couple of days."

Neal reflected on his options and quickly arrived at the conclusion that he didn't have any.

"This is very generous of you," he said.

Steve was already tossing Neal's duffel bag into the truck.

"I'm going there anyway. Wouldn't mind some company for the ride."

"Hold on a second," Neal said. He straightened himself up, tottered over to the Nova, and opened up the trunk. He tore the fabric off the inside of the trunk hood, reached in, and pulled out a stack of bills, the last five hundred dollars of his expense money.

"You may not be as dumb as I thought," Steve observed.

"Don't get carried away," Neal answered. He felt pretty dumb. He'd come on too fast with Doreen. And much too rough. He could have gotten the answers he needed without insulting her, just as he probably could have gotten the truth out of Paul Wallace without slapping him. He had substituted tough for smarts, and that was stupid. And flashing all that cash around had been just plain idiotic. He didn't blame Doreen and her gun-wielding cowboy friend as much as he blamed himself. He'd been trained better.

He hauled himself back into the truck and the resulting pain felt almost like satisfaction.

Steve climbed into the cab and pulled the truck back onto the road. The old truck rattled, rumbled, and roared down the highway.

Neal settled back in the seat and tried to figure out his next move.

I'm headed toward Austin, he thought, the last known location of Harley McCall. I know McCall has hooked up with a rancher, someone he knew from his California days. That's the plus side.

The down side is that I don't have a car or much money, and that Levine and Graham are expecting me to show up in New York any day now. And they're going to be pissed off that I didn't follow orders. But at least I dumped the car.

He was pondering the wisdom of calling the office when he fell asleep. He woke up over an hour later.

"You don't look crazier than a pet coon!" Steve shouted.

"What?" Neal Carey shouted over the noise of the old pickup truck as it rattled over Highway 50.

"I said you don't *look* crazier than a pet coon." answered Steve Mills. His face crinkled into a wry smile. "I was thinking that you'd have to be crazier than a pet coon to be wandering around this country all by yourself with no particular purpose."

"Maybe I am." Neal answered. "How crazy is a pet coon?"

"Pretty damn crazy. Course, anybody who tries ranching Nevada has no damn business calling anyone else crazy. So even if you are crazier than a pet coon, I figure I still got about twenty years of crazy on you! Hold the wheel, will you?"

Neal reached over and steadied the steering wheel as Steve Mills took a pack of Camels from his shirt pocket, stuck a cigarette in his mouth, struck a match, then lit it up.

"Hope you don't mind," Steve said, exhaling a deep drag of smoke, "but since my heart attack the wife raises unholy hell if she sees me with a butt. They had to whirlybird me into Fallon, so I finally got a little of my *in*surance money back! Kind of scared the wife, though. She says if it happens again, and she finds any cigs on me, she's just going to leave me to die in the barn. I told her she might as well bury me there, too, seeing as how I've been ass deep in cow shit most of my life anyway. You don't say a lot, do you?"

"I like to listen."

"Well, this relationship might work out, because I like to talk and the wife and daughter have already heard all my stories—twice. I got a herd of cows rooting for my next heart attack just so they won't have to listen to me anymore. My cattle don't go 'moo,' they go 'Shut up!' "

The truck reached the top of a long, steep grade. Neal could see a broad valley below them. A mountain range formed a backdrop beyond. The valley seemed to stretch endlessly to the south and north.

You can see forever, Neal thought.

"Welcome to The High Lonely," Steve said.

"The what?"

"The High Lonely—that's what we call it around here. You're at about six thousand feet elevation, and it's mostly empty space, as you can observe. Very few people, some more cattle, lots of jackrabbits and coyotes. Back there in the mountains you have cougars, bighorn sheep, and eagles."

Steve pulled the truck off onto an overlook.

It's like being perched at the edge of the world, Neal thought. A great brown vastness under a canopy of startling blue.

"We're sitting on Mount Airy Summit," Steve explained. "Six thousand, six hundred and seventy-nine feet high. Down there is the Reese River valley, although it isn't much of a river as rivers go. That's the Toiyabe Range across the valley. The big peak there is called Bunker Hill. My place sets at the base of it. Believe it or not, I actually climbed that damn thing once or twice with my daughter Shelly."

Steve pulled the truck back onto the road and started the descent into the valley.

"It's mostly cattle country," Steve said, "but it takes a tremendous amount of land for the cattle to graze, it being mostly sagebrush. We grow the best alfalfa in the country up here but it costs an arm and a leg to irrigate and we don't have the water to do more than we're doing. Used to be a lot of gold mining around, but that's about finished."

"So what do people do?" asked Neal.

"Leave, mostly."

Steve pointed to a dirt road off to the right. "Our place is about twenty miles down that way," he said. "You wouldn't believe the winters up here. That's called a non sequitur, isn't it?"

"Right."

"I got a B.A. in English, although that doesn't impress the cows."

"From where?"

"Berkeley. Back before the whole free speech stuff, of course. Which is sort of too bad, seeing as how I'm all for free speech," Steve said. The road took a sudden steep rise, curling through several switchbacks flanked by thick stands of piñon pine. "Now, we're coming up to Austin, which ain't got much except it does have a bar and I thought I should give you the whole tour."

"The wife doesn't approve of drinking either?" Neal asked.

"Well, not since my heart attacked me. Damn doctor . . . nice enough guy, but Jesus, he tells me to give up smoking, drinking, and red meat. I'm a rancher. I raise beef. I smoke and drink and eat my own beefsteak and I might be the happiest man in America. Well, here's Austin, such as it is."

It sure isn't much, Neal thought. The town seemed to cling to one of the gentler slopes on the west side of the mountain range. Route 50 narrowed to make the town's main street, along which there was a raised wooden sidewalk. Old buildings that looked like a run-down movie set of a bad western flanked the street. The buildings were mostly wooden, with a couple of red brick edifices thrown in, and featured classic western facades and wood canopies held up by long poles. There were a couple of cheap motels, a gas station, one restaurant, maybe three saloons, and a grocery store. A few houses dotted the hill that led up from the north side of the road. The hill was sparse except for a few piñon pine.

"Let's go see and be seen at Brogan's," Steve said as he pulled the car over on the side of the road.

He brushed the dust off his pants and old leather boots and ambled toward Brogan's. Neal watched his slightly bowlegged gait and the little hitch in his left leg. Then he gently lowered himself out of the truck and he followed him into the bar.

It wasn't really a bar, though. It was a saloon, as dark and cool as an old cellar. The two small windows were grimy from forty years of collected grease and smoke and let in unsteady streams of filtered sunlight to highlight the specks of dust that floated in the stale air. The low ceiling sheltered cobwebs in each corner and the three small, round tables showed only a nodding acquaintance with anything resembling a rag.

A few stools, a couple with torn red upholstery, were pushed up against the bar, behind which sat an old man, fat and wrinkled as a bullfrog, with jowls to match. His butt sank deep into the cushion of an ancient wing-back chair and he was sipping what looked like whiskey from a jelly jar that was as greasy as the hand that held it. An enormous dog of dubious ancestry and ineffable color lay beside him and raised its gigantic head to see who was coming through the door.

A younger man, tall and wiry, was perched on a stool at the far end of the bar. His sandy hair peeked out under a red gimme cap advertising Wildcat. A spindly mustache outlined the narrow mouth that was bent into a frown. A long red beard hung straight down from his mouth. He was staring into a glass of beer.

"Whoohoo," the fat man wheezed. "I guess *Mrs.* Mills didn't come into town."

"Hello, Brogan," said Steve. "This is Neal Carey."

The man at the end of the bar looked up.

"Steve," he said, nodding his head.

"Cal," Steve nodded back. "What are you drinking, Neal?"

"A beer?" Neal asked.

"I guess Brogan's got one or two. A beer for my friend and I'll have a beer and shot."

"You know where it is," Brogan answered. Neal got the feeling that Brogan didn't spend a lot of time out of that chair. "Leave the money on the bar first."

"You don't trust me, Brogan."

"I trust myself and my dog and I don't turn my back on the dog."

Steve climbed over the bar and reached into an old-fashioned Coca-Cola cooler and pulled out two sweating bottles of beer. Then he took a bottle of Canadian Club out from under the bar, grabbed a shot glass from a rack, and filled it up.

"I wouldn't either if I had that dog," Steve said. "It would probably try to screw you in the ass, and it's big enough to do it."

Neal saw Cal flinch ever so slightly, then bury his head deeper in his beer. The dog lifted its muzzle with somewhat less interest. Steve Mills knocked the shot back, shook his head, turned red, coughed, and set the glass down.

"I love this country," he said. He popped the caps off the beer and handed one to Neal.

Neal sat down on a stool and took a tentative sip of the beer. It tasted bitter and cold. It tasted great. He took another sip, then a swallow, and then tipped the bottle back and guzzled the stuff, savoring the feel of it pouring cool and wet down his throat.

Steve pulled a couple of crumbled bills out of his pocket and laid them on the bar.

"Mrs. Mills letting you have a little of your money?" Brogan teased. His voice sounded like a slow leak from a steam pipe.

Steve turned to Neal. "The missus handles the money, which is kinda funny, seeing as I'm the one who's supposed to have the head for it."

Cal looked up from his beer again and glanced quickly but sharply at Steve Mills. Nobody seemed to notice but Neal, who took an instant dislike to the guy. That felt almost as invigorating as the beer. Neal hadn't allowed himself to feel very much in the way of emotion for a while. He swigged down the rest of the bottle and saw Steve Mills watching him.

Steve lit up a cigarette and took a drag. "Why don't you come out to the place with me? We can feed you and give you a place to sleep and you can sort things out from there."

"I couldn't impose on you like that."

"We are starved for company out there, and I have a teenage daughter who would just love to interrogate you about life in the big city."

He does have a point, Neal thought. I'm hungry and tired, and if I call Friends just now they might send the old van out to haul me back in. And I'm not ready for that just yet.

And after all, I am looking for a ranch near Austin.

"Well, thank you. It's very kind of you," Neal said, feeling like a lying hypocrite.

But that's what undercover work is all about, he thought.

Three more beers met their maker before Steve and Neal got back in the truck and headed out of town. They drove west for a mile or so and then turned south down the dirt road Steve had pointed out earlier. The road ran roughly parallel between the Toiyabe Range to the east and the Shoshones to the west, through pretty flat sagebrush plain broken by deep gullies. It took an occasional dip down into one of the wider gullies but then rose right back up onto the plain.

The terrain was mostly the blue-gray of sagebrush above the yellow-gray of the alkaloid soil, punctuated here and there by a few deep green fields of alfalfa. The mountains in the background, rising as high as twelve thousand feet, were a blend of the darkest—almost black—green, and purple, with patches of gray stone and bright yellow spreads of wildflowers.

Cattle dotted the landscape. Most grazed in small herds far from the road, but a more adventurous few explored the grass along the roadside, stopping to stare indignantly at the truck as it passed by. Steve had to stop once or twice for cows and calves that were standing in the middle of the road.

"Most of what we're on now is Hansen Cattle Company land," Steve explained. "Hansen owns most of this part of the valley. In fact, my spread is about the only piece he hasn't bought up the past few years."

"Does he want to buy you out?" Neal asked.

"Oh, I suppose he would if I ever left, but he doesn't seem to mind my puny presence. Bob Hansen's a good guy, which is a good thing, seeing as how we're each other's only neighbors. His son Jory and my daughter Shelly are the hot item at the high school right now."

The truck lurched down into a particularly bumpy old wash. A jackrabbit, its big ears twitching with anxiety, broke out of the sagebrush and sprang away with long jumps at amazing speed. A skinny coyote appeared at the edge of the road, gave the truck a thanks-a-heap glare, and trotted back into the brush.

They drove for another forty minutes or so before coming to the Mills place. It was a big, two-story log house that sat about two hundred yards east of the road, on the left side of the dirt driveway. An enormous hay barn just to the west almost dwarfed the house. On the side of the barn was an open shed, with two tractors and some other agricultural equipment that Neal didn't recognize. About fifty yards north of the house was a corral made of metal piping. Three horses pricked up their ears at the sound of the truck, saw the vehicle, and trotted to the edge of the fence. There were two other, smaller livestock pens and then another barn beyond that.

"It's beautiful," Neal said as he got out of the truck.

He meant it. The Mills place seemed to stand alone in the sage-brush, the only building within sight in the beautiful valley, framed by the mountains. The stillness was at once soothing and alarming.

"Yeah, well, it has its moments," Steve said. "Of course, it's under about two feet of snow from October to April, then you're knee-deep in mud until sometime in June, then you got your dust until September, and autumn lasts about an hour and a half until it snows again. But goddamn if I don't love it. Speaking of which, here's the missus."

The "missus" was maybe five feet three on tiptoes. Her black hair, cut short just below her ears, framed her strong cheekbones, strong nose, strong jaw, and wide eyebrows. Her face wasn't pretty. It was handsome, and its beauty wasn't diminished by the laugh lines and worry lines etched by twenty years of crazy on an isolated ranch twenty miles from nowhere.

She was wearing a red shirt tucked into trim blue jeans over white sneakers. Her sleeves were rolled up and the whole effect was one of energy, efficiency, and strength.

She kissed her husband on the cheek and offered Neal her hand.

"I brought home a stray," Steve said to her. "This is Neal Carey."

"I'm Peggy Mills. Welcome."

If she was surprised or annoyed at having a strange guest sprung on her, she didn't show it. Neal had the feeling that he wasn't the first stray that Steve had ever brought home.

"Thank you."

"Has Steve been showing you the sights?"

"Some of them."

"I'll bet. Come on in."

She led them into the kitchen and sat Neal down at a wooden drop-leaf table. The kitchen was small but uncluttered. Pots, pans, and spoons hung from a metal ring above the sink. Checkered contact paper covered the counter.

"Where's Shelly?" Steve asked her.

"Riding around with Jory Hansen. She should be back soon."

Steve chuckled. "Jory's old man won't like him wasting a Saturday afternoon." He poured himself a cup of coffee from a pot on the counter and sat down.

"Don't get too comfortable," Peggy said. "I think Eleanor's sick."

"Oh?"

"She's been bawling all afternoon."

Steve sipped his coffee, set his cup down, and headed for the door.

"There is no rest for the weary," he said. "See you in a bit, Neal."

"I'll be right back," Peggy said. "Grab yourself a cup." She followed her husband out onto the small enclosed mud porch where he was putting on a pair of rubber boots.

Neal figured that Steve was filling her in on their visitor. Neal took the moment to look around the house.

It was basically a square. The walls were made of big, dark logs with white mortar in between. The kitchen occupied a narrow rectangle on the north side of the house. The table was set by a big window that looked out to the mountains on the east. Three other windows gave a view to the north, to the horse corral and the barns. Closets and a stairwell made up the south wall of the kitchen. On the other side was a large living room that made up the rest of the first floor.

The living room was terrific. A stone fireplace took up most of its north wall. A big sofa stretched along the south wall, and two big easy chairs on either side, by the fireplace, created a conversation area. There was a big, dark blue Indian rug on the floor and a large glass coffee table in the center.

The east wall was a beauty, being mostly a huge picture window that afforded a wonderful view of the Mills ranch. Beyond the porch that wrapped around the east and south sides of the house was a small lawn that had been laboriously nurtured and carved out of the surrounding sagebrush. Beyond the lawn the land sloped gently for hundreds of yards down to what appeared to be a creek bed, judging by the thin scattering of pines along its side. The land rose again on the other side of the creek, particularly on a big spur that ran down from one of the bigger Toiyabe peaks.

The mountains were a revelation from this perspective. What had looked from a distance like a solid mass was actually a series of separate peaks joined by saddles along the top. Each peak had a spur that ran down onto the flat, forming a wedge where the mountain met the sagebrush plain. Parts of the mountain were thickly wooded, other sections looked barren and rocky, still others were abloom in enormous fields of wildflowers. Clouds were beginning to wrap around the mountain peaks, obscuring the summits and softening the sharp lines of cliffs and ravines carved in the western face of the mountain.

It was a view, Neal thought, that seemed to build in evocative layers—the homey porch, the struggling lawn, cattle grazing out on the plain, and the dramatic mountains in the background.

"Pretty, isn't it," Peggy said as she came back in.

"Pretty doesn't begin to say it."

She stood beside him and looked out the window. "Sometimes," she said, "I just pull up a chair and sit. How's your head?"

Better than it's been in a long time, lady, just looking out this window, being here. "It's okay."

"Sounds like you ran into some bad luck."

"I feel like it ran into me."

She gazed out the window for a few more seconds, as if she were thinking about saying something and wondering whether she should.

"What would you like to know, Mrs. Mills?" Neal asked.

"I'm not much for small talk, Neal. I'm the mother of an impressionable teenage girl and I need to know who's in my house. So, is there anything about you I should know?"

Where to begin, where to begin . . . "I've had some troubles."

"Drug troubles?"

"No." Well, not *my* drug troubles, anyway.

"Troubles with the law?" Peggy asked.

"No."

Neal felt her eyes like laser beams, looking right through him.

"So you're just trying to find yourself?"

No. I'm just trying to find Cody McCall. "Something like that," Neal answered.

She looked at him for another moment and said, "Well, there are worse places to find yourself."

Steve came back in the door.

"How's Eleanor?" Peggy asked.

"Even nastier than usual. She's got too much milk for that calf and her udders are real swollen. You'd bawl, too."

"So are you going to Hansen's?"

"I guess so," Steve sighed. "Actually, it's okay. I wouldn't mind getting another calf."

"I'll get some boots on," Peggy said.

"No," Steve said. He turned to Neal. "You want to play cowboy with me?"

The turnoff to Hansen's place was about two miles farther south down the road. The big white clapboard house was set about a half mile east of the road. It had a two-story central section with two one-floor wings coming at forty-five-degree angles on either side.

The ranch had none of the casual, loose charm of the American

West but an almost obsessive air of efficiency and order. White fences bordered the long driveway. The clapboard house gleamed with a recent coat of white paint and shiny red shutters. Two large barns were painted orthodox red, as were several equipment sheds, a garage, and a big bunkhouse that was set several hundred yards east of the house. A large lawn, green from fertilizers and neatly trimmed, was protected from the road by a perimeter of crushed limestone. A heard of holstein cattle, uniformly black and white, grazed in a rectangular pasture. A smaller herd of light brown Swiss Charolais patrolled the next enclosure.

"Bob Hansen is a model rancher," Steve explained to Neal as the old pickup rumbled up Hansen's drive, "and I mean that sincerely. He scratched this place out of the rabbit bush and he gets the most out of every inch. Now, Bob doesn't have what you'd call a scintillating sense of humor, and he isn't the kind of guy you'd sit and have a beer with, but he's a hell of a cattle man and a fine neighbor. When I got my leg broke, Bob or Jory or one of the hands was over my place every day feeding the cattle and chopping the ice out of the creek."

Steve gave the horn a beep before pulling into the crushed rock parking circle outside the garage where two green tractors were parked side by side, as shiny and bright as if they had just come out of the John Deere showroom. A minute later a short, middle-aged man dressed in a light khaki shirt over khaki slacks and a big gray Stetson hat came out of the barn. He had the gait of a bantam rooster. His short blond hair was carefully combed and his blue eyes high-lighted a handsome face. He looked like the second lead in a forties movie, the guy who gets the money but loses the girl.

"Hello, Steve," he said.

"Bob. This is Neal Carey." Steve said.

Bob took off the canvas glove and offered his hand. "Nice to meet you. What can I do you for, Steve?"

"Got a calf you can sell me? I got a cow giving too much milk."

"Well . . . I don't have anything really good I can spare."

"Don't need anything really good."

"Well . . . then I got a mixed-breed Angus and Charolais heifer

I could let you have, might be good for some table beef down the road."

"She'll do."

"Come take a look at her."

He led them to a corral behind the barn where a few cows and calves were lazily swatting at flies with their tails. Hansen pointed at a long-legged calf the color of mud.

"That's the one," said Hansen.

"How'd she happen?" Steve asked.

"Ohhh, back up in the mountains during spring pasture, I suppose," Hansen said with an edge of irritation. "The two hands I had up there weren't too careful about keeping the herds separated. You know cowboys these days, they know it's a cow and that's about all they know or want to know. Half of them move on after the first payday."

Say, Mr. Hansen, Neal thought, you wouldn't have a cowboy named Harley McCall working for you, would you?

"How much will you take for her?" Steve asked.

"Hardly worth me feeding her—she'll never do much. A hundred?"

"Sounds fair."

Steve opened his wallet and handed Hansen two fifties.

"Thank you," Hansen said. "I do appreciate it."

"How's the bull business these days?"

"Terrible. Federal government's going to put me out of business. They make all these regulations that mean I have to buy new equipment, but then the bank won't give me the loan to buy it."

Steve Mills took his cap off, shook his head, and then put the cap back on. "That's ridiculous, Bob. Bill Bradshaw knows that you're one of the best ranchers in Nevada."

"Bill don't own the bank anymore. It got bought by some California outfit."

Steve shook his head again. "Things change, don't they?"

"Too much. Had some government inspector from Reno out here

snooping around my dairy, saying it's a health hazard. Saying my milk's 'unsafe.' "

Neal heard the indignation in the man's voice.

"Shit," said Steve.

"Of course," Hansen continued, his voice starting to rise, "with the price you get for milk these days—and I mean the price *I* get, not the middlemen—I might as well go out of business, maybe just sit around and drink whiskey."

"Hey," Steve asked, "would you mind giving Neal here a tour of your place? He's from New York City. It'd be an education for him. While you're doing that, I'll wrestle this calf here into my truck."

"Oh, a man from New York wouldn't be interested in my operation."

Actually, Mr. Hansen, this man from New York would be very interested in looking around your operation. Neal said, "I'd like to see it if you feel like showing it to me."

Hansen shook his head a little but looked pleased nevertheless. "Well, come on."

When he stepped into the livestock barn Neal wished that Joe Graham were there with him. Graham would have loved it—the long narrow building was immaculate. The floors had been scrubbed and disinfected, the stanchions shone from metal polish, the equipment glistened.

"This is really something," Neal said. And he meant it—anyone could see the dedication and hard work that went into Hansen's operation.

"Thank you. Care to see the rest?"

"Yes, please."

Hansen gave him the tour. He showed Neal the neatly laid out barns, the tool shop, the equipment shed. He took him along the different pastures that separated the breeds of cattle and explained how he rotated the grazing schedules to let the land refresh itself. He pointed out the wooded slopes above the pasture that he had left pristine so he could hunt deer for the meat locker and take firewood from the deadfall.

He took him around to the large garden—almost a farm in itself—behind the house where he grew all of the vegetables for their table.

"How many people work here?" Neal asked.

"Oh . . . that depends on the season and the economy. Right now only about twelve. That's not including my boy Jory and the cook. My wife used to do the cooking, but since the cancer took her . . ." His voice trailed off. "We ought to get back to Steve."

"Thanks for the tour."

"My pleasure, young man," Hansen answered. Then he added shyly, "Thank you for your interest."

Steve was leaning against the truck. The calf stood trembling in the truck bed.

"Sorry you had to load her yourself," Hansen said. "The hands are up bringing a herd in for inoculations and I think Jory's out running around with your Shelly."

He chuckled a little and Steve joined in, a shared joke between fathers of teenagers.

Steve said, "Youth will be served."

"I suppose."

"Aw, Bob, it's just one of those homecoming king and queen things. They ain't gonna run off and get married or nothing."

"No, I guess not."

"Well, you take care, Bob."

"Yup. Nice to meet you, Neal."

"Nice to meet you, sir."

Bob's head came up a little on the "sir" and he gave Neal an evaluating look before he turned around and headed back to the barn.

"Climb in the back and hold on to that calf, will you, Neal? Steve asked.

"Do you have a rope?"

"Yep. At home where I forgot it. Just get a headlock on the calf and keep it from jumping out or tumbling around."

Neal found that the only way he could get a headlock on the calf was by kneeling on the metal bed of the truck. This wasn't too bad until the truck got bumping down the road, bouncing Neal's knees off the steel studs with every rut, rock, and jolt, of which there were about two thousand. Neal winced, groaned, whimpered, and finally cursed every time his kneecaps slammed into the steel, but he held on to the calf.

The calf wasn't all that thrilled either. Bawling and trembling, she let loose a stream of urine all over both of Neal's pant legs. Neal could feel it soaking through and sticking to his legs, but he held on to the calf until the truck took a particularly daredevil bounce and the calf squirmed out of Neal's hold and attempted to jump over the back end. Neal sprawled on his stomach and managed to get a hold of her left rear leg.

This was a tactical error, because it left her right rear leg free. Not a calf to miss an opportunity, she hauled off and gave him a Bruce Lee to the diaphragm. Neal got a grip on the hoof implanted in his chest and managed to flip the calf over onto his lap, discovering that a baby cow weighs a lot more than the baby person he'd probably never be able to have, judging by the sudden pain in his crotch. But he held on to the calf.

He could hear Steve happily singing along to some tune on the radio about a mother not letting her babies grow up to be cowboys or something, which Neal didn't think was very funny. But the calf must have liked it, because she let out a big sigh and relaxed in his lap. She felt so relaxed she let loose the contents of her bowels on those parts of his pant legs that she'd missed soaking with urine. Neal kind of wished that Steve had remembered that rope, but he held on to the calf, stroked her neck, and cooed soothing endearments. He hurt like crazy from the earlier beating, but he held on to the calf.

Steve stopped the truck by the back of the Mills' house, got out, and took a look at Neal and the calf.

"She piss and shit on you?"

"Yeah."

"Yeah, they'll do that. Do you two want to snuggle some more or shall we introduce her to her new mama?"

He dropped the back gate and the calf scrambled out the back end.

Steve opened a rickety wood and wire gate and shooed her into the small corral behind the barn.

Neal stepped in behind him. The sun was getting low and the sky was turning a soft salmon pink. The air was crisp and cool. Neal could see how you could fall in love with all of this and never want to leave.

"Now the fun begins," Steve said.

"I don't know if I can stand any more fun."

"See, Eleanor has a calf of her own and she's too dumb to figure out we're trying to help her by bringing in this young interloper. So even though she needs another calf to suck on those udders, she's going to resist. She'll try to kick that calf, and if I know Eleanor like I do know Eleanor, she'll try to kick it square in the head."

No, Neal thought. She's not going to kill that calf. I have two broken knees, a purple chest, I'm covered with shit and soaked with piss, and I've become kind of possessive of that calf.

"So what do we do?" Neal asked.

"Well, we do a number of things. See, these are range cattle. They're about half-wild anyway, and long about dusk they hide their calves in the brush on the lower slope. So first we have to find Eleanor's calf before the lions or the coyotes do—"

"Lions?"

"Mountain lions—and then drive the little thing back to the barn. Eleanor'll follow even though she already suspects an ambush. Then we finagle Eleanor into a stanchion, sneak around her backside, and tie a rope around her hips so it pinches a nerve and hurts if she tries to kick. Then we introduce the new calf to its new lunch counter, which won't be difficult because a calf will just naturally go for it, if you know what I mean. After the new calf sucks for a while, Eleanor'll forget it ain't really hers and then she'll take care of it."

"Lions?"

"They're scared of people."

Oh, good.

"However," Steve said, "I'm going to bring the rifle along, just in case."

"In case of what?"

"In case we run across a psychotic one or some goofball survivalist who figures that taking my calves is cheaper and easier than raising his own. I could use your help. Two is a lot better than one when you're trying to drive cows on foot, and it would save me the trouble of saddling up a horse. Besides which, the doctor told me I should take a daily constitutional."

"Sure." I would never pass up a chance for a sundown confrontation with a lion and/or goofball survivalist rustler, Neal thought.

They walked back to the house and Steve took a 30.06 lever-action rifle off a rack in the kitchen. Then they hiked for about ten minutes down through the sagebrush toward the base of the mountain. They came to the tree line Neal had seen from the window, and sure enough, it screened a shallow creek that ran at the bottom of a deep gully. Sandbars flanked the creek on both sides and it was easy to cross the stream by stepping on rocks and then jumping onto the sand.

They walked a couple more minutes and reached the bottom of the big spur of the mountain.

"The mountains themselves are government land," Steve said. "The spur here is the southern boundary of my land and Hansen's."

At the base of the spur, almost dug into the north slope, was a small log cabin.

"Whose is that?" Neal asked.

"It's ours," Steve answered. "It was here before I was. Probably an old miner's place. You'll find abandoned shafts all over these hills. Or it was a station for the cowboys to sleep in when they came to get the cattle down from the hills for the winter. We've had a couple of hired hands stay in it from time to time."

They didn't run across any mountain lions or beef-crazed survivalists. They did find Eleanor, an enormous black-and-white cow, who promptly led them in the wrong direction.

Or tried to, anyway.

"Eleanor's getting predictable in her middle years," Steve said. "If she heads east you can be damn sure that junior's lying under a bush somewhere to the west."

He was. A cute, big-eyed little squirt who looked a little grateful to have the game of hide-and-go-seek end so quickly. He got up on shaky legs as Eleanor trotted over protectively. Steve gave her a poke on the flanks with the rifle butt.

"To the barn, dumb ol' Eleanor."

It took about forty minutes to drive the cows back and another twenty to lure Eleanor's head into the stanchion by putting a big handful of aromatic alfalfa into the trough. Eleanor took the bait and Steve slammed the stanchion shut, just getting his hand out of the way before Eleanor swung her head in a violent effort to crush his fingers.

"We're both getting a little slower, old girl," Steve said without any bitterness Neal could detect. Then Steve snuck around her backside, dodged her kick, tossed a rope over her hips, grabbed it behind her udder, and pulled it tight. He tied it off on a post and stood back. She started to give a kick, suddenly changed her mind, and gave an aggravated bellow instead. Then she settled down and started chewing on the hay. Her calf instantly slid in and started to suck.

"Go get the new one, will you?" Steve asked. He took a quick look around, reached behind another stanchion, and pulled out a pack of Luckys.

Neal walked out into the corral, found his calf huddled up against the fence, and shooed it into the barn. It took one look at Eleanor's swollen udder and nuzzled up. She tried another feeble kick, gave up, and apparently decided that she was the mother of twins as the calves happily nudged, pushed, and nuzzled against her.

Steve took a contented drag on his cigarette as he watched the scene.

"I love this country," he said.

He had loved it from the moment he saw it, he told Neal over dinner, twenty-odd years ago when he and Peggy had given up the ghost trying to grow lettuce in California. They had packed what little they owned into their "Fix or Repair Daily" and headed east to Reno, where Steve drew a ten to a king down. This started a streak that

Peggy capped off with a hot hand and three straight dice rolls that each added up to seven.

They thought they might treat themselves to a little vacation and headed east out of Reno, finally ending up in the Reese River valley. She loved it too, so they ended their vacation early, bought this chunk of land, got a good deal on an old trailer, and settled in.

Steve got a job driving a mining truck over on Round Mountain and Peggy waited tables at the one diner in town. They used their spare hours to clear enough land for a corral and a barn.

Peggy started the garden, lost most of it to bugs and rabbits, and then started it again behind a wire fence that represented about a month of tip money. Steve joined a few of their new friends on some jack-lighting expeditions and put a winter's worth of venison in the freezer he'd bought fourth-hand from Brogan's place in town.

They lived in the trailer for two years before they saved enough money for a house. Two years of his wrestling trucks around treacherous switchbacks. Two years of her pouring coffee, flipping burgers, and putting down whispered remarks about her "neat little rear" with a withering glance, and once twisting the arm half off a trucker who gave her neat little rear a pat. Two years of saving every penny except for their twice-a-month expedition into town—twenty miles away—to drink a few beers and dance a few dances at Phil and Margie's Country Cabaret to the country tunes of New Red and the Mountain Men. (Old Red having been caught with half an acre of marijuana behind his house and the Mountain Men being composed of two men and two women.)

Steve and Peggy built the house themselves after Kermit Wolff had put in the foundation. They started in May and had the roof party in mid-September, about half of north central Nevada showing up to help them raise the damn thing and polish off the beers chilling in ice in the horse trough. They had one hell of a party, and Peggy shed a few tears when the young Shoshone from down by Ione hauled off the old trailer. Steve got real busy finishing the house when Peggy came home from Fallon with the news that she'd done in a rabbit with something other than her pellet gun.

Shelly was born in the middle of winter. There were problems with the birth and weren't going to be any more babies. Peggy was pretty down about that, but Steve didn't care because he loved that little girl positively to distraction.

Neal could see why just as soon as Shelly came bursting in the door a good minute before dinner hit the table.

She had her father's eyes and smile and her mother's strong features. Her chestnut hair was shoulder length and thick—Peggy swore that she had broken scissors trying to trim it once. She dug into her steak and baked potato with the voracious appetite of the young, guileless, and guiltless.

She was a junior in high school. Biology and chemistry were her best subjects, English and history her worst, meaning that she had to work for her A's in them. She wanted to go to the University of Nevada and then on to either med school or vet school, because she couldn't decide which she wanted to help more, people or animals. She had succumbed to classmates' pressure and become a cheer-leader, although she thought it was pretty boring and a little silly. She'd rather have spent the time with one of the horses, or helping out on the place, or taking long rides with Jory up on the trails in the mountains.

She was a secure kid from a secure home. She knew her parents loved her and each other, and she loved them back.

She also loved Jory Hansen. They planned to go to Reno together and get married after they established their careers, she a medico of some type, he a crusading district attorney. Her parents didn't disabuse her of her plans by telling her all of the things that usually happened to a relationship on the long trek through college. She was a level-headed kid and she'd take it all in stride.

She had clearly been told by her mother to suppress her natural curiosity about their house guest, and for the first twenty minutes avoided asking Neal the three thousand questions she had about the world outside of Austin.

"How was your afternoon with Jory?" Peggy asked her between bites of cherry pie, by way of rescuing Neal.

"Fine," she answered.

Peggy picked up on it. For her exuberant daughter, "fine" was a barely positive description.

"Why? What's wrong?" Peggy asked.

"I don't know. He's been a little quiet lately."

"Jory Hansen's never been exactly a chatterbox," Peggy said.

Shelly hesitated. "He seems angry," she said.

"Honey, I think he's been a little angry since his mother died," Peggy answered.

Peggy knew how he felt. She was angry too. Barb Hansen had been one of her closest friends. They had raised their babies together, helped each other through all of the childhood illnesses and injuries, sipped on a little wine together when the men were up in the hills cutting timber or hunting. They had spent long summer afternoons down at the creek, watching their kids splash around in the water and trading notes on marriage, business, cooking, ranching, and just plain stuff. She missed Barb Hansen too.

And Jory—short for Jordan—was such a sensitive kid. Much more like his mom than his dad. It was a hard loss for him.

"That's three years, Mom."

"I know."

"He talks strange lately."

"Strangely," Peggy corrected, "and what do you mean?"

"I don't know. Politics. How the country's changing. He talks like a right-wing Republican or something."

"I knew there was a reason I liked that boy," Steve observed.

"He just seems angry," Shelly repeated. "It scares me a little."

"Maybe you ought to go out with other boys," Steve suggested, ducking his head closer to his pie to avoid his daughter's sharp eye.

"What other boys? Jory's the only one around here who thinks that there might be more to life than roping cows," Shelly answered. "Besides, I love him."

"There's always that," Steve answered and the conversation turned to the local economy, politics, and the usual topics that people discuss when they're getting to know one another.

And then the conversation turned to Neal.

He pretty much made the cover story up as he went along, letting it out little by little, playing at being shy and embarrassed but always observing the number-one rule of a good cover: stay as close to the truth as you can.

So he told them he'd been in graduate school in New York, that he'd fallen in love with a woman who broke his heart, and how all of a sudden life didn't make any sense anymore and he just needed to get away to think.

So by the time he was into the second piece of pie and the third cup of coffee he was telling them how he'd flown to the West Coast, hadn't found what he was looking for there, and decided to buy a cheap car and work his way back east.

All of which was technically true in its parts and a complete lie in its whole. The essence of a good cover story.

After dinner they repaired into the living room. Shelly went upstairs to take a shower and go to bed early.

Neal sank into the sofa and took the glass of scotch that Steve handed him. It smelled a little like the smoke from the charcoal fires in the monastery kitchen. He took a sip and let it linger in his mouth a moment before he swallowed it. It felt like a blanket wrapping around him.

"You look like you've been rode hard and put up wet," Steve said to him.

Neal had no idea what he meant but nodded anyway. He took another swallow of the whiskey and drew the blanket a little tighter around himself.

Peggy came in from the kitchen. She had a drink in her hand and a serious look on her face. She sat down next to Neal on the sofa.

"Steve and I were thinking," she said. "Steve could use a little help around the place. Winter will be here before we know it and we have a lot of hay to put up, that sort of thing. We'd probably need to hire someone anyway, and as long as you're here . . ."

"We couldn't pay much," Steve said. "But you can have the spare bedroom here, and the food is great."

And so is the location, Neal thought.

"How about if I lived in that cabin up on the spur?" he asked.

The Mills laughed.

"You don't want to live out there," Peggy said. "It's filthy, for one thing. It's cold, it's isolated . . ."

Well, I'm not going to be here long enough for it to get cold, Mrs. Mills, and isolation is just what I need to conduct my little search for Harley and Cody McCall.

"Neal might want some privacy, Peggy," said Steve.

"There's not even any electricity. Just that old wood stove."

"I'll be fine," Neal said. "And I'll work for the rent on the place and a few supplies to get me started. I have a little money in the bank at home I can have sent out."

"Are you sure?" Peggy asked.

"I think this is what I've been looking for," Neal said.

Or it's damn close, anyway.

4

*T*he next morning Steve and Neal drove into town to get supplies.

They didn't have to do a lot of walking around; the town had one store. It didn't have a name—people just called it "the store." Even Evelyn Phillips called it "the store," and she had owned it for thirty years. She figured that if another store ever came to town, then she'd give her store a name, although Steve allowed that if that unlikely situation ever came to pass, people would probably still call Evelyn's store "the store" and call the other store "the other store."

Evelyn also owned the town's one restaurant across the street. It even had a name: Wong's. Wong's had red paper lanterns, Chinese fans on the walls, and a big dragon textile inside the front door and it didn't serve a smidgen of Chinese food. Hadn't since Wong died back in 1968 and Wong's wife and children eagerly moved back to San Francisco. Evelyn bought the restaurant and, at the prompting of grateful customers, changed the menu. Everyone had always liked the decor, though, so that stayed.

"Worst Chinese food in the West," Evelyn told Neal.

"God awful," Steve agreed.

She hadn't gone in much for decorations in the store, though. People didn't come in to browse, they came in to pick up things they needed. The men who came in just wanted to get their stuff and get back to work—or steal an hour at Brogan's. The women had already memorized the inventory, so they spent their time in the store talking—exchanging news and gossip. Most of the places outside of town didn't have telephones yet, so the store was the place for a catch-up with the neighbors.

With Steve's advice, Neal picked out a couple of pairs of heavy jeans, three denim work shirts, a pair of work boots, and a hat. Steve had cajoled him into trying on a cowboy hat, but Neal looked so embarrassed—with good reason, Steve agreed—that they settled for an Allis-Chalmers ball cap. Then they picked out some canned goods, cooking stuff, frozen meat, and that sort of thing.

"Is this cash or on your tab, Steve?" Evelyn asked as they set the stuff down on the counter. She was a tall woman in her early sixties. She'd played trombone in an all-girl band in California back in the old days and then figured she wanted something a lot different. She never married, although the rumor was that she had regular alliances with a couple of the businessmen who traveled through periodically.

Steve looked over to Neal.

"Cash," Neal said.

Evelyn didn't flinch at the hundred-dollar bill he laid down.

"Speaking of tabs," she said to Steve, "you haven't seen Paul Wallace around, have you?"

Say what? Say who? Whom? Neal slowly put his change back in his wallet and examined his purchases. Which Paul Wallace is she talking about?

"Paul Wallace . . ." Steve said, testing the sound to see if it rang a bell.

"I believe he's one of Hansen's hands," Evelyn said. "Came in here and ran a tab against his pay, and I haven't seen him since. Been about three weeks. Hansen pays every two, doesn't he?"

"Yeah. Kinda tall? Blond? Nice-looking guy?" Steve asked.

Harley McCall. Neal wished he had a chance to slap the real Paul Wallace all over again. Son of a bitch should have told me that they *switched* identities. Then again, I should have thought to ask.

"Yeah, that's him. I usually don't give credit unless they've been around awhile, but he had this cute little boy with him, and he was buying kids' stuff—cereal, cookies . . ."

Neal wondered if they noticed the bass drum banging in the room—his heart beating a fast, steady boom-boom-boom.

Steve said, "Sorry, Evelyn, I haven't seen him around in at least three weeks. Course, there's no reason I would. I'm not over to Hansen's much. I can ask Shelly to ask Jory if you want."

Evelyn shook her head. "No, I don't want to embarrass the man. But if you run into Hansen, tell him to tell his cowboy to come see me. Course, he's probably moved on somewhere and stiffed me."

I hope not, Evelyn. Boy, do I hope not.

"Cute kid, though," Evelyn observed.

Neal put his stuff in the back of the pickup as Steve looked over to Brogan's.

"I hate to waste gasoline on one errand," Steve said.

"I'll meet you over there," Neal answered. "I want to make a call."

He walked down to the gas station, where there was a phone booth. He dialed an 800 number.

"Give me one reason I shouldn't fire you right now," Levine said as he came on the phone.

"I think I've found McCall," Neal answered.

"Okay, that's one reason. Tell us where, we'll have a crew on the next plane."

"Too soon," Neal answered. He told him about his conversation with Paul Wallace, his visit with Doreen, his luck with the Mills family, and what he had found out at the store.

"He may have moved on or he may be just lying low at the ranch," Neal said. "Wait until I find out which."

Joe Graham came on the line. "Where the hell have you been? I've been worried sick."

"Sorry, Dad. Ed can fill you in. I'm fine."

"Let me put a crew in place, anyway," Ed said.

"There's nowhere to put one, Ed. You'd spook everybody. I have to get going."

He saw Cal Strekker coming. And there was something . . . just something . . .

Ed said, "Now Neal, just try to locate him. Don't do anything, you got that? We've done some research on the True Identity Church, and—"

"Ed, activate that cover story."

"Neal, what are you doing?" Ed demanded.

Strekker was getting closer.

"Ed, just get me covered! I have to go!"

"Carey, you don't—"

Neal hung up the phone. Cal Strekker was walking right past him.

"Bitch!" Neal shouted to the phone.

Cal stopped and sneered. "Woman trouble?" he asked.

"Is there any other kind?" Neal answered.

"Stick to whores," Cal answered. "You pay 'em, you poke 'em, they give you any shit, you smoke 'em."

Okaaaay, Neal thought.

Levine buzzed down to the operator.

"Where?" he asked.

"Austin, Nevada."

Levine looked at Graham. "It's possible."

Graham nodded. Since the failed bag job they had devoted their energies to researching Carter's church. What they had learned was disturbing.

"We should start working the other end," Levine said.

"Yeah. But carefully. If we screw up we could get the kid killed," said Graham.

"Which kid?" Levine asked. "Cody McCall or Neal Carey?"

"Both."

Neal walked into Brogan's just behind Cal Strekker. There was a beer waiting for him on the bar. He had to step over a sleeping Brezhnev to get to it. Brogan was snoozing in his chair.

"Get your call made?" Steve asked.

"Yeah."

Neal didn't volunteer any more information and Steve didn't ask for any. Strekker grabbed a beer from the fridge and moved down to the end of the bar to his customary stool.

"Doesn't Hansen expect you to do any work?" Steve asked him. It was a joking tone, but it had an edge on it.

"Got a big load of barbed wire in the truck," Cal answered. "Thought I'd stop off for a beer, if that's okay with you."

"It's okay with me," said Steve. "What's Bob got you doing? Making another breeding pen?"

"I expect if Mr. Hansen wants to discuss his business with you, he will."

Which in that part of Nevada came pretty damn close to rudeness.

Steve nodded. "Cal, I've known Bob Hansen for nigh unto twenty years. I helped him build some of those fences he's got on his place. In those days we used to take turns, helping each other bring our herds down for the winter. That's before he could afford top-talent professional cowboys like you."

"We should be getting back," Neal said.

"No hurry," Steve said. The edge was a little sharper.

"I'm not a cowboy," Cal answered. "I'm a mechanic. And head of security." Steve guffawed and sprayed beer out his mouth. Some of it landed on Brezhnev and he woke up and growled, which woke Brogan up too. He gave Steve an evil eye and settled back into his chair.

"Security!" Steve bellowed. "What does Bob Hansen need security for?"

"Rustlers. Horse thieves."

"Shit," Steve said, chuckling.

"There've been some rustlers around," Strekker said defensively.

Steve downed his whiskey chaser. "Oh, hell, I know that. I lost a cow just last week. I figure it's only some old back-to-the-earth hippies with a flashlight and a truck. Maybe two or three Paiutes from the res who spent their government checks on hooch and need to feed their kids. Hardly the goddamn James gang. And as for horse thieves, why are they going to take a shot at your remuda when the whole valley is lousy with herds of mustangs eating our cows' grass? Thanks to the goddamn federal government, by the way. Head of security.''

Cal Strekker flushed with anger. "You can sure talk, Mills, that's for sure.''

"That's 'Mr. Mills' to you. Or 'Steve.' Now, why don't you do something useful, head of security, and tell Paul Wallace to pay his tab at the store.''

The name struck a nerve.

"Wallace moved on," Strekker said.

Neal saw Strekker's eyes widen just a bit, saw the intake of breath that held just a little too long. You're lying, Neal thought. Harley/Paul McCall/Wallace has not moved on.

"Then tell Hansen," Mills said.

"If Evelyn loaned Wallace money, that's between her and Wallace. It doesn't have anything to do with the Hansen Cattle Company.''

Steve stood up and put his hat on. "I'll tell you what," he said to Strekker. "You tell Bob Hansen what I've told you, and he'll drive in here personally, apologize to Evelyn, and pay the money with interest.''

"You think so, huh?" Strekker sneered.

"I know Bob Hansen.''

I wonder if you do, Neal thought. I wonder if you do. He followed Steve onto the street.

Steve hopped into the truck, pulled a cigarette from the glove compartment, and lit it up. He exhaled some of his anger with the smoke.

"He pisses me off," Steve said. "Bob's hired himself some real losers lately, all right. Come-lately, drifter trash. No offense," he added quickly.

"No problem. I thought for a second there was going to be a fight back there.''

"Me too," Steve chuckled. "Well, it would have sparked up an otherwise dull morning. Let's go back and get you settled in your new home on the range."

Yeah, and then find out just how good security is in the Hansen Cattle Company.

They drove as close as they could to the cabin. The truck bounced and protested but moved across the hard-packed sagebrush. They stopped just shy of the creek and then carried the supplies across.

A big black horse, loosely tied to a branch, was grazing lazily.

"That's Dash," Steve said, "Shelly's favorite."

Shelly and Peggy were in the cabin, cleaning furiously.

They'd done a great job. The cabin was a small, square one room. A metal bed occupied a corner in the back. The bed had just been made up with fresh sheets, an army blanket, and an Indian blanket. An old barrel sufficed for a nightstand. A kerosene lamp on the barrel would serve as a reading light.

On the opposite wall to the right of the door was a counter and a sink with shelves beneath. A plump wood stove sat to the left of the door. Two small screen windows let in air and light.

"You can cover those with plastic when it gets cold," Peggy said, "if you end up staying that long. I brought some old cast-iron pans and a pot we don't use anymore. Also a few plates, cups, silver-ware."

"Thank you," said Neal.

"Glad to get rid of them. There's a lister bag out there for you boys to hang up."

They went outside. Steve took the big green canvas bag, tied a rope to a ring at the top, hoisted it up on a branch near the creek, and tied it off on the tree trunk.

"Just fill it with water from the creek, hoist it back up, turn the spigot, and you have a shower," he said. Then he showed Neal where the outhouse was, behind the cabin hidden in some pines. It was a little bigger than a phone booth and had a bench with a hole in it.

"Here's how you flush," Steve said. He poured a little gasoline down the hole, lit a match and tossed it in. "That usually does it."

Shelly was in the saddle when they got back.

"You want a ride, Neal?" she asked.

"No thanks."

"Have you ever been on a horse?" she asked.

"Sure, and I almost caught the brass ring."

"You're just afraid," she teased.

"You're just right," answered Neal.

"Where are you headed, honey?" Steve asked.

"I'm going for a ride with Jory. Up there." She nodded toward the mountains.

"Where is he?"

"He didn't want to wait. We're going to meet up at the spring below the caves."

"You stay out of those caves!" Peggy hollered from the cabin.

Shelly rolled her eyes in mock exasperation. "Don't worry! They give me the creeps!" she said. She pointed toward the cabin door. "Ever vigilant."

Then she gave Dash a little kick in the ribs and set out at a trot up the lower slopes of the mountain. She waved good-bye without turning back.

"Well," Steve said as much to himself as to Neal, "I suppose it's better than her hanging around some mall all day."

Peggy came out on the porch.

"Do you suppose they're sleeping together?" she asked evenly.

"Peg! Jesus!"

"I'm not saying they are, Steve," she said. "But we should look at the possibility."

"Maybe it isn't better than hanging around some mall," Steve considered.

They tinkered around the cabin for a little while longer, making sure Neal was all set up, and then left to let him get settled in and have some privacy. They invited him to dinner, but Neal said that he might just as well get started in being self-sufficient.

Besides, he had some things to do.

* * *

First of all he laid out his stuff. It didn't take long. He had his new work clothes, some of his old street wear, and his new breaking-and-entering regulation black jersey, jeans, socks, tennis shoes, and cap. He had the dog-eared paperback of Smollet's *Roderick Random* which had saved him from going crazy during his three years' confinement in Sichuan.

He took his collection of racist literature—*The Turner Diaries, The Zion Watchman* newsletter, and a couple of C. Wesley Carter's cheaply printed tracts—and hid them where anyone tossing the place could find them.

Then he unpacked his binoculars, the little Peterson bird glasses that came so highly recommended by one Joseph Graham, and went for a hike.

He climbed up the north side of the spur, pulling himself up the flaky ground by grabbing onto pines, until he came to a shelf of rock on the top. He edged around that, gained another fifty feet of elevation, and walked along until he found what he was looking for.

It was a little outcrop on the south side of the spur. A small grove of aspens provided cover but left enough of the view; a lovely panorama of the main compound of Hansen's a thousand or so yards down and away from his perch.

My hunch was right, Neal thought with an unbecoming degree of satisfaction. Just as the slope of the ground shields my cabin from Mills', so does the same geography create dead ground behind Hansen's. Except the dead ground is quite lively this late Saturday afternoon.

First of all, he could see the construction even with the naked eye. It was a frigging stockade. The center building was a large bunker—basically rectangular, but with circular gun ports built at the corners to provide a field of fire that could sweep all of the ground around it. It was built low to the ground with a sandbagged roof, over which was stretched a net stuffed with sagebrush. Neal imagined that the foundation was dug deep into the ground to protect against explosives.

There were three smaller bunkers on the other side of the main one. They were all circles of poured concrete; two had gun slits barely aboveground. Neal guessed that they were supply dumps of some sort, perhaps for food and ammunition. The other one looked like it might be for prisoners. All were similarly camouflaged in sagebrush.

Somebody knows what the hell he's doing, Neal thought. A casual observer from the trails along the mountain would barely pick this out, and if he did it would look like an old mining operation or cattle pen. The bunkers would be impervious from fire directed from the mountain slopes. You'd need artillery or at least mortars to do any serious damage, and who was going to haul that up here? But the fort clearly had been constructed to defend against an attack coming from the valley, not the mountains. A charge across the flat sagebrush plain into these bunkers would be suicidal folly.

Three sides of the compound were flanked by a twelve-foot-high chain-link fence topped with barbed wire. The fourth side, the one that faced the Hansen house, was the one under construction at the moment. It looked like they were trying to build the fence to allow a gate to open onto a dirt trail that cut all the way back to the main Hansen compound. Even now men were unrolling wire along the trail.

What are they expecting? Neal wondered. Armageddon?

They probably are, he thought. Probably the idea would be to give up the big house and withdraw to the stockade. Fight it out there until the good guys win.

Neal put the field glasses to his eyes and adjusted the lenses for distance. Even with the powerful binoculars, the busy figures were indistinct against the dull gray of the sagebrush-covered ground. Neal could just make out the figure of Bob Hansen, mostly because of the cowboy hat. Neal scanned the compound to see if he could locate the rangy figure of Cal Strekker, but he didn't find him.

Maybe he's in one of the bunkers, Neal thought. Maybe Harley McCall and Cody are too. Maybe I should be as well.

Neal watched for a few minutes longer and then pulled off the outcrop and found himself a place to sit among the pines farther back.

There was no sense in being exposed for too long, and he wanted to wait until the light got a little softer before trying to get any closer.

If McCall and the boy are in that compound, he thought while he sat, it isn't going to be any easy bag job. I don't care how much high-priced muscle Ed can bring in, we aren't getting the kid out of there. We're going to have to find a way to lure Harley and the boy off the place and then take them. And I don't have a clue yet how to do that.

Neal waited for an hour before he got up and started to ease himself along the slope closer to the stockade. He figured that even a couple hundred yards might give him a shot at recognizing faces, primarily to see if Harley was one of them, but also to start getting an idea of just how many people they'd be up against.

Then the thought hit him with almost nauseating force: just how the hell many people know about this? Shit. Jory Hansen certainly, the same kid who is on a trail ride with Shelly Mills, the daughter of my friends Steve and Peggy. Do I tell them?

The second wave hit him: or do they already know?

Old friends . . . good neighbors . . . Steve's remarks about the "goddamn federal government" . . . Steve from California . . . a rancher Harley knew from California . . .

Suddenly he couldn't breathe.

A hand pressed tight against his mouth. A knee pressed into the small of his back while the forearm pulled him up and backward, arching his spine to the breaking point and threatening to snap his neck.

"You're a dead man," a voice hissed. The point of a combat knife pressed against Neal's ribs.

Well, Neal thought, at least I've found Cal Strekker.

To Neal's disappointment, Strekker didn't take him to the compound. Instead he dragged him to a clearing farther along the ridge and slammed him down at the base of a small cedar.

He chose the spot pretty well, Neal thought. You can't see or be seen from here.

Cal talked quietly into a small field radio. Neal made out the word *intruder*.

"Mr. Hansen's on his way up," Strekker said. "But maybe I should just kill you and tell him you tried to escape."

His voice had a dangerous edge to it. His eyes were shining with an excitement that was almost sexual. Psychotic. Neal knew all about psychotic—he had ridden the Broadway local train for years. So he also knew there was only one way to treat this kind of violent crazy, the type that gets his jollies off other people's fear.

Strekker unholstered his pistol and waved it in front of Neal. "Why don't I just blow your face off right now?"

"Why don't you just eat me?"

He watched Cal's face turn red. With the blush and the orange beard he looked like a mutant tomato. He was furious, but Neal saw something else come onto that face: uncertainty.

"You think you're a tough guy?" Strekker asked.

"No, but I'll do until the real thing comes along."

"It has come along, shithead."

Neal laughed. "You?"

There is a definite ebb and flow to this kind of interaction, Neal thought. Cal's tide is going out.

"What are you doing up here?" Cal asked.

"What's it to you?" Neal asked. "Oh, that's right. You're the dickhead of security."

And a pretty damn good one, I must admit. I sure as hell never heard you coming. Fine "operational shape" I'm in. But you're good. You're very good. I'm going to have to find a way to deal with you before I can get Cody McCall back to his mother.

Strekker clicked the hammer back and pointed the gun in Neal's face. "This is a 9 mm. Do you know what that would do to your head?"

Neal felt the almost paralyzing pins and needles of terror. He wanted to curl up in a little ball and cry.

But that would probably get me killed, he thought. So he answered, "Has anyone ever talked to you about handguns as phallic symbols? Listen, Cal, genital size isn't everything. There's also charm, good grooming, a sense of humor . . .''

Cal holstered the pistol.

"Get on your feet," he said. "I'm going to beat the hell out of you."

Neal had no doubt that if he got to his feet Cal would beat the hell out of him, so he stayed on his butt and said, "You're going to do shit. Hansen's on his way here? I'll deal with the boss, not the hired help."

He leaned back against the tree and closed his eyes. He didn't open them again until he heard footsteps.

Hansen wasn't alone. He had brought one of the other hands with him. A thick, broad-shouldered short man with black hair and a beard.

"Get up," Cal barked at Neal.

Neal made himself get to his feet very slowly. He dusted off his jeans and looked at Hansen.

Hansen said, "What are you—"

"Just hold on a second," Neal cut him off. "I have a question for you. I'm out taking a simple walk on public land and your goon here jumps me, holds a knife to my ribs, points his gun at my nose, and holds me prisoner. I make that three counts of assault, plus kidnapping and unlawful detention, and I'm holding you responsible. So you make sure you keep that ranch of yours in good order, because I want it nice and clean when I take possession."

Something Joe Graham taught him: when you're hopelessly on the defensive, attack. When they catch you red-handed, slap them with it. Neal dusted himself off some more and started to walk away. Cal's hand went to his gun.

"Government land starts another two hundred feet up," Hansen said. "You're on Hansen Cattle Company land. I have a right to protect my property against rustlers and horse thieves."

Neal spun around. "Where am I going to put a cow? In my pocket?"

"You could be scouting the place out," Hansen replied.

True enough, Neal thought.

"What are you doing with those field glasses?" Strekker demanded.

Scouting the place out.

Neal made a show of calming down. He stared at the ground as if trying to recover his temper, and then said in a tone of determined reasonableness, "I wanted to see a mountain lion."

Hansen and the black-haired man laughed.

"A mountain lion?" Hansen asked.

"Yeah, Steve Mills said there were mountain lions up here. I'm staying in his cabin, thought I'd take a walk and try to see one. I'm from New York. I've never seen anything like a mountain lion."

Neal watched as Bob Hansen tried to decide how to react. Cal Strekker's lupine grin left him in no doubt as to what would happen if Hansen gave the thumbs down.

"Well, you're a friend of Steve Mills," Hansen said, "so we'll give you the benefit of the doubt. But we'll be keeping an eye on you."

Which is when Neal decided to push it. "Jesus," he muttered just loud enough to be heard. "I might as well be back in the joint."

"What?" Hansen asked.

Neal opened up the tap on his feigned temper a little. "I said I might as well be back in the joint! I came out here so I wouldn't have people 'keeping an eye' on me!"

"Where were you in jail?"

"New York."

"What for?" Hansen asked.

Do I push it some more? Open it up, step on the gas, let it rip? Or do I play it safe? "Shooting a nigger," Neal answered, looking Bob Hansen straight in the eyes.

And the eyes told him that he had Hansen's interest.

"Well, hell," Hansen said. "I didn't think you could shoot a gun in New York and not hit a nigger."

His boys laughed.

"Mr. Hansen, I wish you'd been the judge," Neal said. "He took it pretty seriously."

"Did you kill him?"

"The judge?"

"The nigger."

"No. To tell you the truth, I'm not a very good shot."

More laughter. The atmosphere was starting to change.

We're getting to be buddies, Neal thought.

"What was he?" Hansen asked. "A pimp? A pusher?"

People will always tell you the answers they want to hear, Neal thought.

"Both."

"I'll bet the judge was a Jew," the black-haired man said.

They'll even tell your story for you if you just take the time to listen.

Neal nodded. "The judge and both lawyers. Mine told me to plead guilty. I got six to ten. Served three."

Hansen shook his head angrily. "That's the jew-dicial system we got. I'll bet the nigger is back out selling women and dope."

"I didn't look him up," Neal said. "Parole officers frown on that sort of thing."

"Your parole officer know you left the state?" Strekker asked.

Neal picked up on the tone of doubt.

"What do you think?" he answered sarcastically.

"So you're skipping," Strekker said.

Let's push it a little more, Neal thought. "I'm not going to live my life with Big Brother looking over my shoulder every minute, telling me what to do, what not to do, where I can work, who I can see. Seems like a white man can't be free back East. I thought it would be different here. I guess I was wrong. I'll stay off your land, Mr. Hansen, but you keep your eye on your own business," Neal said. Then he looked at Strekker, "And if you ever lay a hand on me again, I'll kill you where you stand or die trying." And, by the way, don't tread on me.

Strekker leered at him. Hansen was sizing him up as if Neal was a bull he was thinking about buying.

"You're a fighter," Hansen said.

"I don't want to be," Neal answered. "But if I'm pushed . . ."

"We're all being pushed, son," Hansen said. "But some of us have decided to push back."

Neal just shrugged.

"I can check out your story, you know," Hansen continued.

I'll bet you can, Neal thought. "It's not a story, Mr. Hansen. I wish it was."

"And if it turns out you're lying you'd best be long gone from this valley."

Mister, Ed Levine will have this cover story locked down so tight that *I* would believe it if I checked it out.

"And if it turns out to be true?" Neal asked.

"Then maybe I could use a man like you," answered Hansen.

And maybe I could use a man like you, Neal thought. But he said, "What for?"

Hansen smiled. "Depends. Let me ask you, Neal, what did you see from up here with those glasses?"

Do I lie? Do I bluff? If I lie and they don't buy it, I'm dead. But if I tell the truth and they don't like it, I'm dead.

So Neal gave them his best "ink blot" look, an enigmatic expression that allowed the other person to read into Neal's face whatever it was he wanted to read—lips curled into the slightest of smiles, eyes just a shade widened.

"Nothing," he said.

Hansen smiled back at him. "You'll be hearing from me," he said. Then he signaled to his boys to follow him and headed off down the slope.

Strekker bumped into Neal.

"You and me still have a date, shithead," he hissed as he walked away.

That is a distinct possibility, Neal thought.

He waited for a few minutes to let his heart slow down and started the hike back to the cabin.

Steve Mills was waiting for him with a gun.

"I forgot to give you this," he said just as Neal was about to drop into a fetal ball on the ground.

Steve looked at the binoculars. "Sightseeing?"

Neal ignored the question and gestured at the rifle. "What do I need that for?"

"You're a long way from the nearest policeman, Neal," Steve answered. "And a lot closer to the nearest cougar. Not to mention coyotes."

"Or goofball survivalists."

"Or goofball survivalists."

"I don't want to shoot a cougar or a coyote."

"Oh, hell, the noise will scare them away," Steve said.

"In that case . . ." Neal reached for the rifle.

"You know how to shoot one of these things?" asked Steve.

"Something to do with pulling a trigger, right?"

The rifle, Neal learned, was a Marlin 336. It had a lever action, a ten-round magazine, and shot 30/30 ammo. It weighed six pounds but seemed a lot heavier when Neal shot it and it bucked back against his shoulder. And it did make one hell of a noise.

"But don't you need this?" Neal asked through the sound of cathedral bells tolling in his ears.

"No," Steve answered. "I've got a regular arsenal back at the house. You collect these things over the years. You saw the Winchester. I have a Remington, a Savage combination, an old H&R twelve-gauge pump, even a few old handguns until the fed decide to collect them all. I guess I can spare you this one."

I guess you can.

"You oughta practice with this a little bit," Steve advised. "You never know."

"True enough," Neal answered.

He watched as Steve loped back across the sagebrush toward his place.

You never know, Neal thought.

He went back into the cabin, took a half hour or so to get a fire started in the stove, then another forty-five minutes to figure out the intricacies of an old-fashioned coffee percolator. By the time he made a pot it was dusk, and he took his hard-won cup out onto the small porch and watched the hard desert edges turn a soft rose. The Shoshone Mountains across the valley turned into indistinct silhouettes, first charcoal gray and then black. The sun blazed red for a finale and then dropped behind the mountains.

A moment later the coyotes started to howl.

Ed Levine was bored.

He was gazing out his office window at Times Square. He was leaning back in his chair, his feet propped on his desk, a cigarette smoldering in a saucer on the desk.

The flashing lights below were doing nothing for him. Neither were the sounds of the taxi horns and buses, nor the vaguely human sounds that reached up from the streets. He leaned over, took a drag of the cigarette, and leaned back again as the man on the other end of the phone went on and on and on.

The office door opened and Joe Graham walked in.

"Can you hold on a minute?" Ed asked the man on the phone.

He pushed the hold button, looked at Graham, and raised his eyebrows.

"It's all set up," Graham answered the unasked question.

"Good," Ed replied. He took a closer look at Graham. "You're worried."

"The kid hasn't been undercover like this for a long time. It's risky."

Ed nodded. "It always is."

Graham rubbed his artificial hand into the sweaty flesh of his real palm.

"I want to get closer," he said.

"It's too soon."

"I don't want it to be too late."

Ed frowned and gestured at the phone.

Graham set himself down in the chair across from the desk.

Ed frowned more and said, "If we get too close now we might burn him. Just be ready to go."

"I'm ready now."

Ed gestured impatiently toward the phone again. Graham showed no sign of moving from the chair.

"Okay," Ed said. "Start working out a cover for yourself. Now stop worrying and go have a couple of beers."

Graham got up. "I'll have the beers," he said from the doorway, "but I won't stop worrying." He closed the door behind him.

It is definitely time for a change, Ed thought.

He pushed the hold button again and started speaking before the other guy could. "Let's get down to business," Levine said. "Just what is it you need, Reverend Carter?"

Back out on The High Lonely, Jory Hansen sat at the bottom of the ravine. He was watching the moon.

When it was high and full, Jory hopped onto his horse, gave the mare a gentle kick in the ribs, and started across the rabbit brush, dull silver in the moonlight.

He reached the spur of the mountain, stopped for a moment to stroke the horse's neck, and then let the animal pick its way carefully up the slope.

From the brush beside the narrow trail, small eyes glowing red in the darkness watched him. An owl left its perch and flew slowly above and behind him, hoping that the horse would flush a rabbit or a squirrel out of the brush. On a shelf of rock a hundred or so yards above, a cougar flicked its ears as it caught the hated scent of the horse and retreated into a deep stand of cedar.

A half an hour later the cougar growled softly as the horse

passed by, a rabbit squealed in terror as the owl sank its talons into its neck and lifted it into the dark sky, and far out on The High Lonely a coyote sniffed the night air for the distinctive scent of death.

Part Two
Outlaws

5

*N*eal picked up the heavy cast-iron skillet and poured the bacon grease into an old coffee can. He set the skillet back on top of the wood stove. As the thin layer of grease spattered and hissed, Neal broke two eggs on the edge of the skillet and opened them into the pan. He swirled the skillet gently until the eggs were set and put it back down on the cast-iron heater.

On the back burner, the bubbling of the old metal percolator slowed to a single blurp. Neal picked the coffee pot up with a hot pad and poured himself a mug. Prismatic residue floated on top, giving off that oily tang particular to old-fashioned perked coffee. Neal took a careful sip, scalding his lips only slightly as he stepped out onto the cabin porch.

The sun was rising behind him, starting to warm the cabin's tin roof. Neal savored the sounds that he had first heard only as silence. Listening carefully, he now heard the western breeze ruffle the trees, the distinct crackle of the creek as it rushed over rock and sand. He heard that same old ornery crow scolding him from the same pine branch, the hammering noise of a downy woodpecker as it hunted for ants in a dead cedar, the rattling chirp of a ground squirrel.

And there were the smells. The dominant odor of pine needles, distinct from the muskier smell of pine pitch, the warm, acrid smell of the acidic dirt beneath the rabbit brush, the sagebrush itself, dry and sweet smelling in the crisp early morning. And now there was the aroma of the eggs frying in the bacon grease and the wonderful bread smell as it browned on the grill above the stove.

Neal walked back into the cabin and turned the eggs over, then pressed the spatula down until the yolks broke. He took the toast off the grill, buttered it, and placed it on the old, white, chipped plate with the little blue flowers around the edge. He watched the eggs until they turned solid, then flipped them onto the plate, poured himself more coffee, and sat down at the table, three wide pine boards hammered onto a frame of split logs. He pulled up his chair—another primitive pine job hacked out with a hatchet—and opened his *Carson City Gazette* to the sports page.

The newspaper was exactly one week behind. Neal hitched a ride to town with Steve once a week to buy his supplies and stocked up on his newspapers seven at a time. He had disciplined himself to read only one paper a day, and so his news was a week old, but it wasn't long before that didn't matter, and it wasn't long after that that he took to only glancing at the hard news anyway, turning his attention to sports, book reviews, editorials, and the comics. He got very involved with the comic strips, actually feeling suspense at the fate of Gil Thorp's baseball team and Steve Roper.

On this morning, as on every other morning, building a life was mostly a matter of maintenance. Joe Graham had taught him that a long time ago—that managing your life was about doing the small tasks well and doing them when they needed to be done. "People think that they're 'free,'" Joe Graham had lectured one time as he was browbeating Neal into cleaning his pigsty of an apartment, "when they don't have any order in their lives. They're not free. They're prisoners of their own sloppiness. They spend a hell of a lot more time and energy cleaning up their messes than they do having fun, whatever they tell you. Now, if you just do the little boring things every day, in some kind of order, you leave yourself with more time to sit around, drink beer, and watch ball games on TV, which is, after all, what you want to be doing in the first place. Besides which, sloppy detectives tend to end up dead."

It was true in detective work, it was true in scholarship, and it was true in living a reasonably comfortable life on an isolated mountain.

So he finished his breakfast, heated some water, and did the dishes right away, before he lost the ambition to do them. He poured himself a second cup of coffee and went out to sit on the porch. It was the time he allowed himself to enjoy the terrain, think about the upcoming day, and watch the coyote.

The coyote had started coming just a few days after Neal's arrival at the cabin. Apparently it was just as much a creature of routine as Neal was. It would arrive just after breakfast and skitter fifty or sixty yards away from the cabin until Neal came out to start his hike to the Mills place. Then the coyote would fall in behind him, trailing him, always staying well behind and running off if Neal turned around too suddenly.

At first Neal thought he had some kind of Disney experience going for him, until Steve explained that the coyote was using Neal like a hunting dog, staying behind him to pounce on any grasshoppers, mice, or rabbits that Neal might stir up. Also, coyotes were scavengers, just smart enough to learn that human beings left a lot of garbage in their wake. Neal preferred the Disney scenario and came to look on the coyote as a friend.

So he was looking for the animal when he went out on the porch to sip that wonderful second cup of coffee. All the more wonderful because the mornings were now quite cold. The higher slopes of the mountains had snow now, and it wouldn't be long before the first big storm covered the whole valley in white. Neal had spent many hours of his spare time getting wood off the mountain and stacking it on the porch.

The way the job is going, Neal thought, I might need it.

He'd been there for two months and hadn't seen another sign of Harley or Cody McCall.

Maybe they did move on, Neal admitted to himself. Maybe I should too. But I won't be any closer to finding the boy in New York than I am here.

He'd had a tough time selling that concept to Levine and Graham. There had been that difficult conference call about three weeks after Neal had moved into the cabin.

"Get your ass back here," Ed had demanded.

Neal insisted, "I'm staying."

"What the hell for?" Graham asked. "They won't even let you into the stupid compound!"

"I'm still in the probationary period," Neal said, feeling more than a little foolish. It was true. Hansen had checked out his cover story, bought it, and invited Neal to attend the "self-defense" training sessions he held at the ranch. Outside the compound.

Ed broke in. "We're working it from this end now, Neal. You're off the case."

"I'm off the case when I bring back Cody McCall, Ed."

Neal could picture Ed fuming, leaning over his desk, sucking on a cigarette.

Graham said, "Son, come back and go to school. You've done what you could do. We'll try something else, that's all."

"I don't care about school, Dad. I care about the boy. And until I know that he's not here, I'm not leaving."

Besides, I like it here.

Which was true. Neal Carey, denizen of Broadway, inveterate strap hanger, with sidewalk smarts and a three-newspaper-a-day habit, loved his life on The High Lonely. Neal, whose previous experience herding cattle was maneuvering a cheeseburger into his mouth, had come to enjoy bringing Mills' cows down from their summer pastures in the mountains. Neal, who had once seen the Hudson and East rivers as the borders of the universe, now reveled in the panoramic dawns and dusks of the high desert. Neal, whose idea of a dead lift had been restricted to the weight of a large coffee to go, now thought nothing of flinging bales of hay into the loft, or stretching barbed wire, or digging post holes, or wrestling a calf that needed an injection. Neal, who once couldn't wait to get back to New York after his years of confinement in China, now dreaded the idea of leaving his splendid isolation in the Reese River valley for the tight confines of the Big Apple.

So he wasn't going to do it. This was going to be his last job. He'd find Cody McCall, as long as it took. But once that was over, he was staying right here in the valley. Take his back pay and buy himself a little place, maybe even this cabin. He'd have to give up graduate school, but he didn't need graduate school to read books. In fact, he'd had a lot more time to read these past two months than he'd had for the past five years.

So as soon as I find Cody McCall, I'm quitting, Neal thought as the coyote peeked up from behind a clump of brush.

He shucked off his clothes, slipped on rubber thongs, and paddled over to the lister bag. He stepped up onto the wooden platform he had built, opened the nozzle, got himself wet, and closed the nozzle. He soaped up, washed his hair, and opened the nozzle again to rinse off. Then he lathered his face with soap, crouched a little to look into the mirror hanging from the stump of a branch, and shaved.

"Shaving," Peggy Mills had warned him, "is what separates you from the goofball survivalists. As long as you shave, you're a guy who just wants his privacy. When you stop shaving, you've gone a little too mountain man. So shave, Neal, and I won't nag you or worry about you as much."

It was a good bargain, so Neal dutifully scraped his face every day and felt better for it. One of the challenges of living a primitive life was keeping clean, and a beard would make it more difficult, a repository of sweat, dirt, and dead little bugs. Besides, this was his big day of the week, the day he went to town, and he always liked to show the locals that he had it together. It was a point of pride. He put on a reasonably clean denim shirt, jeans, and jacket, and then his brand-new black Stetson. It was Saturday, his big day in town.

He started his hike to the Mills' house. He didn't have to look back over his shoulder to know that the coyote was trotting a good distance behind him.

Far back in the mountains an old man lay in the brush watching a rabbit in the clearing a few feet in front of him. The old man was naked except for a breechcloth made of pounded sagebrush. His long hair was white, as were the few scraggly whiskers that hung from his chin. He was a small man, well under five feet, and his copper skin was stretched tautly over muscles that were still lean and tight. The old man lay perfectly still as the rabbit lifted its head, twitched its nose, and sniffed the air.

The old man was not concerned. He had taken great care to stay downwind of his prey and he had watched the rabbit for many days, learning its habits. Meat was hard to come by, the rabbit was a wary prey, and his own reflexes were not as fast as they had been in his younger years. The old man recognized that the days when he could survive on speed and strength were long gone; now he must make do with experience and craft.

The rabbit put its nose to the ground and hopped slowly toward the bush. The old man released the string of his bow and the tiny arrow went through the rabbit's neck. The rabbit twitched and kicked in its death spasms and then lay still. The old man got up, took the rabbit by its feet, and headed back to the cave to begin the long process of skinning it with a sharpened piece of flint.

Getting food was a full-time effort and would only get harder. The old man was sorry that summer—that time when the Creator stayed close to the earth and warmed an old man's bones—was coming to an end. It was so much easier getting food in summer, when it was easy to dig roots, gather pine nuts, and pull up big clumps of desert grass. Then there were mesquite beans and the reeds that grew along the creek banks, and it was good for an old man to sit on a rock in the sun and grind the beans and nuts into a paste, or sit by the creek and make soup from the reeds and grass.

And there were lizards and rats and birds to catch. And rabbits.

But his favorites were the grasshoppers. The old man remembered the time before he was the last of his people, when he and his brothers and sisters would take their sharpened sticks and dig deep pits in the earth. Then they would form a big circle and pound on the earth with their sticks, driving the grasshoppers into the pit, where they could be easily caught. There were many ways to eat grasshoppers: crush them into a paste, boil them in a soup with sweet grass, roast them on a rock in the fire, or set them out to dry in the sun. Or if they were very hungry and their father was not looking, they would simply pop a live one into their mouths and chew.

But those were memories, and now there were no brothers or sisters to help and it was harder to catch the grasshoppers. And soon the snows would come and he would have to stay in the mountains away from the white men and it would be very cold. He had to kill many rabbits for their warm fur as well as their meat. And perhaps soon he would take his bow and his sharpened stick and try to kill a mountain sheep, because he no longer dared to sneak down into the valley and take one of the white man's calves. Not when he could be easily tracked in the snow.

Shoshoko, "Digger"—that was his name, although he had not heard it spoken in many years—picked up his sharpened stick and headed back toward the cave.

Neal thought that shopping was a wonderful thing. He hadn't thought this when he lived in New York City, three blocks from a grocery store, or even in Yorkshire, where the grocer and butcher were a pleasant twenty-minute stroll away, but he sure as hell thought it now, after two months of having to procure, preserve, and store food. Now he thought the cans of Dinty Moore beef stew stood among humankind's highest achievements, right up there beside the pyramids, the Hanging Gardens of Babylon, and Hormel chili. He had also developed a high opinion of the Jolly Green Giant's cans of green beans, peas, and those peach slices floating in the sweet, sticky juice—especially the peaches, after a day or so in a canvas bag in cold, rushing water.

And what genius, Neal wondered, had come up with peanut butter? Could it really have been some dork named Skippy? Never mind, it was a major cultural advance. Let the food critics, the health food nuts, and the yuppies whine and scoff at canned food. To Neal canned food meant freedom, the ability to live at arm's reach from civilization and still survive. Canned food let him live in his cabin and have plenty of time to read great books, fish, and take naps instead of spending all his time scratching in the dirt, or hunting, or guarding his crops from vermin.

Steve Mills thought so too.

"I'm happy to see," Steve had said when he saw how Neal had stocked his larder, "that you're not one of these purists we get up here who arrive with their Whole Earth catalogues and plans for a geodesic dome. They figure they're going to grow their bean sprouts and their organic vegetables and live in harmony with nature. Only thing is, nature never read *Diet for a Small Planet,* so the deer and the rabbits and the bugs eat the whole crop instead of restricting themselves to their socially responsible share. Then one of these 'alternative life-stylers' kids named Sunshine or Raven gets an ear infection that herbal tea can't cure, and so I find myself hauling them to the doctor in my air-polluting, gas-guzzling truck so he can write them a prescription for some nonorganic chemicals they can't pay for anyway, so half the time I end up writing a check from the capitalist profits I make from selling my murderous, unhealthy red meat. And about the only thing that grows naturally up here that the animals don't like is dope, so these purists are stoned half the time anyway, unless they have the sense to sell it instead of smoking it. So they end up either starving, dirty, malnourished drug casualties or wealthy capitalists running bales of marijuana into Reno in custom vans that cost more than my whole house. So I'm glad to see that you like Dinty Moore stew."

Joe Graham had a different take on the purity issue. "You heard that saying about not taking the easy way out?" he'd asked Neal. "Sometimes the easy way is the best way. A lot of smart people have put in a lot of time making things easier. People who tell you not to take the easy way out are the same people who'll then get on a plane to the West Coast instead of taking a covered wagon, which would be a lot harder."

Neal didn't care much about the philosophy of the whole thing. He just wanted to live in the cabin, not see people unless he wanted to, and read books. So he stocked up on his favorite canned food, bought a six-pack of bottled beer, and picked up his week's supply of newspapers.

Steve Mills pulled his truck up alongside the sidewalk. He'd been down at the gas station, stocking up on surreptitious cigs.

"You ready to head back?"

"Why not?"

Neal slung his pack into the bed of the pickup and hopped into the passenger seat.

"Thought I'd work on my fluid intake at Brogan's for a minute," Steve said.

"Sounds good to me."

Brogan was asleep in his chair. Brezhnev was asleep at his feet. The flies on the window screen were awake, though.

Brogan cracked an eye open as the door shut. "Help yourselves, leave the money on the bar, and remember that Brezhnev can count," he said, then shut his eyes again.

Brezhnev raised his heavy head at least a centimeter and looked at Steve and Neal with a proprietary interest. Neal hopped over the bar, poured two bourbons into greasy glasses, and left a five-dollar bill on the bar.

Steve tasted his drink, decided he liked it, and tossed it down. "There goes another year of my life. I think I'll give 'em my ninety-ninth, what do you think? So what are you planning on doing up there in January when the pump freezes and there's two feet of snow on the ground?"

Neal sipped at his drink, savoring it. He'd decided against buying any hard booze for the cabin precisely because he thought he'd use it. Like every night. But the one or two he had at Brogan's, or the odd drink at the Mills' house sure went down well.

"I'll let January worry about January," he said. It sounded just as stupid out loud as it had in his head.

"Well, you know I ain't much for worrying, but now is the time to start getting your firewood together and figuring out a dry place to store it. You're going to need a hell of a lot of it. And then there's cabin fever."

"I won't get cabin fever."

"Tell me after you've spent a winter by yourself out there. That is, if you're not still talking to little men who live in the walls."

"Oh."

"Everybody around here gets it to one extent or another. It's the cold, the wind, the darkness, the monotony of snow, snow, and snow. Hell, I get it, Peggy gets it, Shelly would get it if she wasn't teenage crazy already. But I've seen some of these survivalists and Vietnam vets and hippies who've tried to winter it alone around here. By the time spring springs, they're already sprung, you know what I mean? Do you suppose Brogan has any more bourbon, or did we drink it up already?"

Steve took Neal's glass with him and came back with two more drinks. He sat down, lit up a cigarette, and tilted his chair back against the wall.

"Why don't you come down and stay with us for the winter? I could use the help, Peggy would like to hear a new set of lies for a change, and Shelly thinks you hung the moon anyway."

"What help do you need in the winter?" Neal asked doubtfully.

"Well, I can't drink *all* the bourbon myself."

"I'll be okay, Steve. I'm used to being alone. I like it." Besides, he thought, I need my privacy.

"Suit yourself. But I can tell you right now, Peggy's not going to let you sit up there during the holidays. She'll come after you with a gun, tie you on the back of a horse."

They finished their drinks and got back in the truck. Thirteen bumpy, dusty miles later they pulled into the Mills' driveway. Shelly and Jory were in the front corral. Shelly was throwing a saddle on Dash. The horse was doing his distinctive little shuffle dance like a prize fighter in his corner before the first-round bell. Jory was cinching up the docile mare with the appropriately soothing name of Cocoa.

"Hey, Neal!" Shelly hollered. "Want to ride?"

It was a joke between them. Shelly had been trying to get Neal on a horse since his first morning in Nevada. Sometimes she would ride Dash up to his cabin, trailing Cocoa or the equally tame Dolly, and try to get him to go for a trail ride. Neal thought that riding on the spine of a horse along the spine of a ridge was a double jeopardy he wasn't eager to pursue in the name of recreation.

"I'll leave you two lovebirds alone," Neal answered.

Shelly laughed and flashed him a brilliant smile. Then she stuck her foot into the stirrup and swung up onto the horse.

"What's the matter? Afraid to ride?"

Neal was tempted to tell her that he had ridden the IRT number two train, otherwise known as the Beast, thank you very much. He was also tempted to make some smart crack about teenage girls and horses. But he thought better of both remarks. Shelly was a great kid who just wanted to share the fun.

Yeah, right.

"Hi, Neal," said Jory.

That was a long-winded anecdote for Jory.

"How's it going?" Neal asked.

"Just going riding," Jory answered as he got into the saddle.

Shelly gave Dash a sharp kick in the flanks and the horse tore out of the corral like it was a dog food factory. Jory snapped his reins and Cocoa trotted after them.

Steve watched them ride off. "Now at Berkeley that's what we'd have called life imitating art. I'm afraid that boy's going to be eating her dust for as long as he stays on her trail."

"Is she leaving him behind?"

"Oh, I think so. I think they might make it through their senior year, but when she gets to college and sees what all is out there . . . and lately Jory doesn't see much beyond his dad's ranch. I tell you, I hope Shelly calls us from college one summer to try to convince we should let her spend the summer riding a bike around Europe, or looking at naked statues in Italy or something. We'll put up a little struggle just to make it more fun for her, but I do hope that's what happens."

"She loves it here, Steve," Neal said.

"She can always come back. You want to stay to dinner? I'm just going to throw some steaks on the grill."

"I better not. I have stuff to get done."

"Lot of work, being a mountain man. Well, come in and have a cup of coffee with Peggy, or you'll get me in trouble."

Peggy didn't have any coffee on. She had a pitcher of sun tea, a bottle of vodka, a stack of magazines, and a firm intent to sit out on the porch with her feet on the railing while reading nothing more complicated than a photo caption.

"I figure it might be the last afternoon warm enough to do this. You can join me," she said to Neal, "if you promise to speak in short sentences."

"Thanks."

"Good start," Peggy said. She poured three glasses of tea over ice, topped two of them off with a shot of Smirnoff, and handed her husband the unloaded one.

"You're a terrible woman," he said.

"Hmm. Is our one and only off leading Jory Hansen on a merry chase?"

"Merry for her, anyway. Why, did you have something for her to do?"

"Well, she could toss a hand grenade into her room by way of cleaning it . . . but no, not really. Come on, boys, the porch awaits."

She picked up her magazines and pushed the screen door open with her elbow.

"You two alcoholics go ahead," Steve said. He drained his iced tea in one long gulp. "I want to check on the cattle for a minute. Are those magazines the ones that are mostly advertisements, with little perfume samples and articles about orgasms?"

"Yep," answered Peggy.

"Well, save one for me," Steve said. "I'll be back in a minute."

Neal followed Peggy out onto the porch. True to her word, she pulled up a deck chair, plopped the stack of magazines by her feet, and stuck her feet up on the railing.

"Tough day?" Neal asked.

"Not really. It's just nice to have a chance to sit down and relax, this part of the afternoon. It's my favorite time of the day."

She picked up a magazine, licked her finger, and started to flip through the pages.

"*Cosmo,*" she said. "Well, let's see . . . how *do* high-powered young women executives get satisfaction? Nope, no pictures. Next story."

Neal sat down, drank his tea, and watched the afternoon sunlight start to soften.

"So, Neal Carey," Peggy said as she flipped through the magazine, "what's happening at Hansen's place?"

"I dunno."

"Hmm."

Neal hated her hmms. She could hmm him to death. Her hmms were her way of expressing skepticism. If Peggy Mills were a New York City police detective, every criminal in the city would break down and beg for the old rubber hose before enduring another one of those hmms.

"What does Jory say?" Neal asked.

"Jory says less than Jory usually says. Jory talks like one of those Indians in those old Jeff Chandler movies. Lotsa ughs and uhs."

"Hmm."

"Very funny. Well, something is going on at Hansen's, and I figured because they're just over the spur from you . . ."

"I thought you didn't want a lot of conversation."

Peggy looked up from her magazine and stared out at the trees across their lawn.

"Never mind me. Maybe it's just that it's late in the afternoon . . . and I'm late in the afternoon . . . and winter's coming and my baby's all grown up . . . and my husband has a big, weak heart . . ." She reached her hand out, took his, and gave it a squeeze. He squeezed it back.

"You're just hitting your prime," Neal said.

She squeezed his hand again and then let it go. "You're a good guy, Neal. I know a few single women around here who'd die to meet you. You want to go with us to Phil and Margie's tonight? Big Saturday night out? I'll introduce you to some mountain women with shiny hair and long legs."

"I don't know how to dance."

"I'm sure they'd love to teach you, honey."

"I don't know." I don't know, Peggy. The last woman who taught me ended up dead.

"Well, just come down around eight if you want to go."

"Okay."

Neal finished off his tea and got up. "Thanks for the drink. Tell Steve I needed to go, huh? Maybe I'll see you tonight."

He picked his pack up out of the truck, strapped it on, and headed back up to his cabin. He did have things to do.

If he was thinking of spending the winter here there was something he had to get resolved first.

Neal heard the bullet smack into the tree behind him as he dropped to the ground. He didn't feel any pain, wondered if that's what instant death was like, then checked himself to try to find the gaping hole in his body.

"You're a dead kike," Cal Strekker said as he came out from behind a boulder. He lowered his rifle and grinned.

"That was too goddamn close, Cal," Neal croaked. "Live ammo."

"You oughta be more alert," Strekker said.

"I didn't know the training session had even started," Neal answered.

"We're always in training, Carey."

Well, you are anyway, Neal thought as he looked at Strekker. He was decked out in a tiger camouflage suit, replete with parachute pants, webbed belt, and combat boots. His face was striped with cammy paint and he wore a combat fatigue cap.

Even from my position groveling at your feet, you look stupid, Neal thought. He didn't say that, though. Instead he said, "Well, you owe me new underwear, Cal."

That seemed to mollify him, judging by the lupine grin that parted his mustache and beard. Then he got all man-to-man earnest. "You'll thank me for this when it saves your life one day during the End Time."

The End Time—the period foretold in Revelations that would see the final battle between good and evil, the last struggle between the chosen people and the hordes of Jews, niggers, and race traitors.

"Boy, for a second there I thought it *was* the End Time," Neal said.

Neal got to his feet and offered his hand to shake. Strekker took it. Neal clamped his left hand over Cal's wrist, lifted his arm up, spun underneath it, and pivoted, which locked Cal's elbow up around his ear and going in the wrong direction. Neal took two long steps forward and pushed on Cal's wrist, which took the bigger man off his feet and slammed him hard down on his back. Neal threw a punch that stopped a millimeter from Cal's nose.

"We're always in training, Cal, huh?"

He let go of Cal's wrist and backed away. "You taught me that throw, Cal."

Yeah, you taught me all right, Cal, Neal remembered. You threw me to the ground about five hundred times, always a lot harder than you had to, always giving my wrist that extra little twist. You always picked me as the "kike" in your hand-to-hand demonstrations. The choke holds, the elbow locks, the hip throws. You've been a good teacher. But I know seventy-year-old, five-feet-three, one hundred–pound Chinese monks who would dust your ass without looking up from their rice bowls.

"I'm going to take you to school, boy," Cal growled. He got to his feet, drew his knife, and went into his combat stance.

Neal picked up his rifle and cocked a round into the chamber. "We're all in our places, with bright shiny faces," he said.

Cal started to circle him, passing the knife from hand to hand, making feinting jabs.

Neal braced the rifle stock against his cheek and focused on placing the bead right on Strekker's alleged heart.

He almost did shit his pants when the sound of the gun exploded in his ears. He whirled around to see Bob Hansen standing there, his smoking rifle held at high port, a group of about ten men forming behind him.

"That'll be enough, you two," Hansen said sternly.

"Yes, sir!" Cal shouted.

"Yes, sir," Neal croaked, his head still rushing from the thought that he had accidentally killed Cal Strekker.

Then Hansen's face broke into a delighted smile.

"Do we have us some tigers here?" he asked the group. "They're just spoiling to fight. I almost pity the ZOG race traitor who has to fight one of these fine men! Well, almost."

The men behind him began to chuckle obediently. Cal looked like a German shepherd having his chest scratched. Then Hansen got stern again and frowned.

"But good white men can't afford to fight each other, men. That's what the enemy wants us to do. Let's save that hatred for ZOG, all right?"

ZOG—Neal always thought it sounded like the monster in a low-budget Japanese horror movie, sort of a poor man's Godzilla, but actually it was an acronym for Zionist Occupation Government, the white supremacist name for the federal government in Washington, manipulated by the Jews for the suppression of the true chosen people.

"Now shake hands," Hansen ordered.

Neal gave Cal an ironic smile and stuck his hand out like he was Mickey Rooney coming back to Boys' Town. Cal took it, gave it a hard tug, and stared into Neal's eyes with an unmistakable this-is-a-long-way-from-being-over look.

Hansen stepped back into the center of the group. He wore plain khakis with cuffed slacks and a black baseball hat. He had a webbed belt with a holstered .45 Colt.

Neal had come to know the rest of the men during the past few weeks. There was Strekker, of course. Levine had pulled the file on him—sergeant in the army, ranger certified, dishonorable discharge for beating up a trainee. Served two years in the Washington State pen for knifing a man in a bar fight. Member of the Aryan Brotherhood in prison.

His cell mate had been Randy Carlisle. Rape. About five-six, black hair, mustache. A perpetual expression of feral cunning, the kind of twisted leer that your mother was talking about when she asked you if you wanted your face to freeze that way. A coyote to Cal's wolf.

There was Dave Bekke, the chunky, bearded man Neal had met in his first encounter with Hansen back on the ridge. Part-time mine worker, part-time ranch hand, full-time loser. He had a fat wife he was scared of so rarely saw. He was a follower looking for something to follow, and he found it in the white supremacist movement. No prison but some jail time for DUI and petty theft.

Bill McCurdy was a cowboy first and a cretin second, but it was a close race. He was a runty, bowlegged little bastard with a giggle that could have made Gandhi slap him in the mouth. Neal had never seen him without his cowboy hat, which was a mercy, because the brown hair that hung below his ears hadn't been washed since Jimmy Carter was popular. But the boy was transformed on a horse. On horseback he became a centaur, an idiot savant of the saddle.

Craig Vetter was something else again. A tree with clothes. Six-five with broad shoulders, sinewy legs, and muscles that wouldn't quit. Short blond hair and blue eyes and a face as open as a Bible on Sunday. Guiltless, guileless, fearless. Didn't drink, smoke, cuss, or chase women. There was a wife and five kids back in St. George, Utah, and Craig would still be with them if he didn't feel duty bound to fight for God and the white race. He sent his pay home, though.

And then there was John Finley, tall, skinny, with sandy hair and shit for brains. Finley was a California surf boy who had his cocaine jones and his ass busted in the LA County jail. He'd found religion for comfort and the Aryan Brotherhood for protection and joined the True Christian Identity Church shortly after his release. Carter had shipped him out to Hansen's ranch to keep his nose clean.

The Johnson brothers were bespectacled, benighted behemoths. Neal supposed they had first names other than Big and Little, but he never heard them. And Jory was Hitler's poster boy.

There were a couple of others Neal didn't have a line on yet, but they were pretty much the same type—men who saw an America that never existed slipping away from them, whose childhood horrors, or adult disappointments, or desperate need for pride had been transformed into a hatred for ethnic scapegoats.

Neal had all sorts of cheap psychoanalysis and snotty Freudian concepts to attach to his new playmates, but basically he thought they were scum. These were the men Bob Hansen had brought in to work his place, to turn a model ranch into a survivalist hovel.

Well, that's his problem, Neal thought. I have my own. Come on, Bob, it's dark enough. Let's get going.

It was a night training exercise, because, as Bob Hansen had joked, "that's when night fighters fight."

"One technique you can use," Hansen said, "is to leave out some fried chicken, and when the nigger smells it, he'll smile. Don't fire until you see the whites of his teeth."

The small group gathered at the base of the spur chuckled. Neal joined in the laughter, but his stomach was fluttering.

Enough with the jokes, he thought. Let's get on with it.

"Seriously," Hansen continued, sounding like a fascist nightclub comic, "we're very likely to do a lot of night fighting during the End Time. And even sooner, when we begin the shooting war against ZOG, which should be soon now, we'll favor night attacks to make up for our lack of numbers. We must learn to be swift, silent, and lethal. So no firearms tonight, gentlemen. Just hand-to-hand combat."

They broke up into two teams for a nocturnal, violent version of hide-and-seek. Neal hoped that his luck would hold out long enough to put him on the "hide" side, which would make what he had to do a whole lot easier.

The scenario was that a gang of marauding "mud people" were planning to attack the compound to get its food. The defenders would launch a surprise nighttime spoiling raid to scatter the marauders and track them down one by one.

Strekker said he would lead the defender's team.

"I'll be a nigger," Neal volunteered.

"Figures," Strekker commented.

"See you up there," Neal said, pointing to the spur.

"Count on it," Strekker answered.

You don't know, Neal thought, just how much I'm counting on it, Cal.

Hansen made the rest of the assignments. Neal, Jory, Dave, and Craig made up the marauding band of blacks. Hansen, Strekker, Finley, Carlisle, and Big and Little Johnson were going to track them down and "kill" them.

"You have a ten-minute start," Hansen said. "Make sure you spread out."

You ain't just whistlin' Dixie, Neal thought as he took off at a dead run. I have to put as much space between me and everybody as I can in those ten minutes. Space equals time, and I'm going to need time.

He sprinted across the sagebrush toward the spur until he figured that no one could spot his silhouette. Then he turned right, running parallel to the base of the mountain. He trotted until he found a narrow ravine and dropped down into it. He hoped he had moved enough south to take him out of the main path of the exercise. He crawled out of his denim jacket and baggy canvas pants. Underneath he was wearing a black turtleneck and black jeans. He pulled a tin of black, water-based makeup out of his pocket and spread it over his face and hands. He put a black stocking over his face and then pulled a black watch cap over his head. He took two thin steel cables, each about two feet long, and tied them around his waist. Then he laid flat on the ground and waited.

He thought about chickening out, creeping back to his cabin and forgetting the whole thing. Then he thought about Anne Kelley and Cody and decided to go through with it.

He let a full ten minutes pass before he got up into a crouch and headed west toward the compound. He was hoping that no one would figure him to be this far south, and certainly not to be headed toward, instead of away from, his pursuers. He knew that Strekker was running like a greyhound toward the spur to find him and dispatch him in the most painful acceptable manner.

It took him twenty minutes to make it to the compound fence.

Graham, I wish you were here, he thought. I'm more than a little rusty and could use some coaching. Oh, well, it's no different from breaking into a car lot or a warehouse. Except that if anyone's home here, I'm likely to catch a bullet in the chest while I'm sprawled out on the fence.

He wrapped the denim jacket around his waist and tied up the sleeves at his waist. Then he jumped onto the fence, dug a toe into the space between the links, and began to haul himself up. He was sweating not so much from the exertion as from the thought that a searchlight might hit him at any moment, followed shortly by a large-caliber, high-velocity bullet.

He made it to the top of the fence and paused to catch his breath, get a good toehold, and think about the next step. Then he untied the jacket and laid it over the top of the two-strand barbed wire. He took one of the cables from around his waist and looped it underneath the bottom strand, pulled it tight, and tied it off on top. He did the same with the other cable on the other end of the jacket.

When the wire was pulled up tight under the jacket, he took another deep breath and swung his left foot over the top of the jacket, pivoted his hips, and planted the tip of his left foot into a space on the inside of the chain link fence. Then he lifted his right foot over, balanced himself with his hands on the jacket, and pulled himself over the top.

He paused for a second to listen. He didn't hear any footsteps, or barking dogs, or the sound of a rifle bolt.

Holding himself to the fence with his left hand, he reached up, untied the cables, dropped them, pulled the jacket off, and let it fall to the ground. Then he lowered himself another couple of feet down the fence, listened again, pushed off with his hands, and dropped to the ground. He landed perfectly on the balls of his feet, then fell over backward and hit the ground with his butt.

Rusty, he thought. Definitely rusty. But not bad.

He was still congratulating himself when he heard a deep growl. It was a Doberman, of course. It was advancing slowly in a low crouch, the hair on its spine standing up, its fangs bared, tiny speckles of spit dripping from its mouth.

Neal muttered, "You could have had the decency to growl while I was on the *outside* of the fence."

But it wasn't a guard dog, Neal realized—guard dogs are trained to bark. It was an attack dog, which was trained to . . . well, attack.

And this one had ambushed him.

The dog took another careful step forward. It was sizing him up and quickly arriving at the conclusion that this particular human wouldn't be much of a problem. It showed even more fang and boosted the volume on the growl.

It would leap for his throat at any moment.

There's only one thing to do, Neal thought.

Panic.

Turn and run for the fence and hope you can climb high enough before Hans here rips into your leg, pulls you backward off the fence, and tears your throat out of your neck.

Panic.

No, no, no, no, no. Think. Surely Graham must have covered this subject in one of his endless lectures. He had covered everything else. Barbed wire, alarm systems . . . dogs.

What you have to do, Neal, is pretty goddamn weird and presents an enormous initial risk. . . . What you do is . . .

Neal reached down with a quivering hand and unzipped his fly. Then he assumed the classic men's room position.

Talk about presenting an initial risk, he thought. As for the "enormous," well . . .

The dog kept growling but stopped advancing.

Why is it, Neal asked himself, that when you absolutely have to piss . . . you can't? Like when you're taking a physical and the nurse hands you a jar, or when you're standing exposed to a potentially homicidal canine . . .

Come on, come on, come on.

The dog got impatient and started to come forward. It was staring at Neal's crotch.

Come on, come on, come on . . . ahhhh.

Neal zipped his fly.

The startled dog came out of his crouch. His nose started twitching madly. He bent his head down to get a closer sniff. Then he turned his back to Neal and lifted his leg.

Now you have established—what do you call it—a rapport with Spot. He understands that you understand doggy etiquette. Of course, if he is really well trained, he's just going to piss on your puddle and then kill you anyway. Otherwise, try to show him that you consider yourself lower status than he is. With you, this is no problem . . .

Neal laid down on his back, making himself completely vulnerable to the dog's attack. The Doberman came over, growled, sniffed Neal's crotch and stomach, and then opened his jaws over Neal's throat.

If you move during this part, you're a piece of meat . . .

He felt the dog's fangs press gently onto his skin.

The dog growled again. Then he let go, straightened up, and wagged his tail.

Then lick his ear.

Lick his ear?

Lick his ear! That's doggy talk for telling him that he's the boss. Once he's confident that you admit that, he probably won't attack you.

Probably?

What, you want a sure thing? Go into insurance.

Shuffling on all fours to the dog, Neal slowly put his tongue to its ear, and made a great show of licking. If it can be said that a Doberman can smile, the dog positively beamed. It wagged its stub of a tail and invited Neal to have a look around the place.

Neal made directly for the largest building, the one that looked like a barracks. He trotted down the steps to the sunken entrance. The thick wooden door was unlocked.

Of course, thought Neal. They aren't expecting anybody until the End Time, which is still a few years off.

He opened the door and stepped inside.

It was a white supremacist whacko's dream. The main rectangle was split into three rooms, each of which could be sealed off by a thick metal door in case part of the bunker was overrun. The first section was the barracks. Bunk beds lined the walls between ground-level fire slits that had been dug at angles to ward off shell fragments.

Hoping to see the form of a sleeping child under the military blankets, Neal looked into each bunk. But Cody McCall wasn't in bed.

He went into the next section, which looked like a planning room. A wooden table sat in the center. A U.S. Geological Survey topographical map of the area had been spread on the tabletop. There was a small chalkboard on an easel and about a dozen metal folding chairs in front of it. The walls were decorated with posters—a picture of bodies stacked up outside a crematorium, with the caption "A Good Start"; a religious poster of God talking to Jacob in heaven and pointing to America down below; a framed photograph of Adolph Hitler. A pine bookrack held a section of supremacist writings including some back issues of a newsletter called *The White Beacon,* by Reverend C. Wesley Carter.

Neal fought off the queasy feeling in his stomach and checked his watch. Had it only been half an hour? He figured he had another hour or so before the boys wound up the exercise in the hills and made it back. He checked the gun ports at each corner of the building. No Cody.

He went back outside. The Doberman had brought a stick to play with and Neal obediently threw it. He had to check each of the smaller, circular concrete bunkers. The first held a survivalist cache—stacks of canned food, bottled water, and fuel. The second one was an armory, surprisingly skimpy. There were a few civilian rifles and pistols, one M-16, and what looked like some Korean War vintage land mines. Neal ran to the last bunker.

It was a jail. Iron rings were bolted to the walls. Chains and shackles were run through the rings. Neal felt his skin tingle with revulsion. He could smell the fear in here. Traces of stale sweat clung in the closed air. Bloodstains marked the concrete floor. Something horrible had happened in this place.

Neal felt the chill of a pervasive evil and backed out the door. That's when he heard the dog barking joyfully. A greeting. Because his master was home.

"You think it's late for *you?*" Ed complained into the phone. "How do you think I feel?"

Ed drummed his fingers on the desk. He was hungry. He wanted a pastrami on rye with mustard and a beer—and not a lite beer, either, but a full, dark beer with some heft to it. And a bag of potato chips.

"So tell me," Ed said, then listened while Carter told him what he needed.

"Reverend, we're talking a tall order here," Ed said when the man had finished. "I mean, you're asking me to take a terrible risk. We're talking big bucks."

"How big?"

"Like you-pull-up-truckloads-of-money-and-I'll-tell-you-when-to-stop big."

The man bitched and moaned and Ed bitched and moaned back and they finally settled on a number.

"Do we have a deal?" Carter asked.

"We have a deal," Ed answered.

Hell of a deal.

He hung up, lit a cigarette, and dialed another number.

Neal listened to the voices and the footsteps coming toward him. They were laughing, speculating as to how Neal had gotten lost, where he was, and how long he'd be wandering around the sagebrush before he got back.

The door opened and Cal Strekker came in, followed by Craig Vetter and Randy Carlisle. Neal could see that the two Hansens and Dave Bekke were right behind them.

When they were all inside, Neal threw the door open and lifted the pistol he'd taken from the armory.

Strekker started for him.

"Please keep coming, head of security," Neal said as he pointed the gun at him.

Strekker froze.

"You're not supposed to be in here," Vetter said.

"No kidding."

"What are you doing, Neal?" Hansen asked.

It's fourth and long, Neal thought. Nothing to do but throw deep.

"Well, Mr. Hansen," Neal answered, "I'm just trying to show you what I can do . . . what kind of man I am. I'm the kind of man who can get into places, past twelve-foot fences, barbed wire, and attack dogs. I'm the kind of man who can penetrate security and take what I want—witness the gun in my hand. I'm the kind of man who wants to lay a hurting on ZOG. I want to fight for the white race, and I'm smart enough to figure out that you have more going on here than hide-and-go-seek games. I want to be a part of it. You were right the first time, Mr. Hansen, you can use a man like me."

Neal flicked the clip from the pistol and tossed it to Hansen.

Cal Strekker sprang toward Neal. Hansen's sharp voice brought him up short.

"Hold it, Cal."

Hansen turned to Neal. "We call ourselves the Sons of Seth. The Reverend C. Wesley Carter himself gave us that name, so we wear it with great pride. And you're right, Neal, we're training to be the fighting arm of the True Christian Identity Church. We're training to strike a blow against ZOG and to serve as a base of operations when the End Time comes.

"But you can't just become a Son of Seth, Neal, just because you have some useful skills, and may I add, one hell of a nerve. You have to earn the name."

Neal gave him his best flinty-eyed look. "Just give me a chance, sir."

"I will, Neal," Hansen said. "You can count on that. You'll get your chance to show us what kind of a man you really are."

I'm really a jerk, Bobby. Because Harley McCall isn't in your damn compound and neither is Cody. I've wasted two months being stupid, stubborn, and selfish.

That's the kind of man I really am.

"He's cute," Karen Hawley said to Peggy Mills, "but isn't he supposed to be nuts or something?"

"No, he just needed some time alone."

"Well, I guess he has it, living up there in that cabin. I don't know if I'm up for another survivalist type, Peggy."

"Just dance with him."

"He hasn't asked me."

"True."

Peggy Mills and Karen Hawley were having one of those ladies' room conversations, if you could call the women's lavatory at Phil and Margie's Country Cabaret a ladies' room. There was no pink wallpaper, plush banquettes, or mirrors framed in makeup lights. Instead there were two stalls divided by paneling, a sink with a rubber stopper on a broken chain, and a mirror that teamed up with a fluorescent light to tell some harsh truths about the cosmetic effects of long months and short paychecks.

Peggy and Karen were hip to hip, leaning in to share the single mirror as Peggy dusted her face with a little powder and Karen replaced some of the lipstick she had left on her beer glass. Lipstick was one of the few concessions Karen made to the magazine image of femininity, that and a little eyeliner on Saturday nights. She'd long ago taken an inventory of her physical features and found them quite acceptable on their own. She had thick black hair, cut just above the collar, and blue eyes as deep and sparkling as a lake on a brilliant winter day. She had a long face, a strong jaw, a sharp chin, and if some guys thought her nose was a little big, too bad. She had come to like it, even the little bump right there on the bridge. Her mouth was wide and her lips a little narrower than she'd ideally like, but her smile had been known to turn big lumberjacks into little boys, and if those little boys could turn back into men they'd find she was a great kisser.

She liked her body, too. She was tall—even taller now, in her cowboy boots—with long legs made taut and muscular by a lifetime spent hiking in these mountains. And if her hips were a little wider than you'd see on a Paris runway, she didn't want to be seen on one anyway. Her jeans fit her real nice, thank you, and the white western shirt she was wearing had to stretch over breasts to tuck in over a tummy that owed her, dammit, for all the sit-ups. It was a good body, Karen thought. Good for backpacking, good for dancing, good for whatever the dancing led to, good for having babies. Except she hadn't met a guy who wanted to settle in long enough to have a baby with her.

"I just don't want to get involved with another 'I have to be free like the wind, darling,' 'Love me, love my dog,' guitar-strumming, moon-howling, living-in-his-car-and-my-kitchen cowboy mountain man who's going to make me fall in love with him and then leave for California to 'find himself,' " Karen said.

"You can screw him without falling in love with him."

"He is cute."

Peggy Mills took a brush to her hair. "He reads books," she said.

Well, that is interesting, Karen thought. She had been teaching third grade in Austin for five years now and had heard more than one parent tell her that his son didn't need to know how to read in order to rope a calf or dig gold. That was, of course, when she could even get a parent to come to one of the conferences. A lot of the parents were great, but there were also a lot she had never seen, not even once, not even for the Christmas pageant, when half of central Nevada came to town to see their kids dressed up as reindeer or the Virgin Mary or something. And while most of the kids in her school were happy, healthy, well-scrubbed kids, there were also a sad number who were dirty, malnourished, and just plain sad looking, and there were those kids who had bruises they didn't get playing kickball at recess. And when one of her boys had shown up with actual burns on him, it was Karen Hawley who had driven up to their remote shack, woke his daddy up from his alcoholic stupor, stuck a shotgun into his crotch, and explained precisely what would happen if Junior didn't stop "falling against the wood stove." Word on The High Lonely was that you didn't mess around with Karen or with anyone Karen put her arms around, and she definitely had her arms around the kids in that school.

"What kind of books?" Karen asked. "Remember Charlie? He read books. They were mostly about Swedish stewardesses."

"Neal was working on his master's degree in English."

"Another hard-core unemployable."

"You're a hard woman, Hawley."

"I'm a marshmallow."

"Too true."

"If he asks me, I'll dance with him, okay?"

"You're glued to that chair like you're paying rent on it," Steve Mills was saying to Neal Carey.

Neal was drinking beer straight out of the bottle, munching on peanuts, and feeling about as comfortable as a eunuch at an orgy.

Neal Carey had been in some bars in his life, early and often. He had been in Irish pubs in New York on Saturday nights when both the booze and the blood had flowed, when on- and off-duty cops laid their revolvers on the bar while they knocked back double shots, when the band had led the crowd in cheerful sing-alongs about martyred heroes and killing Englishmen. None of it had prepared him for Phil and Margie's Country Cabaret.

First of all, there was the location. Austin, Nevada, could have been built by a Robert Altman set crew. Its broad main street was mostly mud, flanked by wide wooden sidewalks. Phil and Margie's was a large, low, ramshackle building with a classic western facade, heavy screens over the small windows, and swinging doors, and if Gary Cooper had come through, Neal wouldn't have been at all surprised.

They hadn't arrived until after nine, and by that time the crowd had a good start on the drinking, smoking, and dancing, so the air in the place was a rich mixture of second-hand alcohol, smoke, and sweat with a heavy overlay of perfume, cologne, and failing deodorant. The delicate scent of grilled hamburgers and deep-fat french fries wafted from a grill in the back. The ceilings were low, the room was dark, and Neal knew that if any of his white-wine-sipping, vegetarian, rabidly antismoking Columbia friends could be condemned to a Saturday night in hell, this would be it.

The noise was literally earthshaking as about fifty pairs of cowboy boots, miner's boots, and hiking boots pounded on the sagging floor to the beat of the Nevada two-step and the bar glasses rattled and the walls trembled. What conversation there was got shouted at full voice and close range and wasn't really given to serious dialogue about deconstructionism in literary analysis or pithy interplay about what James Joyce may or may not have said to Ezra Pound.

They had elbowed their way to a table in the back, Steve exchanging back slaps and Peggy swapping hugs with just about every person in the place. Peggy insisted on making the first trip to the bar and returned with four beers and Karen Hawley.

Peggy made the introductions, Karen and Neal shook hands, she sat down in the chair next to him, smiled, and Neal found that he had a sudden fascination with the band.

Not that the band wasn't fascinating. To Neal, country music had meant anything sung or strummed in New Jersey or Connecticut. So he wasn't ready for New Red and the Mountain Men. New Red was the lead singer and rhythm guitar player. He was a young guy with sandy hair and a beard. He wore a Caterpillar gimme cap, plaid shirt, black logger pants, and tennis shoes. He had a face as friendly as an old pair of socks. The drummer was a woman with waist-length blond hair, a black cowboy hat, black western shirt with red roses on the chest, tight black jeans, and black cowboy boots. Neal sensed a sartorial theme and wasn't surprised to find out from Steve that her name was Sharon Black, aka "Blackie." She was a good drummer, anyway. The bass player was a big guy with curly brown hair falling to his shoulders and a bushy beard, bib overalls over a denim shirt, and cowboy boots he probably hadn't seen for a while. The violinist ("That's a fiddle player, Neal") was a woman in her indistinct forties who looked like the kind who had about twenty cats at home and wind chimes. She wore a flower print blouse, painter's pants, and sandals, and her hair was a wild quarrel between the colors gold and gray.

Whatever they looked like, they could play. Over the din of the pounding crowd Neal heard music as sharp and clear as the creek that rippled down by his cabin, each note distinct but blended into one stream. And just about as effortless. Neal watched the guitarists' fingers sliding over the strings, pressing down strong and precise chords, or flying over the frets to pluck individual notes. He watched Blackie's hands flash patterns with the sticks on the drumheads, her hips bobbing as she stepped on the bass pedal. He watched Cat Lady nestle the . . . fiddle . . . into her cheek as if it were a baby, but stroke the strings as fast and hard as if she were trying to start a fire. He watched it all the harder as he felt Peggy watching him and Karen trying not to.

He was doing all right until Steve, the dirty turncoat, stretched out his hand to his wife to fight their way out onto the dance floor.

Which is a lot worse than you leaving me in the back of a bouncing pickup with that calf, Neal thought.

Then he realized he hadn't really talked with a woman for years, except for Peggy and Shelly Mills, which didn't count.

"Where are you from?" Karen shouted.

Well, I've been living in a Buddhist monastery for the past three years, and on a Yorkshire moor the year before that . . . "New York," he shouted back.

"City or state?"

"City!"

So far so good.

"Where are you from?" he asked, realizing that his voice sounded as high and narrow as one of Cat Lady's strings. She thinks I'm an idiot.

"Here," she said, "I'm from here."

"Austin?" Great. Now she knows I'm an idiot.

"I think that's where we are."

Duhhh.

"What do you do for a living?"

I was sort of an unlicensed private investigator, a troubleshooter for a secret organization. But right now I think I'm unemployed.

"Nothing much lately. What do you do?"

"I'm a teacher."

Oh?

That's when the music stopped, the band took a break, and Peggy and Karen went off to the ladies' room together, a ritual that is constant throughout the world.

"You're glued to that chair like you're paying rent on it," Steve was saying.

"It's a nice chair. I like it."

"You're scared shitless."

Steve grinned at him. He almost looked like Joe Graham, who also had a habit of grinning at Neal when he was being nasty.

"Of what?" Neal asked.

Steve roared. Actually sat back in his chair and guffawed. "Of Karen! Nothing to be ashamed of—Karen has scared a lot of good men."

"Good for Karen."

"Ask her to dance, moron."

"I can't dance," Neal said.

"War wound?"

"I don't know how."

"Nothing to it. You just get up and move," said Steve.

"That's what I don't know how to do."

"Get up, or move?"

"Both."

Steve leaned over the table to give Neal one of those soulful cowboy looks. "It's not like you're Fred Astaire and she's Ginger Rogers or anything. You're not dancing for the artistry of the damn dance. You're dancing to, you know . . . move around together. Get close."

Yeah, right—get close. Getting close isn't exactly my best thing,

Steve. The last woman I got close to did a triple gainer off a big cliff.

Neal worked at finishing his beer. If he could do that fast enough, he'd have an excuse to escape to the bar to buy the next round.

"You ready for another one?" Neal asked as he got up.

"Coward."

"Well, will you let a coward buy you a drink?"

"I'm not particular. You better hurry, though, I see the women coming back."

Neal worked his way to the bar, got a pitcher of beer, and bumped right into Cal Strekker.

"Doing a little honky-tonkin', New York?" Cal sneered.

"Leave your knife at home, Cal?"

"Nope."

Great. "Where do you have it hidden?" Neal asked. "Up your ass?"

"In my boot."

"Well, be careful dancing."

"You want to dance with me, New York? Maybe finish what we started?"

"Gee, I'd love to, Cal, but my beer is getting warm."

"You're a chickenshit bastard."

You're half right, Cal. Okay, maybe all right.

"Jesus, Cal, I told you I'm busy tonight!" Neal shouted. "I'll dance with you another time, all right?"

Cal turned a color that would have drawn a charge from a bull as a whole bunch of people turned around and looked. "I'll be seeing you, New York," he hissed.

"In your worst dreams, shithead."

Neal set the pitcher on the table and sat down. Steve, Peggy, and Karen were staring at him.

"Cal Strekker giving you trouble?" Steve asked.

"How much trouble could he give?" Neal answered as he started to fill their empty glasses.

"A lot," Peggy answered. "He did time in prison for killing a guy in a bar fight in Reno."

It wasn't Reno, Neal thought, it was Spokane. But the bottom line is the same.

"Newcomer trash," Karen said. Then she quickly added, "No offense meant."

"None taken," Neal said. "I'm here for the long haul."

Karen gave him a long look and said, "Then you'd better learn to dance."

She grabbed his hand and pulled him out of his chair just as the band struck up a snappy little number about eighteen wheels rolling down two-lane blacktops.

Karen held Neal by two outstretched hands and did a little hopping step that he did his best to imitate. He could feel his hands getting sweaty in her amazingly cool, soft palms, and he felt as awkward as he knew he looked. Especially in contrast to the beauteous Karen Hawley, with her long legs and wide mouth and big blue eyes.

"Relax!" she shouted to him. Her smile turned his knees to Jell-O, so it looked like he was more relaxed, anyway. He started to let go a little, actually moved his feet more than two inches at a time, and let her swing his arms around in time with Blackie's drum strokes. He was doing all right when that treacherous cretin New Red switched to a slow song.

Neal and Karen looked at each other for an awkward moment. Jesus, Neal thought, I'm blushing.

He looked at her, laughed a little bit, shrugged, and held his arms out. Scary, tough Karen Hawley settled into his arms as soft and gentle as a cloud, and much, much warmer. She didn't bother with any of that hand-held-out-like-a-guitar business, just put both hands on the small of his back, and settled her head into his shoulder. He laid his hands just under her shoulder blades, realized that his hands were quivering, then left them there anyway.

What is it, Neal thought, about the smell of a woman's hair? How it spins around your brain, then rushes straight to your . . . no, don't think about it . . . and the feel of her breasts just grazing your chest . . . or her thighs just brushing against yours . . . don't think about any of that.

The whole thing was an erotic charge, and then she nestled right up against his erotic charge and tightened her hands on his back and let him see the corner of her mouth curl into a little smile and Neal thought he was going to die on the spot. Or get arrested for indecent exposure once the dance was over and they parted hips, even though he was completely dressed.

He looked over her shoulder and saw Steve and Peggy slow dancing, both of them grinning at him. Karen must have seen them too, because the edge of her lips against his neck widened into a chuckle.

"Peggy's subtle," she murmured.

"Like a sledgehammer," Neal agreed.

"I don't mind. Do you?"

"Yeah, I'm real pissed off."

She pressed her hips forward a little. "I don't think you are," she said.

"Sorry about that."

"No, no, no, no. And you *do* know how to dance."

"Yeah?"

"Oh, yeah."

Her head sank a little deeper into the crook of his neck, filling his nostrils and his brain with her scent. Something made him kiss her hair where it fell over her ear.

"Damn hair," she whispered, "always in the way."

He started to brush it off her ear, but she lifted her head to look at him and said, "Later."

"Sorry."

"Don't be sorry. I want you to do that later."

She must have seen the doubt in his eyes, because she leaned forward and gave him a quick, soft kiss on the mouth, her tongue lashing between his lips before her head dropped back on his shoulder and her hips made the subtlest possible circle against his groin.

A big hand grabbed his shoulder and spun him around. Suddenly Neal was looking up into the red, drunken face of one big, angry cowboy.

"What are you doing with my woman?" he yelled.

The dancers around them stopped dancing and backed away. The band kept playing, although they watched the developing altercation with great interest.

"Charlie, get out of here!" Karen yelled.

Neal felt the circle widen around them. Here we go, Neal thought, they're giving us room for a fight. He saw Cal lean against the bar, smiling his feral smile at the thought of Neal getting pounded into hamburger by this animal. Except that under the red face, the drunkenness, and the fury, Charlie didn't look like an animal. He looked like kind of a nice guy.

"Or is she *your* woman now?" the nice guy demanded.

"I think she's probably her own woman," Neal said, trying to keep his voice low and calm, because maybe if he kept it low enough, no one would hear it shaking. He saw Steve Mills work his way toward the front of the crowd and place himself between Cal Strekker and the impromptu boxing ring. The band had come to the end of the slow song and didn't bother to start a new one. New Red was probably searching his memory for a country-western dirge.

"You want to take this outside, or settle it right here?" Charlie demanded.

"Uhh . . . what's behind door number three?"

There was a titter of laughter from the crowd, but no one stepped forward to stop the upcoming fight.

I don't believe this, Neal thought. Stuff like this just doesn't happen. This is so goddamn stupid.

"I'm going to beat the shit out of you," said Charlie.

Why does everybody want to beat the shit out of me tonight? "Too late," Neal said. "You already scared the shit out of me."

Another chuckle from the onlookers. Charlie wasn't laughing, though, he just looked puzzled.

"Are you afraid to fight me?" he asked. It was the ultimate challenge.

"Of course I'm afraid to fight you. I'm a lousy fighter and fighting hurts, even when you win. I never fight unless I absolutely have to."

"You're chicken, yellowbelly!"

"You're not really getting it, are you, Charlie? And by the way, that was a mixed metaphor."

Neal felt that awful sensation of having every eye in the place on him, including Karen's.

"Hold on a second, Charlie," he said, giving him the time-out signal before turning back to Karen. "Do you want me to fight him? Something about your honor or my honor or something?"

"Of course not. Would you fight him just because I wanted you to?"

"Of course not. Do you want to just get out of here?"

Charlie put his hands up and started forward.

"Just a second, Charlie," Neal said. "Can't you see I'm having a conversation here? Jesus."

Charlie stopped cold, his hands still up in the fighting position.

"Yes," Karen said, "I would like to get out of here."

"Let's go," Neal said, taking her arm. As they walked past Charlie, he said, "See? You lost."

As they went through the swinging doors into the street, Neal could hear the roar of laughter from the bar and the music starting up again. Well, he thought, John Wayne might not have approved, but Cary Grant would have loved it.

Karen pushed him up against a pickup parked along the sidewalk.

"That," she said, "was great."

She grabbed his face with both her hands and kissed him long and hard.

"You're not going back to that stupid cabin tonight," she said.

"I'm not?"

"No, you're not."

"Tell me," she said as she nestled in his arm under the sheets of her old iron frame bed, "if it isn't too personal a question, how long has it been since you . . . uh . . ."

"Since I was with somebody?"

"Okay."

"Almost four years."

She thought about that for a couple of seconds.

"Well, that explains it," she said, and then she started to laugh. She laughed until her body shook and he started laughing, and they laughed until she reached for him and observed, "Well, there are some good things about this four-year gap, too. Lucky me."

So much for my monklike existence, Neal thought. Good riddance.

Joe Graham meandered out of his cheap room into downtown Hollywood, which looked like a lot of downtowns on a late Saturday night. The winners had already gone home, the losers sulked in anticipation of the dreaded "last call." The cops pulled out of the doughnut shops to collect their quotas of DUI's along the strips, the emergency room crews took a breather in the last quiet minutes before closing time brought the rush hour of stitches and cold compresses. On the sidewalks, the working girls circled like vultures, waiting to feed on the defeated men who were skulking away from the singles bars still single. In the back rooms of the biker clubs the boys made low-ball dope deals, while heavy metal teenagers in sleeveless T-shirts scuffled to pick up nickel bags of grass. In gravel parking lots old rivalries burst into new fights, and in the AA club the old-timers and the newcomers drank coffee, smoked cigarettes, and thanked their higher powers that for this twenty-four hours, anyway, they were out of it, out of the old cycle of fresh hopes and stale disappointments that was Saturday night in America.

Back on The High Lonely, Neal Carey slept in Karen Hawley's warm arms and warm bed, while out on the sagebrush flats the coyotes sniffed, pawed, and whined in an excitement that turned into a howling frenzy.

6

Neal found Harley McCall the next afternoon.

He might have found him in the morning, except that he stayed late in Karen Hawley's bed. He woke to the sound of wind chimes and water. The chimes jangled in Karen's small backyard; the water came from Karen vigorously brushing her teeth in the bathroom two giant steps from the bed.

Karen's house occupied a little knoll on the north edge of town. It was a small, white one-story clapboard affair, a little ramshackle on the outside but clean and well furnished. Her small kitchen had all of the modern appliances, the living room had a sofa that looked new, an expensive stereo system, and well-framed Gorman prints on the wall. The bedroom was just large enough for the bed and a chest of drawers.

"Can I give you a lift back out to the Mills'?" she asked as she came back into the bedroom. Then she added, "I have lesson plans to do."

"If you don't mind."

"I don't mind. After all, I practically kidnapped you."

She gave him a breakfast of blueberry muffins and coffee, then gave him the ride back out to the Mills' place.

"You don't mind if I don't come in," she said as she pulled into their drive. "I don't think I could stand to see Peggy's smug smile."

"Your honor is safe with me."

"Better not be." She kissed him lightly. "So I think one of us is supposed to say 'When will I see you again?' "

"When will I see you again?"

"When do you want to?" Karen asked.

"I usually get into town on Saturdays."

"You should get a car."

"I should."

Somehow they had started kissing again, and somewhere in there they agreed to see each other on Saturday, unless Karen had a chance to pop out to the ranch before that. And somewhere in there— maybe it was while looking at her smiling eyes—Neal felt a tug he hadn't felt in a long time. Maybe he had never felt it before.

Neal got out of the car, Karen put the Jeep into a swift and skillful K-turn, and Peggy Mills made a precisely timed appearance on the porch under the guise of shaking out a rug.

"Next time you see Karen," she said as Neal tried to sneak past the house, "you tell her I said she's a coward. You are seeing her again, aren't you?"

"Saturday."

"You'd better work that smile down before your face breaks in half," Peggy said. "You be good to her."

"Yes ma'am."

Peggy rolled her eyes, smiled at him, and disappeared back into the house. Neal figured that she wouldn't let Steve come out and make any smart remarks.

Neal hiked back toward the cabin. He was almost there when the coyote appeared.

"Sorry I'm late," Neal said.

The animal ignored him. It was acting strangely, prancing around the brush, tossing its head and celebrating like a dog with a bone. Neal looked closer and saw that it did have something in its mouth. The coyote tossed its head again, almost as if it were trying to show off its acquisition.

Neal trotted into the cabin and got his binoculars. It took a moment for him to find the coyote again and another moment to focus the glasses, and then he saw what the coyote had in its mouth.

A human arm. Half a human arm, anyway, from the elbow joint down.

Neal struggled to hold the focus as his own hands shook and the coyote jumped and danced in triumph. He twisted the focusing dial again and then could make out the distinct shape of human fingers against the coyote's white teeth.

Neal ducked back inside the cabin, grabbed the Marlin, jumped off the porch, and ran toward the coyote. The animal dropped down on its forelegs like a dog getting ready to play a good game of keep-away. He waited until Neal got within twenty yards and then sprang sideways, let Neal get within ten, and then juked the other way.

But the forearm was a heavier load than the coyote was used to managing, and it fell out of his mouth. He picked it back up as the man kept charging, then decided it was time to get out of there. He started straight away at a trot, dragging the arm, the elbow joint bouncing in the dirt.

Neal raised the rifle and fired.

The coyote jumped at the noise, gave Neal a look of betrayal, and scampered off at full speed.

Neal took a deep breath and walked over to where the arm lay in the sagebrush.

It was badly decomposed, a putrid gray-green. Neal could tell that the coyote had dug it up from the dirt that still clung to the rotting flesh. Neal forced himself to get down on his knees to examine the arm more closely, and that's where he saw the stain of color showing up through the putrefaction. It was a tattoo: "Don't tread on me."

Neal turned away and vomited.

When he was finished, his eyes watering from his retching and the stench of the severed limb, he took off a shoe and a sock, put the shoe back on, and slipped the sock over his hand. He picked up the arm, fighting back another round of vomiting, and carried it back to the cabin. He wrapped the arm in one of his T-shirts, dug a deep hole on the slope in back of the cabin, and dropped the arm into it. He put some rocks in, filled the hole back up, and then put some more rocks on top.

Thus Neal Carey buried what was left of Harley McCall.

"Why do you think Hansen or his men were involved in the killing?" Ethan Kitteredge asked. "How do you know it was a homicide at all? McCall might have wandered off into the wild and met with some mishap."

He was sitting in an enormous leather wing-back chair in his study at the family house on the east side of Providence, Rhode Island. Ed Levine sat uncomfortably in a matching chair. A fire of birch logs crackled in the fireplace.

One reason for Ed's discomfiture was Kitteredge's dress: pajamas, a maroon robe, and slippers. Levine had called him in the middle of the evening—as soon as he got Neal Carey's call—and Kitteredge had sent a helicopter for him, insisting that he come right away. Ed had never been to Kitteredge's home before and felt awkward from the moment Liz Kitteredge, the former Liz Chase, answered the door. She greeted him warmly, ushered him into the study, inquired if he preferred coffee, tea, or a brandy, and padded off to fetch Ethan.

Now Levine was sipping coffee, hoping not to spill any on the priceless Oriental rug at his feet and trying to brief his boss on the intricacies of a very complicated case.

"Neal thinks that Strekker was lying when he said that McCall had moved on. That, combined with the fact that Neal found the body just a couple of miles from the Hansen place," Ed answered.

"But what would be the motive?" Kitteredge asked. "Wasn't McCall one of these people?"

"Sir, we're not talking about rational men here. We're talking about a virulent combination of racism and religion. The picture that's beginning to emerge here is that Carter's church has combed the prisons and jails for violent men to match a violent creed and placed them in these 'cells' in remote parts of the West."

Kitteredge raised his eyebrows. "The church militant."

"Exactly," Ed answered. "Right now we can only speculate as to how McCall fell afoul of these people, but there are some questions we need to address immediately."

"Quite."

"For one, do we alert the authorities?"

"We have found a body, here, Ed. We do have certain responsibilities as citizens."

"Absolutely. On the other hand, sir, do we really want local cops, state troopers, or the FBI to go plodding in there? That might get these nuts edgy enough to kill the boy."

"Assuming he's still alive."

"And assuming they have him."

Kitteredge looked into the fire. "But you think he's dead, don't you?"

Ed shifted in his chair. "Yes, sir," he answered, "I'm afraid I do."

"Tragic," Kitteredge said.

Ed didn't think that required an answer. He knew Kitteredge's expression well enough to let the silence go on. He knew that Kitteredge was analyzing the information, sorting out fact from supposition, testing various possible actions against the duties and responsibilities Friends of the Family had to its clients.

Ed munched on a shortbread cookie while Ethan Kitteredge thought.

"You say that Neal Carey has penetrated this group?" Kitteredge asked.

"Yes and no," Ed answered. "Neal likened it to circles within circles. He feels that he has penetrated the first circle but is nowhere near the center."

"And you trust his analysis."

"Yes, sir."

"Scottish," said Kitteredge.

"Sorry?"

"The cookie."

"It's very good."

"Yes," Kitteredge said. "Carey's been undercover for a long time, hasn't he?"

"Three months or so," Ed admitted.

"Is it your evaluation that he is capable of sustaining this role for another extended period of time?"

Ed took another long sip of coffee and another bite of the cookie before answering. He had to be careful here, because he knew—and he knew that Kitteredge knew—that three months was a long undercover assignment, movies and television notwithstanding. And Carey had been out there alone with no handler to talk to—no human contact. An undercover operative tends to forget what's real and what's make believe. He gets lonely, insecure, and paranoid. But not Neal Carey.

"Neal Carey," Ed said, "is the perfect undercover. He has no character."

Kitteredge raised his eyebrows at the supposed insult.

"Neal has lots of personality," Ed explained, although he felt that most of Neal's personality was more or less hemorrhoidal, "but no character of his own. He was just a kid when he started with us. When other kids his age were building character, Neal was building cover stories. He's a chameleon—he takes on the coloring of his surroundings. In that sense, sir, Neal is always undercover, whether he's on assignment or not."

"Is he capable of carrying out this assignment?"

"If anyone is."

Kitteredge lapsed into silence.

When he started to speak, he put the tips of his fingers together in front of his lips in an unconsciously prayerful gesture. Ed knew that he had made his decision.

"Yes . . . ahhh . . . I despise these creatures, Mr. Levine. They are an offense to our flag, to our religion, and to our humanity."

"Yes, sir," Ed answered, ignoring the religious reference, or assuming it referred to a general Judeo-Christian tradition.

"Therefore I am authorizing your plan. Infiltrate them totally, ascertain the fate of Cody McCall, then destroy them."

Ed felt a wave of relief sweep through him. Something else, too. Excitement.

"Yes, sir. Thank you."

"Do have another shortbread."

"I'm on a diet, sir."

"I did think you looked a bit thin."

Ed set his coffee down and heard the cup rattle in the saucer. He realized that there was a tremor in his hand.

"Sir," he asked, "are you authorizing the use of terminal remedies?"

"If necessary," Kitteredge answered.

In fifteen years with the company, Ed had never received, nor had he sought, permission to kill anyone.

Kitteredge selected a shortbread cookie, bit off a tiny piece, and chewed it twenty-eight times before swallowing. "And if it develops that any of these creatures are culpable in the death of Cody McCall, then a terminal remedy will be necessary. Do you understand?"

"Yes, sir," Ed answered. I understand perfectly. We're talking Old Testament justice here.

"Will you be staying the night or should I ring for the helicopter?" Kitteredge asked.

"I should get back to New York," Ed said. He had a lot of work to do.

"Of course," Kitteredge answered.

"Uh, sir . . . should I call Anne Kelley, or would you prefer to do that?"

"I don't see any purpose to be served by terrifying Miss Kelley at this point, until we know about the fate of the boy."

"Yes, sir. Uh, may I use the phone?"

"Of course."

Joe Graham picked up the phone. He usually didn't like calls, but this one came as a relief. The small room in the cheap SRO hotel was beginning to close in on him. The rug needed a shampoo, the mattress was mushy and the springs were shot, and about all he could see from his window was a fire escape and the doughnut shop and liquor store across the street. The guy in the next room sounded like he was going through the heebie-jeebies, the toilet was running, and a car alarm had been going off now for at least ten minutes.

"Hello," Graham said sourly.

"Hello, sweetheart."

"Get bent, Ed."

"We're operational."

Graham sat straight up in the bed. "What?"

"We're operational," Ed repeated.

"How's our boy?" Graham asked. If they were operational it meant that Neal had orders to take the operation into an active phase. A dangerously active phase.

"I haven't heard from him," Levine said.

Graham felt the sticky, nauseating anxiety come over him. He didn't like this at all. I'm Neal's handler, not Ed, he thought. Ed is good, Ed is thorough and careful, but he doesn't know Neal as well as I do. Nobody does. And now the kid's out there—he's rusty and he's hurried, and that's a bad combination. You hurry and you make mistakes.

"Are you monitoring?" he asked Levine, even though the answer was obvious.

"Of course."

"You—"

"I'll let you know the second I hear. Get ready to move."

You're damn right, Eddy boy.

"Another thing," Ed added. "We might be going in heavy."

"How heavy is heavy?"

There was a pause. Graham heard Ed sucking on a cigarette.

"If our client is terminal . . . very heavy."

Jesus Christ, Graham thought. This started as a simple custody bag job. Now Ed is talking about killing people. If the boy is dead.

Another thought hit him. "Hey . . . what if *our* boy doesn't make it out? Do we still go in heavy?"

Another drag of smoke.

"No," Ed replied. "That's just the business, right?"

Graham hung up the phone. No, Ed, he thought. That isn't right.

* * *

Neal Carey stood inside the gas station and fed nickels into a slot machine. His mind wasn't on the game, it was on the telephone outside.

Finally it rang. He listened to it ring for thirty seconds before it stopped. He glanced at his watch. Thirty seconds later it rang again.

Once: ditch the operation, come back.

Twice: stay in place and wait.

Three times: destroy them.

He walked out and got into Peggy's Volvo. He thought for a couple of minutes and then drove up to Karen's house, where Peggy had assumed he was going anyway when he asked to borrow her car. He sat outside for a minute, got his nerve up, and knocked on her door.

She was wearing a gray sweater over old jeans. She was barefoot. She had her glasses on and a pen stuck behind her ear. He could tell by the look on her face that she didn't know whether to be pleased or annoyed.

"Did I give you my phone number?" she asked. "I'm in the book, anyway."

"I'm sorry. I should have called."

"Now that we've agreed on that, would you like to come in?"

"Just for a minute."

He stood awkwardly in her living room, not knowing what to say or do, not knowing why he was even there.

"You interrupted my work," she said. "You at least owe me a passionate embrace. Come here."

He held her as tightly as he could.

"What's the matter?" she asked.

He shook his head.

"Dark night of the soul?" she asked.

"Yeah."

"No fun. You wanna mess around?"

"I want to make love."

"Darlin', don't you know it's the woman who's supposed to use the L-word first?"

He shrugged. "I don't know much about this at all."

She took him by the hand and headed for the bedroom. "Then it's a good thing you got yourself a teacher," she said.

They got up an hour or so later, she to go back to her work, he to go back to his.

The woman smiled her professional smile as she opened the door. "Hi, I'm Bobby, what's—" She stopped suddenly as she saw that the three men in the doorway were wearing masks.

Neal stuck a pistol under her nose. "Hi, Bobby. This is a stickup."

Randy Carlisle grabbed her, swept her out of the doorway, and put a forearm choke hold around her neck. The bouncer in the black hat and shades woke up and tried to get his boots off the footstool as he reached for his gun.

"Uh-uhn," Cal warned. He was pointing his own pistol at the bouncer's head. He stepped into the room and ripped the phone cord out of the wall.

The bouncer put his hands up. Neal walked over, took the bouncer's cowboy hat and shades off, and pushed him to the floor. Then he stepped on the shades, crushing them under the heel of his boot.

"We just want the money," Neal said. "We don't want to hurt anyone."

Bobby warned, "You don't know who you're messing with."

"Yeah, yeah, yeah, you're mobbed up, right?" Neal asked. "Isn't everyone? Where do you keep the money?"

Bobby made a show of folding her arms across her breasts and clamping her mouth shut.

Neal pointed his revolver at the bouncer's head and cocked the hammer. He smiled at Bobby and said, "Your choice."

Bobby let out a disgusted sigh. "A safe in the office."

"Show me."

She led Neal down the hallway into a cramped office. He held the gun to her head as she dialed the combination.

"Put it in the bag," he said as she pulled stacks of bills from the safe.

She did what he ordered but said, "You're really getting into big trouble, cowboy."

"I'm terrified."

"Y'oughta be."

When they got back to the corral, Neal leaned over the bouncer and asked, "You live here, stud?"

"No."

Neal put his boot down on the bouncer's hand. "Maybe in a trailer out back?"

"Maybe."

"Let's go." Neal gestured to Cal. "Come on."

The bouncer walked them back to a cheap aluminum trailer. Cal opened the door and pushed the bouncer inside. Doreen was asleep on a hide-a-bed. The bouncer shook her awake.

"We got company," he said.

Cal covered them while Neal searched the trailer. He found what was left of his money, about three hundred dollars, on a shelf in the bathroom.

Doreen gave her boyfriend one withering dirty look when she saw the cash.

"They got the drop on me," he explained.

"You was asleep, I'll bet," she accused.

As they marched the bouncer back out Neal heard Doreen mutter, "This ain't no life for a white girl."

They went back to the corral. Randy left as Neal and Cal covered him. Cal went out next—Neal didn't want him shooting anyone just for laughs. With Bekke and Vetter covering him from the car, Neal backed out and then jumped in the front seat.

"Head west," he said to Dave Bekke, who was behind the wheel.

"But—"

"Do what I tell you," Neal ordered. "They're going to figure the robbers came from Reno. Might as well oblige them. We can double back later."

"Whooee!" Randy hollered. He was counting the money.

Neal asked how much.

"Looks like about eleven thousand!"

"Not bad," Neal said.

"Not bad?"

"Not bad," Neal repeated, "for a warm-up."

"But we're only going to rob from vice mongers, Jews, and race traitors, right, Neal?" Craig Vetter asked anxiously.

"You bet, Craig," Neal answered. He and Cal exchanged amused looks.

Craig added, "Otherwise it would be immoral."

"We sure wouldn't want to be immoral," Cal said.

The occupants of the car broke into laughter, yells, and whoops of general merriment as they rolled down the highway.

Thus the Sons of Seth struck their first blow against the Zionist Occupation Government in the form of a low-rent cathouse, and Neal Carey touched off the great north central Nevada crime wave.

7

*I*t was modest at first. They did another shabby cathouse down by Luning, then hit an after-hours card game in Battle Mountain. They found a marijuana runner in Elko and hijacked his truck on a switchback at Antelope Pass. A long weekend in Reno netted them a pimp's money roll as well as the worldly wealth of a pickpocket whom Neal lured and then followed back to his stash.

They chose victims unlikely to complain too much to the cops and who were themselves engaged in some form of evildoing, at least in the minds of True Identity Christians. They worked fast and clean and used enough force so that they didn't have to resort to actual violence, a condition Neal enforced because he was ''not going to do any more hard time just because any of you guys get scared or triggerhappy.''

As the money came in, Neal's stock rose. He was becoming what he needed to be to get on the inside: a necessity. He was getting the group hooked on money. What had first seemed like a windfall was becoming an expectation. They were becoming junkies to his pusher.

It wouldn't be long before he had enough on them to put them all away. Having lured them into committing crimes they never would have thought of, he would then turn state's evidence, testify, and disappear again. But not yet. He still had to make the crucial connection between Hansen's boys and C. Wesley Carter. Ed wanted the whole enchilada.

And of course there was Cody. Or there wasn't Cody, more to the point. Through the weeks of planning, practicing, and carrying out the robberies, Neal had seen no sign of the boy. He could be anywhere. Farmed out to some Identity family in northern Idaho or Washington State or Arkansas someplace, or left in the care of somebody's loyal woman in a dingy trailer court anywhere west of the Missouri. Or he could be dead.

Neal didn't want to accept that possibility, although he knew that Strekker and Carlisle, at least, were capable of killing a child to cover up his father's murder. But it seemed too much, somehow. Too much to deal with, too much to believe and still keep going on. And he had to keep going on.

He knew it was only a matter of time before the boys in the bund brought him into the inner circle. Only a matter of time, and not much time at that before they'd give anything—even their secrets—to keep the money flow coming in. But time was an enemy to young Cody McCall, if he were indeed alive.

And time is certainly an enemy when you're undercover, and Neal soon came to realize that he was under a kind of double-cover, living one life with the Sons of Seth and another with the Mills and Karen Hawley.

It was a tough thing to juggle, working with Steve then sneaking over to Hansen's for a training session or a lecture. Going to Brogan's for a beer and trying to ignore the gang in the corner. Having dinner at Wong's with Karen, then making some excuse for leaving so he could run with the wolf pack that night.

There were a few close calls, like the time he was in Strekker's pickup headed to Reno and just saw Peggy's Volvo coming the other way from a shopping trip to Fallon. Or when Karen had slept over in the cabin for a change and the boys had come to get him at six in the morning for a little dawn training patrol.

Then there was the time he showed up at Phil and Margie's all bruised, stiff, cut up, and bowlegged from riding that damn horse.

This particular beast's name was Midnight, and it was black all right, all the way down to its malevolent soul.

"Why do I have to learn to ride?" Neal asked as he sat on a corral rail. Midnight stood in Gandhiesque tranquility next to him.

"Might need to someday," Bob Hansen answered cryptically. "Besides, Midnight here is the gentlest gelding we have."

Midnight looked up at Neal and whinnied softly in reassurance. He did look gentle, Neal thought. He was small as horses go, and skinny. And he had soft warm eyes.

Neal lowered himself into the saddle. Midnight turned his head and looked back at him and nuzzled the rein.

"Take him for a spin, Neal," Billy McCurdy urged as he smiled his cretinous smile at the rest of the gang.

Neal picked up the reins. "Is this the steering wheel?"

Jory swung open the corral gate.

Midnight looked back at Neal with a gentle are-you-ready expression.

Neal gave the horse a slight nudge in the ribs.

The horse took off like he had a rocket up his ass. His soft eyes now burned with a demonic fever as he headed straight for the nearest barbed-wire fence.

Neal wanted to get off, but the horse didn't feel so small anymore and it seemed like a long way to the ground, especially at this speed. So he just held on as Midnight found the fence, turned left, and galloped alongside the wire, leaning in ever so slightly to graze Neal's leg on the barbs.

Neal heard the roars of laughter from the corral, and Billy's proud voice warbling, "Yep, that damn horse is doing it again! You can't teach that, you know—he comes by it natural!"

"I wish you still had your balls, Midnight!" Neal hollered as he felt his jeans rip on a barb. "So I could cut them off myself!"

Midnight responded by racing beside the wire for another hundred yards or so and then bearing down toward the trees by the creek bed.

Or more accurately, one particular tree. A scraggly old pine with the dead limb sticking out, the limb about as high off the ground as say, a man on horseback.

Not being as smart as the horse, Neal didn't see it coming until they were about fifty yards away.

He pulled back hard on the reins but Midnight plunged ahead like a New York cabbie at a yellow traffic light.

Neal jerked back harder.

Midnight ignored it and pulled his head down.

"Have you ever heard of Alpo?" Neal yelled.

Midnight was so intimidated that he sped up as he galloped under the limb. Neal managed to get his hands up over his face as he smacked into the tree limb, did a little trapeze dismount, and landed on his back on the ground.

As Neal struggled to get some air back in his lungs, Midnight walked over and gently nudged him with his nose, like Fury trying to wake up Joey.

Then he bit him.

It was just a nip, but it was a nip that hurt, goddammit, and Neal was just pissed enough to get up, dig his foot into the stirrup, and swing back up into the saddle.

Midnight stood still during all of this and then headed out at a tame walk when Neal nudged him. After a while, Neal got brave enough to take the horse to a little trot, and eventually cantered back into the corral as the boys reassembled to watch his triumphant return.

"Just a matter of showing the animal who's boss," Neal announced as he brought Midnight to a stop.

That's when Midnight started whirling in a violent circle, sending Neal spinning off the saddle like a Frisbee and skipping across the ground like a stone on water.

So Neal was a little sore when he met Karen that night, and she had some questions as to why he was learning to ride at Hansen's.

And, of course, the crime wave was the talk of the town. Over beers at Phil and Margie's, or coffee at Wong's, or cheap whiskey at Brogan's, people talked about the robberies that were starting to become the stuff of legend. It seemed like everyone knew about the holdup at the Filly Ranch, and suddenly it seemed like there was a gang sticking up every drug dealer in the Great Basin, and most folks heartily approved. And there was talk that the police were turning a blind eye to these activities, and there was even talk that it was off-duty cops who were pulling them off. And there was titillated talk that the Mafia down in Las Vegas—which most people considered a colony of California and not part of Nevada of all—was getting a little unhappy and was out hunting the robbers themselves.

And Hansen's boys heard the talk too. They started walking with that little extra swagger when they came to town and started smiling smug, knowing smiles when the robberies came up in conversations and people started to joke about the James gang and the Daltons. Neal about choked on a green chili when that bone-stupid David Bekke said something about this gang being more like Robin Hood, "robbing from the Jews and giving to the poor."

Soon the whispering started. A few fingers discreetly pointed at the backs of the boys as they walked through town, and there were murmurs beneath the music at Phil and Margie's; Neal even imagined he heard his name spoken as he sidled to the bar to get another pitcher for the table. And maybe it was his imagination that Steve looked at him a little funny from time to time, or that Peggy's "hmms" took on a more serious tone. And maybe it was only in his head that Karen was getting a little reserved, would start to say something and then stop, as if a question was caught in her throat.

Neal thought that his life was like one of those drawings of railroad tracks stretching out over a horizon. The illusion is that the tracks stay separate, but in reality the lines come closer and closer until, at some point over the horizon, they have to meet.

They absolutely collided one cold Saturday night at Phil and Margie's.

Neal and Karen had gone with Steve and Peggy to drink and dance, to chase away the blues that came with the first snowfall of the season. The snow had hit the valley that morning, not an honest-to-goodness kick-ass storm or anything, but enough of a dusting to let them know that the long winter was on them.

So Neal had crowded into the pickup's cab with Steve and Peggy and they had no real trouble rattling into Austin. They met Karen at Phil and Margie's. The place was already crowded with like-minded celebrants, including Cal Strekker, Randy Carlisle, Dave Bekke, and Craig Vetter—the whole gang.

The trouble didn't start right away. Like a lot of trouble, it needed to get fueled up by alcohol, so for the first couple of hours Neal danced with Karen, Steve spun a few with Peggy, and the boys stayed bellied up to the bar. Steve was refreshing himself liberally between dances though, so the alcohol level rose steadily to the point where all it needed was a spark.

Which happened when Steve and Cal scraped together.

Steve was turning away from the bar with a fresh beer in his hand and he happened to slosh some on Cal's boots.

"Sorry about that," Steve said.

"If you can't hold your liquor, Mills, you shouldn't be here," Cal answered.

Cal's boys turned from the bar to look, other heads turned at that, and then it seemed like the whole crowd was watching.

"What's going on over there?" Peggy asked as she looked toward the bar.

Neal got up and made his way through the crowd.

"Well, now," Steve was saying, "I never knew of a cowman who got too upset over a little beer on his boots. Then again, you're not a cowman, are you? You're the shithead of security."

"Let it go, Cal," Vetter said, seeing the murderous look come into Strekker's eyes.

But Steve Mills was interested in pouring a little more gas on the fire.

"And I told you before," he said, "to call me Mr. Mills or Steve. And while you're at it, you don't tell me where I should or shouldn't be, you jailhouse punk."

Neal grabbed Steve by the elbow and tried to pull him away. "Come on, Steve," he said.

"You better go with him, old man," Cal smirked.

Steve tried to yank free of Neal's grip. "Don't let age stop you," he said to Strekker.

"Let him go, Neal," Cal said.

Steve turned to Neal with a surprised look. "Are you guys buddies now?"

Neal tightened his grip. Steve pulled free easily this time, just to show he hadn't been trying before. He set the beer back on the bar and then launched a wicked roundhouse right at Strekker's head. Strekker stepped back easily and the punch whooshed two inches in front of his nose.

Strekker smiled his psycho smile. "You all saw it," he said. "He swung first."

He brought his hands up and stepped back into a fighting stance.

Strekker will kill him, Neal thought.

"Get out of the way, Neal," Randy Carlisle said. He was grinning like the sycophantic fool he was, eager for his dominant half to shed somebody's blood.

Peggy Mills sat frozen at the table. She was helpless. If she let the fight go on, her husband might get hurt bad. If she intervened, she would hurt him worse. When Karen started to get up, Peggy took her wrist and pulled her back down.

The music stopped. The crowd made a circle around Steve, Cal, and Neal. Steve took another swig of beer and put his hands up.

"Get out of the way, Neal," Randy repeated.

Neal stood for a long second between the two would-be fighters. Then he shrugged, got out of the way, and walked over behind Cal. Randy and Dave slapped him on the back. Karen gave him a look of astonishment and outrage. Neal shrugged again, picked up a barstool, and smashed it over Cal's head. Strekker dropped like he'd been poleaxed.

"Fight's over," Neal announced.

"Whose side are you on?" Carlisle yelled. He grabbed Neal by the front of the shirt.

"My side," Neal answered.

Carlisle punched him in the eye, threw him to the floor, and hit him twice more in the side of the head. Steve jumped on Carlisle and hit him with a tremendous right uppercut that sent him sprawling unconscious into Vetter's arms. Vetter set him down, stepped up, and punched Steve in the jaw. Dave Bekke jumped Steve from the side.

Neal got to his knees, saw Bekke hanging from Steve's back, and tackled Bekke's legs, pulling the man down on the floor with him. Bekke rolled him over, got on top, and started punching. Neal got a leg between Bekke's legs and drove his knee up into Bekke's balls, which discouraged the punching.

Steve and Vetter were holding each other with one hand while exchanging haymakers with the other when Bob Hansen walked through the door.

"Knock it off!" he yelled.

Dave Bekke was rolling on the floor gripping his crotch just as Randy Carlisle got up and charged at Neal. He hit him in the midsection and drove him back to the floor. Craig had Steve bent backward over the bar and was cocking his fist for the coup de grace.

"I said that's enough!" Hansen hollered.

Steve reached up, grabbed Vetter's fist, and pulled back like he was flipping a calf to the ground. Both men went over the top of the bar and landed with a crash on the floor. Neal had managed to pull Randy's denim jacket over his head, trapping his arms. As Steve and Craig got up punching, Hansen pulled a pistol from his belt and shot a hole in the ceiling.

The roar stopped them all in mid-punch, and they looked sheepishly over at the rancher.

Hansen surveyed the damage and said, "You need to leave me with a hand or two, Steve."

"Then you need to teach 'em some manners, Bob."

"I expect you're right about that."

Hansen looked quizzically at Neal.

"Carey coldcocked Cal from behind, Mr. Hansen," Carlisle accused.

"That right, Neal?" Hansen asked.

"You bet."

Hansen holstered his pistol. "Seems we have us a few things we need to get resolved."

You ain't kidding, Neal thought.

Cal Strekker pushed himself up onto his knees. He shook his head a few times as Carlisle and Vetter grabbed his arms and helped him to his feet.

"Let's get going, boys," Hansen said. "We got work to do tomorrow. Neal Carey, I'll be talking to you."

Neal nodded. And I'll be talking to you, he thought. Because it looks as if we'll have to speed things up a little bit.

Hansen looked around at the broken glasses and the pool of blood on the floor where Strekker had been taking his nap.

"I'll take care of the damages," he said to the bartender.

"No you won't," Steve Mills said. "We will—me and Neal Carey."

"You're a traitor," Carlisle snapped to Neal as he walked out.

I wish you hadn't said that, Neal thought. I really do.

The band started up again and Steve threw his arm around Neal's shoulders.

"Goddamn, it's been a long time since I been in a fight like that!" he whooped. "Goddamn that was fun! But you shouldn't have hit him with that stool like that. I would've held my own with him."

"Aww, I know. I've just been wanting to hit him with a stool for a long time. Seemed like the right moment to do it."

They were back at the table now and the women were looking them over for damage. There was a lot to look at. Steve had a split lip, a nasty cut over one eye, and a cheek that was swelling up like a squirrel's in the fall. Neal's right eye was beginning to close and a lump was starting to rise up from his forehead.

"Barbarians," Peggy muttered. "Karen, we're sleeping with barbarians."

"That has yet to be seen," Karen answered. She had a severe, schoolteacher frown on her face.

"Which part?" Steve asked. "The barbarian part or the sleeping-with part?"

"I don't think there's any question about the barbarian part," Karen answered.

Steve winked at Neal. "Uh-oh," he said. "I believe we're in trouble."

But Peggy was looking over his shoulder at Neal and mouthing the words "Thank you."

"Let's get these barbarians home," Peggy said aloud. "I'm married to one, but the other is optional."

"I'll take him," Karen said. Then, in a lower tone to Neal, "Besides, I have some questions to ask."

Uh-oh.

Joe Graham watched as the pretty boy prostitute settled on a price and got into the front seat of the Mercedes. The car sped off, leaving the sidewalk in front of the True Christian Identity Church empty. Graham slipped into the alley and shuffled through the garbage and the stench of stale urine until he came to the fire door.

He looked around once, then pulled a thin metal strip from his coat. The lock gave up without a fight and Joe Graham was inside the building. He listened for a second, heard no human or animal sounds, turned on his flashlight, and headed up the stairs.

He had the place pretty well memorized from weeks of coming to the damn services, drinking the weak coffee, and eating the cake at the social hour afterward. The price you pay, he thought. He'd heard more damn Jewish jokes than he would at a Catskill weekend.

He found Carter's office with no problem. The door was unlocked, so he walked right in. Trust in the Lord is a wonderful thing, he thought.

There were three horizontal file cabinets plus the vertical files in the desk drawers. None of them were locked, which Graham found discouraging. He was looking for something that Carter had to hide.

There was another door in the back and it opened to a smaller room with a desk, a couple of chairs, and a safe.

That's more like it, Graham thought. He knelt down beside the combination lock and got to work.

* * *

"Why did he call you a traitor?" Karen asked Neal as she placed a cold washcloth on his eye.

"I dunno. He was drunk."

"He wasn't that drunk. And why did that one with the beard ask you whose side you were on? And how do you know those guys, anyway?"

Neal took the washcloth from her and held it himself. "Jesus! Are you sure you don't want to shine a bright lamp in my eyes? Beat me with a rubber hose?"

"Maybe."

"Lay off." *Because I'm in a tough position here, Karen. By the strict rules of the game I should have let Cal do a number on Steve back there, but something in me couldn't let that happen. So I stepped in and committed a cardinal sin—I compromised my cover. And I have to figure out how to put that back together again. Then those assholes had to open their big dumb mouths and undermine me on the other side.*

"Just tell me the truth," Karen said.

Which is just the thing I can't do. To tell you drags you into it, puts us both at risk. "Shit, Karen, they live next door."

"Two miles next door."

"It's still the next door," Neal said grumpily.

She had made up another ice pack and held it to the lump on his head as she sat down next to him on the sofa.

"Are you hanging out with those guys?"

Never deny what can't hurt you, Neal thought. *There's nothing worse than getting caught in a lie you don't have to tell. Save your lies for the important stuff.*

"We've had a couple of drinks together," he said. *After knocking over a whorehouse or two.*

"Hmm," she said.

"Did you learn that from Peggy?" he asked.

She shook her head. "Bad company."

You bet. "Anyway," he said, "they probably won't be too friendly after tonight." *Which is something of a problem, actually.*

"Don't bet on it," Karen said. "Out here, little brawls like that don't get in the way of being men together. Just a little bloodier-than-usual male bonding. You know, shake hands and laugh it off. 'Boy, you really hit me a good one there, har-har-har.' That sort of thing."

"You sound pissed off."

"I guess I'm just jealous. I want you to do your heavy-duty bonding with me," she said. She reached down to his lap by way of illustration.

Neal groaned. "Karen, not that I don't appreciate the sentiment, but my eye hurts like crazy, my head is throbbing, and my ribs feel like someone took a hammer to them."

She kept stroking him and said, "Aw, the poor baby. You know, if you're going to be a rootin'-tootin', two-fisted drinkin', barroom-brawlin' cowboy, you'll have to learn to climb back in the saddle after you've been thrown."

"Really?"

His voice was strangely high-pitched.

"Mm-hmm," she said, unbuckling his belt. "Hurt or not, you have responsibilities."

"Responsibilities?" he asked over the metallic zing of the zipper.

"To me."

"To you." He ran a hand through that beautiful hair and touched her neck.

She looked up at him and asked, "How are those ribs now?"

"I don't feel a thing."

"Yes you do," she said, softly laughing.

"Yes, I do."

And he did. He felt wonderful and guilty at the same time, because he knew that a relationship is based on trust and honesty, and he could never give either.

Jory Hansen was thinking about a woman too, as he guided Cocoa up the slope of the spur. He was thinking about Shelly Mills, how he had left her on the couch in her living room, about her disheveled hair and clothes, and about how it was he who had put a stop to it with the feeble excuse that her parents could walk in any second.

She had wanted to do it, too. She had told him straight out, and he had been shocked and thrilled, but there was something that stopped him. He wanted to tell himself that it was his morals, his concern for her, his fear that she would hate him later when she was more in control, but all of that would be lies.

Truth was, he knew, that he had something laying heavy on him. Something terrible. Something that he had to hide but couldn't hide from God, from Yahweh.

He knew it was this secret that stopped him. Stopped him even though he loved Shelly, even though she was so beautiful, even though he wanted to spend his life with her.

There wouldn't be much of a life now. Not with the secret, not with the End Time coming.

But only Yahweh knew when that would be. Yahweh and maybe the old Indian.

The old Indian knew these things. It was the old Indian who had shown him the paintings in the cave, told him what they were and what they meant. Told him how they showed the beginning and the end.

Which is why Jory had done what he had done. Why he had the secret. Why, as he picked his way along the snowy ridge toward the cave, he prayed that he was right. Or that Yahweh would forgive him if he was wrong.

Then he could hear the Indian singing softly. A song older than sin.

Jory got down and slipped the pack off the horse's rump. He asked Yahweh to forgive him for stealing the meat and canned food. He slipped the strap of the pack over his shoulder and hefted the bundle of firewood. Then he started up for the cave.

To see once more the end and the beginning.

Graham opened the file on the desk, pulled the gooseneck lamp over it, and photographed the file. He took special care to focus on the picture stapled to the top right corner of the first page.

The picture of Cody McCall.

---

*   *   *

Peggy could tell that her daughter had been crying. Not that she had ever been very good at hiding her feelings, but now her eyes were red and puffy.

"What happened to Dad?" Shelly asked as Steve snuck upstairs with the briefest of greetings.

"Feeling his age," Peggy answered. "Acting like a colt because he feels like an old horse."

"Huh?"

"He got into a fight in a bar."

"Daddy?" Shelly asked. "Is he okay?"

"He'll feel worse tomorrow. Now, what's going on with you?"

Shelly turned away and went to sit down on the window box. She stared out in the darkness toward the mountains. "Nothing," she said.

Peggy sat down beside her and stroked her hair. "Why don't I believe that?"

"Because it's not true."

Peggy put her arm around her daughter and held her quietly.

After awhile Shelly said, "I wanted to make love to him tonight."

Peggy felt a shot of fear go through her, but she suppressed it. She made her voice as calm as possible when she asked, "Did you?"

"No."

Thank you, God, Peggy thought.

"But only because he didn't want to," Shelly said. "I don't know whether to feel humiliated, or guilty, or relieved . . ."

"I'm relieved," Peggy said, and they both laughed a little. "Why didn't he want to?" Because there's no teenage boy I've ever known who didn't want to.

"He was afraid you'd walk in on us."

"Well, that's silly. You can only hear the truck coming for half a mile."

"I know."

"He was probably scared, honey."

"So was I."

"Me too. Mostly because one of these nights it will happen. You're warm and smart and loving . . ."

"Pretty?"

"Beautiful. But don't be in too much of a hurry, okay?"

"Okay."

"And be careful."

"Mom!"

"Well, I already have at least one more baby around here than I can handle. Speaking of which . . ." She rolled her eyes up toward the bedroom.

Shelly hugged her long and hard and then said, "Go see Daddy. Tell him I hope he won."

Steve was in the upstairs bathroom, looking into the mirror and steeling himself to apply peroxide to the cut over his eye.

"Give me that," Peggy said. She took the bottle and dabbed a corner of the washcloth with the disinfectant. "Tell me something. Did you pick that fight with that asshole?"

"I suppose I did."

"You shouldn't drink at all, you know that."

"I know."

She dabbed at the wound. Steve hissed.

"Oh, don't look so hangdog," Peggy said. "You didn't do so badly."

He walked into the bedroom and plopped down on the bed.

"I've been thinking a lot lately," he said.

She joined him on the bed. "About what?"

"About just who the hell I am." He smiled sheepishly. "A little late for a mid-life crisis, isn't it?"

"Just about on time, I'd say. But is this one of those mid-life crisis deals where you leave me for a twenty-year-old cocktail waitress who really understands you?"

He reached for her and pulled her in. "You don't get that lucky."

"Good. Because you can be whoever you want, just as long as you're my husband."

He kissed her with his split lip and winced. But it didn't stop him.

Bob Hansen put down his Bible and turned out the light. Sleep didn't come easily. It hadn't come easy since . . . he pushed that out of his mind. There was no use dwelling on it. Yahweh demanded a lot of his chosen people, and the End Time was coming soon. Bob Hansen was sure of that, just as sure as he was that he was Yahweh's strong arm in the chosen land. Reverend Carter himself had anointed him, and Yahweh's strong arm needed to get things cleaned up in the valley before the manchild came and the End Time started.

I can't hide this much longer, he thought, not with the compound getting bigger and more men coming in all the time. Soon we'll be using this as a base for operations against ZOG, and soon after that we'll be defending it in the End Time, and I'd better be sure that the base is secure. Steve Mills will have to be with us or against us.

But he'll be with us. Steve is a good white man with his head screwed on straight. All he needs is a little education. Then the whole valley will be the haven Yahweh meant it to be.

But sleep still wouldn't come.

Karen lay in bed watching Neal's troubled sleep and wondering just who this man was, this man whom she was in love with. What was he really doing in Austin? His story about a casual friendship with Hansen's boys was bullshit—the Neal she thought she knew couldn't be friends with that trash. What was he hiding? Should she dump him now, before he broke her heart? What snakes twisting in his head gave him such terrible dreams?

In Neal's nightmare he was chasing the coyote across the sagebrush. The coyote had something in its mouth. Something golden. Neal chased it and chased it until he got close, until the coyote turned around and grinned, and Neal saw that the golden object in its mouth was the blond hair on the head of Cody McCall.

He didn't let himself sleep after that until the sun came up.

8

*T*he next afternoon Neal hiked over to Hansen's house and knocked on the front door. He was surprised when Hansen answered it himself.

"You have nerve, Neal. I will give you that."

"May I come in?"

Hansen stepped out of the doorway and ushered him in.

For a large house, it was remarkably simple. The rooms were all rectangles. The walls were eggshell white with western paintings hanging on them. The floors were wide-plank hardwood with bright Indian rugs.

"Come into my office," Hansen said.

Neal followed him into a small room with a plain wooden desk, a swivel chair, and a straight-back cane chair. He gestured for Neal to take the cane chair as he sat in the upholstered swivel. Neal figured that this positioning was used to intimidate employees, let 'em know who was the boss, as if there were any question.

"What was last night all about?" Hansen asked.

"It was about keeping Cal out of prison."

"What do you mean?"

"You know Cal. He would've killed Mills. Then where would he be? More important, where would *we* be? If Cal had any brains he'd be thanking me for jumping him."

"You're a smart man, Neal."

If I were smart I wouldn't be here.

Hansen continued, "But I don't know how committed you really are."

"I'm committed, Mr. Hansen," Neal answered. Or should be, anyway.

Hansen tapped a pencil on his desk as he looked Neal over. Then he said, "It's a dilemma for me, Neal, it is. Because I was about to make you a full member of our brotherhood. We were even planning the swearing-in ceremony."

Great. Terrific. Good job, Neal. Screw everything up in a barroom brawl.

Neal looked him square in the eye. White man to white man. "There's nothing I want in the whole world more than to be a member of the brotherhood, sir."

Hansen nodded. "That's fine, Neal. Because we need you. We need your skills."

Damn right you do. You couldn't knock off a gumball machine without me telling you how.

"We're going to rob an armored car," Hansen said.

Or an armored car.

"A sympathizer in Los Angeles has 'tipped us off' to this opportunity, so it will be an 'inside job,' " Hansen said, his eye twinkling as he trotted out his criminal jargon. "An armored car company services the little banks and the mines around here. It's making a big run in two weeks. I was hoping you could organize the hijacking."

Neal whistled. "An armored car is a lot tougher animal than a pimp or a card game or a pickpocket, sir. I don't know if we're ready for it." He sat quietly for a few moments, thinking it over. "How much money are we talking?" he asked.

Hansen's eyes widened. He leaned forward in his chair and carefully pronounced, "Two to three hundred thousand dollars."

"Two hundred large," Neal said. "That's a lot of money."

Hansen sat back again. "I can't begin to think what getting that money would do for the cause," he said.

"Getting it and getting away with it are two different things."

"That's why we need you, Neal."

Well, come and get me, Bob. Neal stood up and offered his hand. "I'd be real honored to help, Mr. Hansen. I want to fight for my race."

Hansen stood up and took his hand. "I'm so glad to hear you say that, son. And after this mission is over, you'll become a brother. I promise."

Then Hansen bent on one knee, pulling Neal down with him.

"Let's pray together, Neal," he said. He bowed his head and said, "Oh, Yahweh, bless this, your fine young warrior, and bless our common endeavor. Bless our holy war against your enemies. Your will be done, amen."

"Amen," Neal echoed.

Now let's eat.

Two weeks, Neal thought as he walked over to the bunkhouse to make his peace with the boys. I can do another two weeks.

He didn't get it. He got about two hours.

While he was sitting in the bunkhouse with the boys, talking about the swearing-in ceremony, and the End Time, and about the big job they had to start planning, Steve Mills came to call on Bob Hansen.

"It's good of you to come over, Steve," Bob said as they sat in his kitchen. "We been neighbors too long to have bad blood."

They were drinking out of jelly jars. Steve was having some of the scotch that Hansen kept for guests, Hansen was drinking milk.

"I don't have any hard feelings for you, Bob. But lately, the hands you've been hiring . . . they have a certain low tone. Anyway, I was a jackass last night and I apologize. If we can round up your boys, I'll shake their hands."

It seemed like the opening Hansen had been waiting months for. So he told his old neighbor Steve all about it. How he'd first come across some literature from the Reverend C. Wesley Carter, how he'd visited his church while on business in LA, how he began to see his true Christian identity and his rights and duties as a white man. Hell, they both knew what was happening to this country. The damn federal government was taking over everything, telling a man what he could do and what he couldn't.

"It's true," admitted Steve. "You can't raise a cow or cut a tree without seventeen bureaucrats giving you permission."

Wasn't it the truth, Bob continued. The government had already ruined both coasts and was working its way toward the middle. Why, this was the last open, free country on earth, up here on The High Lonely, but it wouldn't be long before the government destroyed what they had here. And he was sure that Steve knew why.

Steve allowed that he had some ideas about the federal government.

Jews, that's why, Bob told him. The Zionist conspiracy to rule the world. That's why they're letting those subhuman niggers run riot. And homosexuals. They're all in on it. The IRS, the Federal Reserve, the FBI—all were riddled with Jews.

Bob told him all about the True Christian Identity Church, how becoming a member had changed his life, made him see things the way they were, and promised him salvation. How Jory had come to see the truth too, and how he now hired only men who were committed to the cause. And as his friend and neighbor for these twenty years, he felt it was his duty to invite Steve to join.

"Well, I don't think I can do that, Bob," Steve said when he was finished.

"I do wish you'd give it a try."

Steve shook his head, finished his whiskey, and set the glass down on the table.

"May I ask why not?" Bob said. He felt his hopes for Steve fading away.

"Sure," Steve answered. "I guess it's because I'm Jewish."

Which stopped the dialogue.

Feeling the need to fill the conversational void, Steve added, "Half Jewish, anyway. On the top side. Mother was Irish as a drunken wake, but my old man's old man came over from Russia. I think the original name was Milkowski, something like that. Got shortened somewhere along the line. Anyway, I don't guess you want me in your church.''

"Get out," Hansen said. His face had drained of color.

Steve stood up. "You bet," he said.

He took his time getting to the door while Hansen sat in his chair, staring at the table.

"Oh, Bob," Steve said from the door. "Shalom."

Hansen sat in a rage for a couple of minutes before the thought hit him. Then he got up and ran toward the compound.

Neal looked up from cleaning his gun as Hansen burst through the barracks door.

"Where's Jory?" Hansen yelled.

All of the men froze at his rage. No one wanted to speak.

"I think he took Shelly to lunch in town," Neal said. "Is something wrong?"

Hansen looked like he might have a stroke any second.

"Steve Mills is a goddamn Jew!" he roared.

Yup, Neal thought, something's wrong.

They all sat there looking at one another for a second.

"Get off your asses and go get him!" Hansen hollered. "Get him away from that Jew bitch! Bring him back!"

Hansen turned and stormed out the door.

"You heard the man," Vetter said.

Cal Strekker let out the whooping laugh he'd been holding in. "Well, how about that! Prince Jory's been cuddling with a Jew! And don't know it!"

"Let's get after it," said Carlisle.

"Let's all go," Cal suggested. "This might be some fun."

They scrambled out of the bunker and ran toward their trucks. Neal followed them.

"We can all fit into two!" Cal yelled as he started his truck. "You coming, Carey?"

"Wouldn't miss it!" Neal yelled. Which is goddamn true.

He hopped in the back of Cal's truck just as Cal hit the gas and sped out.

*　*　*

"I wouldn't have believed that of Bob Hansen," Peggy said after Steve related the story of his visit.

"He told me himself," Steve said. "I was so damn mad I could have punched his lights out right there. But I figured I'd done about enough of that."

Peggy set a plate of chicken-fried steak down on the table and said, "Barb never would have stood for this nonsense."

"Oh, I don't think he'd have ever gotten involved if he still had Barb. Grief does strange things."

She sat down at the table with her own plate and started to cut a piece of meat. "It shouldn't turn a man into a bigot, though. It's going to be awfully hard being neighbors, though, and . . . oh, shit!"

"What?"

"Shelly's in town with Jory."

Steve set down his fork and headed out the door.

The kids were finishing dessert at Wong's when Cal and the boys came through the door.

Neal lingered in the background, trying to fool himself that he could stay close enough to keep things under control but not be seen.

"Hey, Jory!" Cal yelled. "Your daddy sent us to fetch you!"

Cal took a second to grin at Shelly and let his eyes wander over her body.

"Is he all right?" Shelly asked.

"Oh, he's okay, just a little excited at the moment," Cal answered. "Hey, Jory, guess what—"

Neal stepped up to the booth and said, "Jory, your father wants you to come home now."

"Neal?" Shelly asked. Her scared, bewildered look cut into him.

"Yeah, he's got news for you!" Cal said, elbowing his way past Neal. "Seems like your girlfriend here is a Jew."

"Come on, Jory," Neal said quietly.

Jory looked at Shelly. "Is that true?"

She shrugged her shoulders and looked around. The gang had

formed a semicircle around the booth, trapping her in. Evelyn had come out of the kitchen and was standing in the background.

"Yeah, I guess . . . I think Daddy's . . ."

"Think nothing," said Cal. "Daddy's a Jew. Boy, Jory, I hope we got to you in time. I hope you haven't screwed this little—"

Shelly stood up in the booth and slapped him.

Evelyn hurried out the door.

Neal stood in paralyzed horror. He was watching a young girl being tortured and trying to stack that up against the potential life of another child.

Cal rubbed his face and grinned, then said, "I don't suppose screwing a Jew is much different than screwing a nigger."

"Let me out of here," Shelly demanded.

Nobody moved. Jory sat frozen in his seat with his face in his hands.

"Jory?" Shelly asked. "Jory? Jory, for God's sake, say something! Jory?"

He slowly lifted his head and looked at her.

She smiled at him, a don't-we-live-in-a-world-of-fools smile. An it-doesn't-matter-because-we-love-each-other smile. She slid her hand across the table to take his.

"Jew bitch," he hissed. "Goddamn Jew bitch."

The boys hollered and whooped and slapped his back.

"Goddamn Jew bitch tried to get me to screw her last night!" Jory shouted.

There was more whooping and hollering and Shelly just fell apart right there, curled up into a ball and sobbed.

Every human instinct Neal Carey had screamed at him to go hold her and take her out of the restaurant. But he kept his cover and just stood there.

"Let me out," Shelly moaned. "Let me out."

"Come on, Jew," Cal said. "You wanna screw us all?"

"Yeah, you want to screw us all?" Randy Carlisle echoed. "Do you, Jew?"

"Neal, help me!" Shelly cried.

All eyes were on him.

"Neal, please!"

He looked at her and shook his head.

"You know, Shelly," Cal said, "you really oughta let folks know that you're a Jew, maybe wear one of them Stars of David on your sleeve—"

"You let that child up or I'll shoot your damn head off!" Evelyn was standing five feet in back of them, the shotgun at her shoulder pointed straight at Cal.

They all turned to look at her.

"Evelyn, you wouldn't use that thing," Cal said.

"Cal Strekker, I'm an old lady and my hands shake and this is a hair trigger. Now you let that child pass."

Cal and Randy parted to make space for Shelly to get up.

"Come on, honey," Evelyn said. She held the shotgun in one arm and stretched out the other hand to Shelly. Shelly got up slowly and Evelyn cradled her in her free arm. "Now all you scum get out. And don't be coming into my store, neither. I don't want your business."

"If we was Jews or niggers you'd have to serve us," Randy said. "It's because we're white men we have no rights in our own country."

"I'll serve any human being that comes into my place, but you're just garbage." She held the sobbing girl as she turned away. "Come on, honey, I'll take you home."

Cal yelled after her, "You think you can survive without the business of the Hansen Cattle Company?"

She turned back to him. "Stack all of you up against a man like Steve Mills and you don't come to a thimbleful of piss. And everyone in this town feels the way I do. You tell your boss that. Tell him I don't want to see him or his ever again."

She turned to Neal, "And you, Neal Carey. The Mills took you in when you was down and out and this is how you repay them. You're worse than any of these vermin." She spat on her floor and walked outside.

Cal went out into the street after them and the rest followed.

"Jew lover! Jew bitch!"

Neal stood on the sidewalk and watched as the old lady helped Shelly up the street toward her house. Shelly was doubled over, holding her stomach and crying.

Which was the first thing Steve Mills saw as he raced the truck into town. He took one look at his daughter and the jeering gang of Hansen's cowboys, heard the cries of "Jew bitch," grabbed his rifle off the rack in back of him, and jumped out of the cab.

"Look out!" Randy yelled.

The cowboys ran for their trucks as Steve came pacing up the street. Cal grabbed his own rifle and got behind his truck. Vetter did the same. Randy pulled a cheap pistol from under his coat. Dave ducked down behind Vetter's truck and Jory sprawled flat on the ground under Cal's.

Neal Carey stood on the sidewalk.

Steve ignored them, walked straight up the street, and gently took his daughter from Evelyn.

"Did they touch you, darlin'?" he asked.

Shelly shook her head.

He put his arms around his daughter and walked her slowly past the cowboys' trucks toward his own. He opened the passenger door and lifted her inside. Then he started to walk back up the street toward the gang. Cal and Vetter shouldered their rifles and took aim, steadying the barrels on the trucks' hoods. Seemingly oblivious of the three guns pointed at him, Steve walked back up the street toward Neal.

Neal stepped out into the center of the street, trying to put himself between Steve and the guns without making it obvious. Steve stopped a few paces from him.

"You coming with us?" he asked Neal.

Neal felt every eye and ear in the whole damn world on him. He even felt Karen's, and she wasn't even there. He felt Levine's and Graham's and The Man's and Anne Kelley's and Cody McCall's.

"No," he said.

"You with them now?" Steve made a contemptuous gesture toward the men hiding behind the trucks.

"Yeah."

"You were on my side last night."

So the tracks have come together, Neal thought. Not somewhere over the horizon, but right here, right now. And now they'll go in different directions. And you can't have one foot on both anymore.

"Last night," Neal said, forcing himself to look his former friend in the eyes, "I didn't know you were a kike."

Steve looked back at him for a second as if he were going to say something. Then he turned around and walked back to his truck to take his daughter home.

And it isn't over yet, Neal thought.

He was in the cabin packing his stuff when she came.

He was pretty sure it was Karen when he saw the headlights coming toward the creek, because the lamps were set narrow like a Jeep's and he figured she was going to come. But he picked up his rifle anyway before he stepped out on the porch. He watched the car stop on the far side of the creek and saw the flashlight coming toward the cabin.

The light was just a few feet away when he saw for sure that it was Karen. He lowered the rifle and stepped back inside. He was putting his books into his pack when she walked in without knocking.

She started right in. "I had to come tell you myself what a bastard I think you are."

"Thanks for taking the trouble," he said. He kept his back to her and went on working. He couldn't tell her the truth and she probably wouldn't believe it anyway.

"Is that all you have to say?"

There's a lot more I could say, Karen. I could tell you about the lesson I never seem to learn: never get personally involved on the job. Especially not when you're undercover. You only end up hurting people.

And whatever you do, never fall in love.

He shrugged and laid a pair of jeans out on the bed, then carefully rolled them up and put them inside his pack.

"Steve and Peggy want you out of here by morning," Karen said.

"Tell them not to worry. I want out of here."

"Are you going to move in with those racist pigs?"

"Oink."

Having brought her too close, the job now was to drive her far off. Out of harm's way.

"Do you even want to know how Shelly is?" she asked. "Do you care?"

"Not especially."

He'd known for a long time that he couldn't have this job *and* a life. Where he'd made his mistake was in thinking he could leave the job *for* a life.

"You lied to me," she said, the anger and hurt almost palpable in the closed cabin air.

Undercover is a lie, Karen. You start by hiding who you are, and you hide it and you hide it while you become other people, and then when you want your own identity again, you can't find it. It's like that little treasure you store someplace to keep it safe, and a long time later you forget where you put it.

Karen, how would I tell you if I could? It's just that you play so many characters that after awhile you don't have one of your own. Or maybe that's backward. Maybe I never had any character to begin with.

Anyway, he didn't answer her, so she asked, "How long have you been with them? Just recently, or the whole time?"

"Since before I came here," he answered, because this was a chance to push her farther away. "I've been convinced for a long time now that we have to do something to preserve our white race."

"You disgust me."

Get this over with, Neal thought. Because if you don't you might break down and tell her the truth. Shit, if it were an adult involved, a responsible grownup who had screwed up, I'd tell her right now. But it's a kid. It's a little boy who might still be alive and who has only a slim chance, and that has to be more important. If my stupid, messed-up excuse for a life means anything at all, a child has to be more important.

He turned around and said, "And you disgust me, Jew lover."

He saw the tears come to her eyes and saw her face twist in hurt.

"I was ready to love you!" she yelled. "I was ready to love you and now I hate you! Do you understand me? I hate you!"

I understand you, Karen. "So leave," he said.

Those blue eyes sparkled with rage. "Go to hell, Neal," she said. Then she left.

On my way, Karen. I'm on my way.

He finished packing and started the long, cold walk to the Hansen place.

Part Three

Gunslingers

9

*N*eal shivered in the bitter cold. As the wind bit through his denim jacket he tucked his chin a little deeper under his sheepskin collar and pulled his black cowboy hat tighter down on his head.

The sun was a pale circle in a sharp blue winter sky. Sitting on Midnight on the top of the hill, Neal felt as if he could see forever. He was sitting in a stand of piñon pine on the west slope of the Shoshones, looking down about five miles where the little mining town of Ione sat at the edge of a vast desert. He watched until he saw a flash of silver start moving up the slope toward him. He lifted his binoculars and focused on the flash.

"Here she comes," he said to Jory.

Jory shifted nervously on his horse. He checked the big saddlebags again to make sure they were tied on tight.

Neal moved his glasses just down the slope from him, off the left side of the road on the bottom end of a switchback, where Cal and Randy waited in a camouflaged pickup with pine boughs thrown across it. Just a little above Neal, Dave, and one of the new guys were sitting in another truck, waiting for his signal.

Neal focused on the armored car again. He checked it out and then glassed the road behind it.

Nothing.

"They don't have a follow car," he said.

"That's good," Jory said. Neal could hear the tension in his voice. He hoped the boy would be all right. Then again, all he really had to do was ride his horse. Jory had been picked for that job because he was by far the best rider, about the only legitimate cowboy there except for Craig Vetter and Bill McCurdy, who sat on another horse just by.

"Arrogance," Neal responded. "Laziness and arrogance."

It's going okay, Neal thought. They'd picked the spot well. The armored car would be in low gear as it chugged up the heavy grade. The switchback would keep them hidden and give them the privacy they needed. There was a big boulder on the other side of the road.

"I sure hope they don't spot that pickup," Jory said.

"They won't," Neal answered. "Remember, they're not looking for anything. This is just the usual milk run to the little towns to pick up the checks and drop off the money. They'll only get half-alert when they bring the stuff out of the truck. Now shut up, I need to concentrate."

The timing on the thing was delicate, even though they'd practiced on a similar switchback a couple of dozen times. But there was no way to simulate the armored car's exact speed or what its driver might do, and that's what had Neal concerned. If things started to go wrong, people might use guns in place of the plan.

He was particularly worried that Cal and Randy might get hinky, believe they'd been spotted, and just start shooting. But there was nothing he could do about that, so he put it out of his head and watched the truck work its way up the slope.

He felt his chest tighten. There'd be only one shot at this thing and he had a feeling it would be his last shot at finding Cody. If the robbery went off well, Neal would be sworn in as a full-fledged Son of Seth, and as such he would be privy to all of their secrets.

So concentrate, he told himself. Do something right for a change.

The truck was getting closer. Eight minutes, maybe ten.

"Get back some," Neal said. He maneuvered his own horse a few feet back into the pines. It wasn't easy. He still felt about as comfortable riding a horse as he would flying an airplane. Billy and Jory eased their horses into the pines.

"How much longer?" Jory asked.

"Shut up," Neal answered. He didn't dare lift the binoculars again for fear the flash might spook the driver. But he could catch the glare of the armored car's roof as it came around the switchbacks.

More like six minutes now.

"Check your loads," he ordered.

"But we've already checked about——" Jory started to say.

"Do it!"

Neal pulled his Colt from its holster and flipped the cylinder open. He had five rounds loaded, leaving the chamber empty. He didn't want anyone's pistol going off accidentally. He slipped the revolver back into the holster.

"You think they got two men or three?" Jory asked, his voice cracking with tension.

"Will you be quiet?" asked Neal, although it was a good question. If the car was carrying a two-man crew—a driver and a guard—the job should be a breeze. If it was carrying a third man—another guard—things could get tricky. They'd gone through the options many times, but it clearly was weighing on Jory's mind. A third man almost certainly would mean there'd be shooting. From both sides.

Three minutes, give or take, before the truck would pass Cal's position.

"Cover up," Neal ordered.

He pulled up the red bandanna tied around his neck and fitted it high over his nose. He pulled the brim of his hat down so it shaded his eyes, then turned to look at Jory and Billy to see if a stranger could identify them in some nightmare lineup down the road. With the bandannas on, the hats down, and the collars up, their eyes were about all that was visible. Good enough.

Neal looked down to see the car roof shine in the sun. It was just one switchback below Cal now. One more straightaway and one more curve and they'd be in the trap.

He turned to Billy and pointed up the hill. Billy kicked his horse and started to ride up to where Dave was waiting. Jory had to hold his horse back from following.

Great, Neal thought. Even the goddamn horses are nervous.

He watched the metallic flash get closer. It was almost up to Cal now.

He raised his right arm and brought it down sharply. Jory did the same thing and Billy relayed the message. Neal heard Dave's truck start down the hill.

It's going to go quickly now, he told himself. Keep your head. He looked across the road to the top of the boulder and whistled sharply. An answering whistle came back right away. Neal knew it would. Craig Vetter was a solid hand and the right man in that spot.

Neal watched the armored car come up the hill. Come on, baby, he thought. Keep coming . . . keep coming . . .

The armored car's driver didn't see the truck hidden off the side of the road, not that he was looking for it, anyway. He was idly talking sports with the guy in the passenger seat. It made the time pass. The guard in the back contributed a few ignorant comments about zone versus man defenses, but the driver decided that the guard didn't know squat about either.

"What the hell difference does it make?" the passenger asked irritably. He sipped his coffee where he carefully had torn a crescent in the plastic cover. "The Giants can't throw against either."

"I dunno," the driver answered. "If they get single coverage on man—"

"Sure, if the man is Franklin Roosevelt or Ray Charles or maybe . . . look out!"

The driver was already looking. A lumber truck was headed straight for them. Sideways. The driver knew that the silly son of a bitch had taken the curve too wide and lost it. He knew it was going to jackknife the moment he heard the awful whine of the hydraulic brakes.

The driver slammed on his brakes.

The lumber truck jackknifed, just as the driver had expected. What he didn't expect was that the trailer would flip and spill out its load of logs, which came bouncing and barreling straight for the armored car.

"Holy shit!" the driver yelled. "Get down!"

He and the passenger hit the floor just as one big cedar bounced over the hood and rolled into the windshield. They felt four more jarring thumps before the barrage stopped.

The passenger looked at the driver.

"Look at these slacks," he said with disgust. They were soaked with spilled coffee.

The driver got back up in the seat and looked out to see three rifle barrels pointing out from behind the overturned trailer.

"Stay down!" he yelled to the passenger. He threw the car into reverse and started looking for a place to do a K-turn. He was one hot driver, but he knew he wasn't going to make it to Ione going backward. He looked in the rearview mirror and knew he wasn't going to make it to Ione at all. A big old pickup was roaring up the road in back of him. The pickup went into a controlled skid and slid sideways across the road.

I'll give them a run for the money, anyway, he thought. He squared the armored car up on the pickup and punched the accelerator.

"You think he's going to stop?" Randy asked Cal as the armored car bore down on their truck.

"Bail out!" Cal yelled. He grabbed Randy by the collar and hauled him out the passenger side a moment before the armored car slammed into the driver's door. It shoved the pickup a couple of feet back but didn't clear it out of the road. Randy reached over the side of the truck bed, grabbed the gasoline can, and ducked.

"You got 'em behind you!" the driver yelled to the guard. The guard scrambled to pick up the rifle he'd dropped in the collision.

Neal fired his pistol in the air and Craig Vetter jumped from the boulder onto the car's roof. He landed hard, fell forward, got up quickly, and fixed the lasso in his right hand.

Cal and Randy scrambled in a crouch toward the armored car. The guard in the back stuck his rifle out the gun slit and drew a bead on Cal. Craig tossed the lasso over the gun barrel, tightened the rope, and pulled it to the left. Cal stuck his pistol in the gun slit and pointed it at the guard's head while Randy lifted the gas can he was carrying, shoved the rubber tube through the gun slit, and poured the gas into the back of the armored car.

"I'm coming out! I'm coming out!" the guard yelled as he saw Randy strike the match.

Just like we practiced it, Neal thought. He watched the back door open and the guard step out. Cal grabbed him and put him on the ground.

"Stay there," Cal said.

"No problem, no problem," the guard answered. He was pissed off. This was supposed to have been an easy job.

Neal edged Midnight to the side of the road. He pulled his pistol and pointed it at the passenger door.

"Keep your damn hands off the radio! Those rifles pointed at you have jacketed rounds, so forget about your bullet-proof windshield!"

"What bullet-proof windshield?" the passenger yelled.

"Are you the boss?" Neal asked.

"The supervisor!"

"Open the cash compartment, supervisor!" Neal yelled.

The guy in the passenger seat reached under the dashboard and flipped a toggle switch. The compartment unlocked with a loud metallic click.

"Open the door and come out, supervisor!" yelled Neal.

"I have a gun! I'll toss it first!"

"Okay!"

So far so good, Neal thought.

The door eased open and a Colt .45 dropped to the ground. Neal backed the horse up to give himself some room and pointed the gun at the door. The supervisor came out with his arms in the air. He looked at Neal on the horse and asked, "Which one are you, Butch or Sundance?"

"Get down on the ground, smart guy," Neal ordered.

The guy grinned crookedly and let himself down slowly onto the road.

"Now you!" Neal yelled to the driver. The driver eased himself out from behind the wheel and dropped to the ground.

Craig jumped down and he and Randy went into the back of the armored car. They pulled five large white canvas bags out of the cash compartment and carried the sacks over behind the pines, where Billy, Craig, and Jory had brought the horses. They loaded the stacks of money into saddlebags.

"Hurry up!" Neal yelled.

They finished loading the horses, then walked them up through the pines and out onto the road above the lumber truck.

Neal walked over to the supervisor and gave him a little kick in the ribs. "Get up."

"Take it easy."

"I'm taking it easy," Neal said. "Walk toward the lumber truck. You do anything else, I'll put one in your back."

"You won't have to, son." He started walking toward the truck. Dave came out, grabbed him by the arm, and hauled him to the back side of the truck.

Randy and Cal ran back to their pickup and headed down to Ione. They'd take a roundabout route to Austin when they were sure they were in the clear.

"You boys like your boss?" Neal asked the guard and the driver.

They nodded.

"I have him as a hostage," Neal said. "If I even *see* a plane, or a helicopter, or any member of the law enforcement community, I'll leave him for the vultures. Now get up and get your coats out of the car."

He held the pistol on the two men as they got their coats and put them on. Then he lifted the pistol, shot the radio, and took the keys out of the ignition.

"Just to make sure," he said. "Now don't you boys get all-of-a-sudden stupid. No bank's worth dying for."

"You got that right," said the guard.

Neal stepped to the side of the road and threw the keys over the edge.

"Start walking for Ione," Neal said.

"Aw, come on!" the driver protested. "It's freezing out here!"

"It's a lot colder six feet under," Neal answered.

The guard turned and started walking. The driver took a second to give Neal a dirty look and then started down the road after him.

"It's been a pleasure robbing you!" Neal yelled. He jumped back on Midnight and rode back to the lumber truck. "Let's get going!" he yelled.

The boys hopped into the two pickups they had waiting up the road and drove over the top of the hill as Neal, Craig, Jory, and Bill trotted behind. The hostage was tied and gagged in the back of the first truck. A few minutes' hard driving got them to the base of the hill, back in Reese Valley.

Three big horse trailers were parked on the other side of the hill. The captured mustangs snorted and stamped in two of the trailers. The gang started to off-load their own horses from the back of the third.

Neal pointed to the hostage. "Untie him."

Dave looked startled. "Neal, are you sure?"

"Well, he can't ride like that, can he? Besides, he's one of us."

"What?"

"I said it was an inside job."

Dave grinned as he hurried to untie the prisoner. "Neal, boy, damned if you ain't something else . . ."

Damned if I ain't, Dave boy.

"He can ride with me," Neal said, pointing to the supervisor. "Help him up."

Dave pushed the man onto the horse in back of Neal.

"We all ready?" Neal asked. Then he gave a signal and the men opened the trailers. The mustangs poured out and milled nervously in the snow, waiting for their leader.

He was a big young bay stallion, and he reared and kicked as Bekke led him away from his mares and young ones. The cowboys held the herd in check while Bekke pulled the stallion along until there was a space of a hundred feet between the stallion and his herd. The rest of the cowboys eased their horses into this space as Bekke held the stallion, who was trying to crush his handler's head with his slashing hooves.

"Hold on tight," Neal said to his passenger. He nodded to Dave, who gingerly slipped the rope off the stallion's neck, then fired a pistol in the air. The stallion whinnied and reared, saw the way clear to the broad valley to the north, and took off. His mares and young ones followed at a gallop, while the cowboys in the middle hung on to their mounts and tried to stay ahead of the stampede, which was even now obliterating their tracks in the snow.

Midnight surged forward and both riders almost fell off before righting themselves.

"I told you to hang on!" Neal yelled.

"Did I ever tell you I hate you, Neal?"

"Many times, Graham! Many times!"

Joe Graham hung on to Neal's waist as if it were a life preserver. This wasn't far from reality; their horse was laboring under the double weight and losing ground. If either rider fell off he would be crushed by the stampeding mustangs before he could even get to his feet.

Graham closed his eyes.

Neal looked ahead and saw Dave chasing the stallion on, galloping right behind him and keeping him headed south. The stallion was trying to cut, turn around, and get back to his herd, but it was too soon for that. Neal could hear the hooves behind him, what people called a thundering herd. But it wasn't like thunder, the sound was more like a heavy hail storm, like when the sky opens up and beats the earth with hard balls of ice. He risked turning his head and saw the mustangs pounding just behind him. He gripped his knees harder into the horse's side and kicked his heels into the animal's ribs. His left foot slipped out of the stirrup and he fell forward onto the side on Midnight's neck. He could feel Graham's one hand trying to grab his jacket and pull him back up, but Graham had no leverage and they were both slipping.

He gripped the reins tightly in his left hand as he tried to feel for the stirrup with his foot. He got a toehold, then grabbed the horse's mane with his right hand and pulled himself back up.

And then they were just galloping, flying across the sagebrush with the north wind in their faces, and the horses kicking up snow and snorting and the cowboys gasping for breath. One long, beautiful ride on The High Lonely and then it was over. Craig, Jory, and Billy, their saddlebags full of the loot, cut to the east and trotted toward the Toiyabe Mountains, and Dave slowed to a canter and then stopped. The stallion turned, watched him for a wary minute, made a wide circle around the cowboys, and galloped back to his herd.

Neal watched the stallion gather his mares, his fillies, and his colts, snort greetings, and then lead them in a dash back to the south, back to the hard task of surviving winter.

Then Neal looked east and saw the cattle herd a mile in the distance. He watched the three riders cross in front of the herd, which would soon trample their tracks. The riders were headed for the creek. They'd ride their horses up the creek bed for about ten miles, then take them up into the hills where they could see the Hansen ranch. If everything was all right they'd come in at dusk.

The rest of them would join the cattle herd and make their way slowly down to the ranch.

If anyone was looking for armed robbers, they wouldn't think to suspect a bunch of cowboys bringing in their cattle.

Vinnie Pond stamped down the road. He was not a happy man.

"I'm a driver," he said, "not a walker."

Hell of a driver, thought the guard. He'd hit the pickup perfectly—not enough to move it out of the way but hard enough to look real.

"What I want to know," the guard said, "is where Neal got that shit-kicker accent."

"You know Neal," Vinnie said. He blew on his hands to keep them warm.

"Not always a day at the beach," the guard agreed.

They trod on down the hill.

———

When they reached the cattle herd Neal got off Midnight and helped Graham down. "Take a break," Neal said.

Joe Graham sat down in the snow. "How do you keep from banging your balls when you're riding?" he asked.

"You don't," Neal answered. "You just get used to it."

"No thanks. How much farther do we have to go?"

"About ten miles," Neal answered, hopping back in the saddle. "It's not so far on a horse."

"I think I'll walk."

Neal reached down and helped Graham back into the saddle. He maneuvered the horse to the back of the herd, out of earshot of the others.

"It went well," Neal commented. "How much money did we get?"

"Three hundred large plus change."

Neal whistled. "Pretty generous of The Man."

"He wants it back."

That'll be a cute trick, Neal thought.

Graham said, "Nice touch with the logs. You could have told us."

"It was an afterthought," said Neal. "I didn't know it was going to be you."

"I had something to tell you."

"What's that?"

"I think Cody McCall is alive."

"So do I," Neal said.

"But I think I know where he is."

Cal and Randy had driven to Ione, then on up to Fallon, and now were working their way home on Route 50. They'd picked up a couple of six-packs in Fallon, seeing as how alcohol was in short supply back at the ranch.

They were close to the Filly Ranch when Cal said, "You know, we oughta *really* celebrate."

"How do you mean?" asked Randy.

"Thinking of saddling up a filly."

Randy looked at him in disbelief. "Jesus, Cal, we robbed that place!"

"We had masks on!"

"Still and all."

They were still arguing about it when they reached the Filly Ranch and something Cal saw made the discussion moot.

It was a woman standing by the road with her suitcase by her feet and her thumb out.

"Pull over," Cal said. "I mean, why pay for it?"

Randy pulled the truck over and Cal rolled his window down.

"Awful cold to be standin' out there, ma'am."

"You're telling me," she answered.

She's pretty, Cal thought. Long legs, big tits . . .

"Where you headed?" he asked.

"Anywhere away from here," she answered. "This is no kind of work for a white woman."

"We can take you as far as Austin," Cal offered.

"That's a start."

Cal hopped out, threw her bag into the back of the truck, and helped her into the cab.

"My name is Cal, he's Randy," Cal said. "Course, I'm randy too, but my name is still Cal."

She laughed politely but was starting to get a little nervous. "I'm Doreen," she said.

"You sure are pretty, Doreen."

"Hey, I just want a ride, okay?"

It's okay, Cal thought, we just want a ride, too.

A little way down the road he asked, "You don't suppose you could contribute some gas money, do you, Doreen?"

She shook her head. "I don't have no money. That bitch back there wouldn't give me my pay. Said I owed her for rent and towels and shit."

Cal and Randy looked at each other and laughed like banshees.

194

"Well, that's too bad, Doreen, but maybe we could work something out?"

Randy pulled the truck to the shoulder.

"You goddamn men are all the same," Doreen said. "All right, who's first?"

Cal looked at Randy. "Wait outside."

"It's colder than your momma's heart out there. Are you kiddin'?"

Cal took his pistol from his waistband. "I ain't kiddin'."

"At least let me have a cigarette and a beer," Randy grumbled. He lit up, popped open a beer, and got out of the truck. He leaned against the passenger door.

Cal pushed Doreen down on the seat. "You're going to love me," he said.

"I'll bet." She wriggled her jeans down to her boots. "Come on, lover."

A couple of minutes later she said, "Is there something special I can do to help you . . ."

"It's the cold," he said.

"Sure, baby, it's the cold."

Randy rapped on the window.

"I ain't finished!" Cal yelled.

He ain't even started, Doreen thought. It might be quicker to walk to Austin.

Randy rapped again. "Cal!"

Cal looked up. "What?"

"A car's pullin' up!"

Cal zipped himself, tucked the pistol back in his waistband, and backed out of the cab. A big man in a black cowboy hat and shades was getting out of an old Cadillac and coming toward them.

Doreen kneeled on the seat and looked out the window. "Shit, it's Harold!"

Cal thought he recognized the man as the bouncer at the whorehouse, but he asked her, "Who is Harold?"

"What are you doing with my woman!" Harold roared, answering the question.

Randy giggled and Cal answered, "I was just about to make her the happiest woman in America before you interrupted."

"Get out of there, you whore!" Harold yelled. "Your ass is coming back to the ranch! You think I'm paying your bill?"

Doreen looked at Cal.

Cal said, "I'll pay her bill."

"Shut up, cowboy," Harold said, "I wasn't talkin' to—"

Cal looked around at the empty road, pulled his gun, and shot Harold three times in the stomach. As Doreen watched in shock, Cal and Randy dragged the writhing, moaning man off into the sagebrush.

"Finish that up for me, will you, Randy?" Cal asked as he walked back to the truck. He climbed in and pushed Doreen back down. "I guess that makes you my woman now," he said.

He didn't need any special tricks this time, and Doreen lay on the seat listening to his grunts and Harold's whimpering. Then she heard the shot and felt Cal finish.

They were a few miles up the road when Doreen said she had to take a pee.

While she was squatting behind a bush, Randy said, "She saw you kill that man, Cal."

"Us. She saw *us* kill that man, my friend."

Randy pulled his gun. "This is as good a place as any."

"What's the hurry?" Cal asked. "We're having a party tonight."

Randy frowned. "Hansen ain't gonna like us bringin' no whore to the ranch."

"He don't have to know. We'll sneak her in."

Randy slipped his gun back inside his jacket as Doreen walked to the truck. Cal opened the door and Doreen climbed inside.

Steve Mills stood on the penultimate step of the ladder, gathered the lasso, and tossed it over the chimney. Then he took the other end, tied it around his waist, and hauled himself up onto the slippery roof of his house. He stood for a moment to get his footing and watch the snow of the valley turn sparkling orange as the sun blazed in the late dusk. Then he got to work; he didn't have a hell of a lot of time.

"Carter seeks out these custody cases," Graham told Neal. "He encourages the father to skip the state, cool out for a while, and then enter one of the cells. Once Daddy is completely committed to the cause, Carter persuades him to give the child up for 'racial adoption.' A boy Cody's age will be hidden somewhere until he forgets he ever had a family outside the Identity movement."

Neal pulled on the reins to slow his horse down. He wanted to stay in back of the herd, well out of earshot of the rest of the gang.

"The idea," Graham continued, "is to raise the perfect Aryan warrior. A child completely indoctrinated in Identity philosophy. Someone without personal connections or loyalties to anyone or anything except Reverend Carter and the white supremacist movement."

"Are there many of these kids?"

"About a dozen so far," Graham answered. "As soon as we're finished here we'll turn the files over to the Feds."

Neal felt a chill go through him that didn't come from the sharp north wind.

"Maybe Harley wouldn't give them his son."

"And they whacked him and took the boy."

"So where is he, Graham?"

"I'm not sure," Graham answered. "But Carter likes to use a child in these swearing-in ceremonies."

Meanwhile, back at the ranch, Bob Hansen guzzled coffee to try to soothe his nerves. It didn't help much that his house guest was a model of serenity.

"Trust to Yahweh," Reverend Carter said once again. He sat at the kitchen table. The three bodyguards he had brought with him from Los Angeles stood in each doorway and beside the window. They were wearing their uniforms—starched khakis with crossbelts and red Nazi armbands.

Bob looked out his kitchen window to the south. The boys should be coming in now, if everything went as planned. If . . .

"If Yahweh means us to have the money, we'll have the money," Carter intoned.

"I have a son out there," Hansen reminded him.

"They're all my sons," Carter replied. "And Yahweh's."

But Carter was edgy too. The money would mean so much for the cause. It would give them the ability to wage a holy war.

He watched Hansen as Hansen watched the south pasture.

Craig Vetter looked down from the Toiyabe slopes. He thought he saw something coming up the valley from the south, but he couldn't be sure it was the herd. He wasn't worried. He had a good view of the ranch and could see that it was in the clear. If the law had set up a stakeout, he would have seen it.

He turned to Jory and Bill, who sat shivering beside their horses. The boys were beat, but they had done well. They'd ridden hard across miles of frozen sagebrush, then down into the creek, where they'd first headed south, then turned around in the water and worked their way back north. It was hard, cold work, especially when they'd come out of the creek into thick pine and had to walk their exhausted horses up to the lookout. And now the sun was setting, and even though the fierce wind was dying down, it was bone-aching cold. Craig wished they could make a fire.

He looked south again.

No doubt this time, it was the herd.

He kneeled down and offered a quiet prayer of thanksgiving to Yahweh. Then he turned to his comrades and said, "Let's go home, boys."

The two cowboys got up stiffly, then started down the mountain.

They came home to a hero's welcome.

Hansen shook their hands, and the Reverend C. Wesley Carter himself embraced each and every one of them and just couldn't stop gushing, "Wonderful, this is just wonderful. God bless you brave men. You Aryan warriors."

Hansen introduced Neal to Carter, "This was the mastermind, Reverend."

Carter shook Neal's hand, hugged him, shook his hand again, and said, "Your name will take an honored place in the roll call of those who stood and fought for our race."

"Thank you, sir. It's a great joy to meet you," Neal answered. He pushed Graham forward. "I guess you know this guy."

"Joe Gentry," Carter said. "We did it!"

Graham grinned. "Yes, Reverend, we did."

Carter looked around at the group. "This man sat in the back of my church twice a week for months . . . and never put anything in the plate."

They all laughed.

"Well, isn't this wonderful?" Carter asked. "Isn't this Yahweh at work? You put a little in the plate today, didn't you?"

"We should put that money away," Neal said to Hansen.

"It can go in my office safe," Hansen said. "That way it'll be handy for tomorrow."

Say what? Neal made himself not look at Graham.

"What happens tomorrow?" Neal asked.

Hansen and Carter smiled at each other as if they'd been caught planning a surprise party.

"I guess we can tell them now, Reverend. What do you think?"

I guess you goddamn can.

"I think it's okay now," Carter answered. "Tomorrow the arsenal of Yahweh comes."

Crates of Bibles? Swastika stencils? A singing group?

"M-16s, rocket launchers, land mines," Hansen explained. "State-of-the-art modern fighting equipment. Everything we need to start the shooting war against ZOG."

Carter added, "And it is heroes like you who have provided the money to wage this holy war."

Great, Graham thought, The Man will be delighted to hear he just laid out 300K to arm a band of violent, neo-Nazi loonies.

Neal could feel Graham's eyes boring through the back of his neck.

"And I have even more good news for you," said Hansen.

More?

Hansen beamed and said, "Neal, Reverend Carter is here to personally swear you in as a Son of Seth."

"I'm honored," Neal said.

"You've earned it, my son."

No shit, Reverend.

"Go get cleaned up," Hansen ordered. "We're holding the ceremony tonight."

Tonight, Neal thought. A few more hours is all we need.

"He was a real son of a bitch," Doreen said as she knocked another whiskey back. "Left me just cuz I did a nigger."

Brogan opened his eyes and leaned forward in his chair to check this one out. Brezhnev shifted and whined at the unaccustomed activity.

Cal filled her glass from the bottle on the bar.

"You gonna want another one?" Brogan asked.

"This oughta do her," answered Cal.

Brogan leaned back in his chair and closed his eyes. "She looks done to me," he muttered.

Brezhnev looked at her a little longer before he set his head back on the floor.

"So, Doreen," Cal asked, "what do you think about my proposition?"

She snorted. Wasn't much of a proposition. Go out to some shit-kicking sagebrush ranch to pull a train for a bunch of cowhands. But it wasn't like she had a whole lot of options, and she would need some money if she was ever going to get off The High Lonely. Besides, if Cal here liked her enough to shoot Harold over her, maybe he'd give her a ride down to Vegas, where she could get a fresh start. There was only one problem.

"I'll do it," she said, "if you can promise me *he* ain't there."

"He who?" Cal asked.

"The son of a bitch," prompted Randy. He'd had enough whiskey to almost forget what they were planning for Doreen. And to hope that he had a chance with her before they did it.

"Harley McCall," Doreen stated with the exaggerated pronunciation of the defensive drunk.

Which was when a little chill came over the party.

Cal looked at Randy. "Harley McCall."

They both knew. They both remembered "Paul Wallace," his legs propped up on saw horses, Cal standing over him with a sledgehammer, *screaming* his real name.

"Harley McCall," Randy repeated.

"—is a son of a bitch," muttered Doreen.

Cal put his arm around her shoulder and said, "Darlin', I can absolutely, positively guarantee you that this Harley McCall won't be at the party."

Randy giggled. He remembered Cal swinging the hammer down on Harley's shin, first one and then the other. Harley had stared down at his bones sticking out of his flesh and howled like a coyote in a trap. They'd stuck a rag in his mouth when the screaming stopped being funny.

"You know," Doreen blubbered. She started to cry. "I'd like to find that son of a bitch. I loved the son of a bitch. And the little boy. Maybe you could help me find him?"

"You bet we could," Cal answered. He looked over her shoulder and grinned at Randy. "I'll bet we could take you right to him."

"Come on," Randy said, "we'd better be gettin' back to the ranch."

He hoped he'd have a little time with Doreen. They'd have to sneak her into the bunkhouse so Hansen didn't see, and then they'd have to go to the ceremony. But he hoped that left a little time before they killed her.

* * *

Neal and Graham walked toward the bunkhouse. "Okay, okay," Neal hissed, "no problem. After they teach me the secret handshake we get the boy, slip away in the darkness, get to Austin, and phone Ed. He calls the FBI, they roar in, get the gang, the money, *and* the arms. It's a cinch."

Graham grabbed his crotch. "Now I know why cowboys walk the way they do. Here's the deal: you go to the frat party and I'll do some snooping around. If I find Cody and can get away with him, I will. Otherwise I'll get out of here and get someplace I can call in an army. You stay in place."

They stopped walking and looked at each other in the gathering darkness.

"And if we don't find Cody?" asked Neal.

Graham started to grind his artificial hand into his real one. "Hansen has a kid, doesn't he?" he asked.

"Yeah."

"We snatch him and trade. Beautiful business we're in, isn't it?"

"Lovely."

Then Neal asked, "Think we stand a chance?"

"Sure I do."

"Neither do I."

They started walking again.

"Maybe," Graham said, "it'll be like one of those old movies. Maybe the cavalry will ride in."

They looked at each other again and laughed.

Hansen finished recounting the money again and put it into his office safe. Carter sat at the desk watching him, his bodyguards watching the door and window.

"Do you trust them?" Carter asked.

"I trust Neal. I don't even know the other one," answered Hansen.

"Gentry is white trash," Carter said. "A low-life drifter and a cripple to boot. His usefulness is at an end. Your Neal Carey I'm not sure about."

"You can count on Neal," Hansen said. He was ready to dig his heels in on this one.

"I don't know, Robert, I don't know. That's what you said about McCall. Maybe you're wrong again."

Hansen flushed, thinking about everything that had happened because he'd been wrong about McCall. "What do you suggest?" he asked Carter.

Carter looked up at the ceiling and stroked his chin. "A test," he said. "Now that I think about it, maybe Gentry can do one more thing for us."

Shoshoko crawled to the mouth of the cave and sniffed the north wind. There was time, but not too much time. He wrapped his blanket around him and went to gather more wood for the fire.

A storm was coming, and it was almost time for him to die.

10

*F*ear none of those things which thou shalt suffer: behold, the devil shall cast some of you into prison, that ye may be tried; and ye shall have tribulation ten days, be thou faithful unto death, and I will give thee a crown of life,' " Carter intoned.

He stood by the third door in the bunker. The gang lined up on either side, forming a corridor for Carter and Neal to walk down. They were wearing the official uniform of the Sons of Seth—khaki shirts and trousers, brown leather belts and shoulder harnesses, Nazi campaign caps. Nazi-style daggers hung from their belts. On their left sleeves they wore a red armband with the swastika, on the other sleeve a black armband with the SOS symbol, a Christian cross with a flaming sword through it.

Carter opened the door and walked through. Strekker, playing the sergeant-at-arms role, gestured for Neal to follow.

Neal looked straight forward and started to march between the line of men. As he passed, each one touched him on the shoulder and intoned, "Brother."

Brother, indeed, thought Neal. He felt stupid in his new khaki uniform. He was glad Graham hadn't been invited to the service, because he never would hear the end of it.

He entered the secret chamber.

It was a chapel. A cross with a sword superimposed hung on the wall above a small altar. The altar was draped in white silk, embroidered on the front was the cross-and-sword motif with the legend "Sons of Seth." Seven gold candlesticks were set on top, their flames casting the room in a warm, golden glow. A gold plate and a Luger automatic pistol with SS insignia were set in the center.

"Kneel before the altar of Yahweh, brothers," Carter said. He stood behind the altar. Strekker and Carlisle stood off to the side behind him. The rest sat on the benches arranged like church pews.

" 'I am Alpha and Omega, the beginning and the ending,' saith the Lord, 'which is, and which is to come, the almighty.' " Carter said.

Where's the boy? thought Neal. Bring out the boy.

"Who sponsors this man to become a brother?" Carter asked.

Hansen stepped forward. "I do."

"Are you bonded in blood?" Carter asked Hansen.

Here we go, Neal thought.

"I am bonded with my brothers in blood," Hansen said.

Yippee for you. Now bring out the kid.

Carter looked at Neal and said, "Speak your name before Yahweh."

"Neal Carey."

Carter looked a little embarrassed, leaned over, and whispered, "Do you have a middle name, Neal?"

"Not that I know about."

"Okay," Carter answered. He looked up at the ceiling and intoned, "Oh, Yahweh, look down upon this son of Seth, this child of the white race, this warrior in the struggle for your chosen people, and bless him. Make him brave for battle and give him the strength to do those things which he must do. Amen."

"Amen," responded the congregation.

"Neal Carey, do you solemnly swear to devote your life to Yahweh, to his son Jesus Christ, to his apostle and martyr Adolf Hitler, and to the chosen people? If so, say 'I do.' "

"I do."

"Do you solemnly swear your loyalty to these assembled brothers, your Aryan kinsmen and fellow warriors?"

"I do." I do already. Where is Cody?

"Repeat after me: I, Neal Carey, do swear to fight to the death beside my Aryan kinsmen, to share their travails and their victories, to keep the code of honor of the Sons of Seth. . . ."

And on and on, as Neal repeated each phrase . . .

"To never—upon pain of hideous death—divulge the secrets, to never betray my brothers, to wage relentless war on our racial enemies and on race traitors, to avenge my fallen brothers, and to keep Yahweh's commandments first in my mind and heart."

Carter mumbled a whole bunch of stuff, then asked, "Has Neal Carey been bonded in blood?"

"He has yet to be bonded in blood," Hansen recited.

But he thinks he's about to be, Neal thought. Then he had a delightful thought: maybe Graham has the boy already. Maybe he's picked every lock in the place and is already on the road with Cody tucked under his arm. Maybe . . .

"Arise, Brother Neal, and approach the altar."

Neal stepped up.

Carter picked up the Luger. "Behold the sword of Yahweh. Before you may become a true Son of Seth, you must be bonded in blood with your brothers."

Swell, Neal thought. Well, drag it out. Give Graham all the time you can. I wonder how's he's doing.

"Behold the blood of your enemy."

Then he knew how Graham was doing, because Carlisle and Strekker brought him out from behind the curtain. He was gagged and his hands were tied behind his back.

They brought Graham to the front of the altar, facing Neal, and removed the gag.

"Yahweh has revealed this man's treachery. Yahweh has exposed him as a traitor to his race!" Carter yelled.

Neal read Graham's eyes. He had seen the expression a thousand times, ever since he was a kid. It said *do your job.*

"It is now time," Carter said, "for you to prove your loyalty and bond in blood with your brothers."

Neal felt the sick, dizzy feeling of terror. This has to be a nightmare, he thought. Any second I'll wake up screaming.

"Prepare!" Carter ordered.

The boys drew their daggers and stood at attention. Strekker stepped behind Graham and threw him to his knees.

Wake up, Neal told himself. He saw Graham's jaw tighten and lock.

Carter stepped off the altar, stood beside Neal, and handed him the pistol. Hansen came up on his other side.

"Shoot him," Hansen instructed in a whisper.

"No."

"You have to," Hansen said. "We all have before. You have to kill in front of your brothers to prove your loyalty."

"I've proven it already." Come on, God. If you're up there, it's time to get in the act now. Time to get off the sidelines and make a play. Please, God.

"You won't be alone," Hansen urged. "We'll each stab him after you do it. The final dagger will be yours. That's what bonds us."

Neal could feel Graham's eyes on him, the eyes that said *do it, do your job. That's what I've always taught you.* Yeah, but you also taught me to think.

"You guys have this all wrong," Neal said. "He's one of us. He was in on the job, remember?"

"Sometimes," Carter said, "ZOG sends agents to trap us. They appear to help us and then testify against us later in ZOG show trials. I prayed to Yahweh and he told me this man was sent by ZOG. But he will not live to set the hounds on us, to reveal our haven. There will be no one to testify. Unless you are a ZOG agent as well, Neal Carey."

You heard the man, son, Graham thought. Do it. There's no point in both of us dying. Let's get it over with. I'm scared shitless here.

Neal avoided Graham's eyes and looked over his shoulder. Strekker was grinning. *Grinning.*

The pistol shook in Neal's hand.

"We caught him snooping around the compound, Neal," Hansen whispered.

Neal looked back at Graham. Graham stared at him.

"It's true, kid," Graham said. "The feds had me on a counterfeiting charge. I couldn't do another long stretch, not in federal. I agreed to set you up on the robbery."

Neal read the words behind Graham's words: *the boy, Neal. The boy may still be alive. Focus on the boy.*

Neal gripped the pistol handle and raised his arm. These guys aren't this crazy, he thought. This must be some kind of a test; the gun must be loaded with blanks. They must have given Graham his "confession," to test whether I'd execute a traitor.

"Do it, Neal," Hansen whispered. "Then all things will be revealed to you."

So I pull the trigger, it's blank, we all have a laugh, and they bring Cody out here. Do it. Pull the trigger.

He pointed the pistol at Graham's chest.

And if it's not a blank? Focus on the boy. The boy.

You always taught me precision, Dad: *do a thing right the first time and you won't have to do it again. That'll leave you time for the important things, like sitting in your easy chair, drinking beer, and watching the Rangers blow a two-goal lead.* God, Dad. How many times did you save my life? From the moment you rescued me from the streets to now? How many times?

Neal looked into Graham's eyes, trying to tell him, I love you, Dad. I love you.

Graham nodded. Then he smiled and said, "Come on, son. Do it. The Yankees suck anyway."

You are one brave, tough SOB, Joe Graham, Neal thought. He wiped the tears from his cheek with his forearm and aimed the gun again. God, let me be accurate and fast.

He swung the pistol around just as he reached out with his left hand, grabbed Carter by the neck, and hauled him into a forearm choke. He brought the barrel up to Carter's head.

"Anybody moves, I kill him."

Nobody moved.

Cal Strekker started to laugh. "There are no bullets in the gun, Neal. It was just a test."

He dropped into a fighting stance, knees flexed, dagger blade held sideways by his waist. "Looks like you and me is finally going to finish that dance, Neal." Strekker lunged forward.

Neal started to shift his aim, but Hansen grabbed his wrist and then Strekker was on top of him. Strekker pressed the dagger against Neal's ribs and took the pistol from him with his free hand. He put the pistol barrel to Neal's head and said, "I think you flunked the test, Neal buddy."

Strekker pulled the trigger.

A dry click.

I can still talk myself out of this, Neal thought, even as his knees turned to water.

He heard the door open and saw a drunken women lurch into the room. Doreen stood at the back for a second and surveyed the scene.

"This is some kinky goddamn party you boys is having!" she bellowed. "Remember, I charge extra for this kind of stuff!" She weaved down the aisle.

Her eyes narrowed when she saw Neal. "Hey, I know you! You're that uppity son of a bitch who was looking for Harley!"

But I don't think I can talk my way out of this.

"Who are you?" Hansen asked Neal.

Neal was trying to come up with a suitable lie when Doreen staggered into Cal's arms. "And you," she said. "You promised to take me to see Harley and Cody. When do I get to see that son of a bitch and my sweet little boy?"

"Right now," Cal answered. He held her firmly by the back of the neck and drove the dagger into her stomach.

Neal saw Doreen's eyes widen and her mouth drop open. He watched her stagger backward and heard her gasp. He saw her hold herself and look down where the blood was flowing over her splayed fingers.

Then her knees buckled and she collapsed. She lay rasping on the floor as Cal said, "Harley and your sweet little boy are in hell, honey. And I think you're almost there."

"Whore of Babylon!" Carter bellowed. He spat on her, stepped over her writhing body, and walked out.

Hansen followed him, yelling behind him, "Lock those bastards up! I want to find out what they know!"

Neal felt his arms being pinned behind him.

Randy looked at the woman still quivering on the floor.

"Shit, Cal!" he yelled. "I didn't even get to—"

"So go ahead," Cal said.

He grabbed Neal and threw him toward the door.

Steve Mills poured a slug of scotch into Karen Hawley's coffee. She tasted it, made a face, then took another taste. One more of these and she just might accept the Mills' invitation to spend the weekend.

Besides, it was so damn comfortable in the Mills' living room. A big old log blazed, hissed, and spattered in the fireplace. The lamps cast a soft glow in the room and the Indian rugs seemed to mute the already quiet evening.

Karen sat on the couch, her stockinged feet tucked underneath her. Peggy sat beside her, sipping a glass of red wine and watching the fire. Steve was in and out of the big chair, alternating between bartending and fire tending.

And there was Shelly. Karen looked over at her as she lay by the fireplace with some thousand-piece jigsaw puzzle of chocolate chip cookies. That might be another reason to stay, Karen thought. To try to engage Shelly in a late night conversation about everything that had happened. Peggy had told her that Shelly was doing all right, but just all right. Peggy and Steve had thought about taking her to Reno or even San Francisco to talk to a professional, but Shelly had said it was silly. She didn't need a therapist because of a bunch of jerks.

But she was quiet. Quiet and sad, which was to be expected, of course. They decided just to give her time. And keep talking about it. That's what Shelly probably needed, what they all needed, and most likely the unspoken reason for their get-together this night.

And I need to talk about it, Karen thought. She had buried it deep, the hurt, the anger, the disappointment. They had talked about everything else, about racists, white supremacists, the Hansens, the True Identity Church, Cal Strekker. But they hadn't talked about Neal Carey. Nobody had mentioned Neal.

"I didn't even know," Karen said after another sip of coffee, "that you were Jewish."

"I barely knew it myself," answered Steve. "My father was an atheist. We didn't talk about it."

"His old man was thrilled when we got married by a justice of the peace," Peggy said, and she and Steve chuckled at the memory when she added, "My parents weren't so delighted."

Steve said, "I mean, we didn't go to synagogue, we sure as hell don't keep kosher . . . I don't wear one of those beanies—"

"Yarmulke," Shelly corrected, not looking up from the puzzle.

"Shelly brought some books home from the school library," Peggy explained to Karen.

Well, that's a good sign, Karen thought. "Do you see Jory in school?" she asked.

"I think he dropped out."

"Such a waste," said Karen. She decided to jump in with both feet. "And how are you doing, kid?"

Shelly craned her neck up from the puzzle. "I'm doing okay. I'm not very happy . . . and I don't feel like a teenager anymore and I'm mad about that . . . but I'm doing okay. How are you doing, Karen?"

Well, I guess you're not a teenager anymore, Karen thought. And I guess I owe you an adult answer. "I'm doing lousy. I feel awful about what happened, I feel awful Neal was . . . is . . . part of it. To tell you the truth, Shelly, he broke my heart."

"Mine too."

There was a long silence before Peggy said, "The valley doesn't seem the same anymore."

"It isn't," answered Steve. "It's infected. It's sick."

"God damn Bob Hansen," Peggy said.

Karen had never heard that kind of anger from her before. Sure, she'd heard Peggy bitch about Steve smoking, or seen her blow up at Shelly for some teenage sin, but she'd never heard the cold bitterness she now heard in her friend's voice.

Steve said, "I think Bob just couldn't handle it after Barb died. He was angry and confused and looking for something to hold onto, and unfortunately, the first thing he came to was this church and this race thing. You know Bob, when he does something, he does it all the way."

Peggy rolled her eyes and looked affectionately at her husband. "Steve would make excuses for the devil."

"Well, he'd need some help if you got on his tail."

"I don't know," said Karen, "it just feels like we should do something."

Steve answered. "We're doing it. We're going on with our lives, just like always. Only better—because this year I'm buying Christmas *and* Hanukkah presents. Double holidays from now on. Hell, maybe I'll find out great-grandma was a Buddhist or a Hindu or something, and then we can have those holidays too."

Shelly looked up from her puzzle and gave him an "Oh, Daddy" look.

"Well, I said I was a Jew," Steve answered. "I didn't say I was a good Jew."

"Speaking of which," said Peggy. "Tomorrow night we're having a little celebration."

A celebration? Karen thought. She didn't feel much like celebrating, but she knew that's exactly when you should. And maybe there was something to celebrate. After all, she'd found out about Neal Carey before it was too late.

She lifted her cup and said, "So, long, Neal. Good riddance."

11

Neal's hands were cuffed to a ring bolted into the wall of the small bunker. They'd taken his watch, but he figured it was somewhere near morning. He sat shivering on the concrete floor, listening to Joe Graham nag at him.

"You should have pulled the trigger, son," Graham was saying. He also was chained to the wall.

"I know."

"You should have gone through with it."

"You're right."

"I've told you a million times, the job comes first."

"Let me ask them," Neal said through clenched teeth. "Maybe they'll give me the gun back—loaded."

They sat quietly for a few minutes. Then Neal asked, "Are you scared, Graham?"

"Out of my mind."

Me too, thought Neal. But so far it just doesn't seem real. They've thrown us into the old prison bunker, chained us to the wall, and just left us in here to freeze. And there's nothing we can do about it.

"What are we going to do?" he asked Graham.

"Well, when they come in, and they will, they're going to start working on us. They'll probably start with one of us first and let the other watch. The guy watching sees what's happening to his partner and starts thinking, Do I really want them doing that to me? Maybe I can make a deal. So that's what we do."

"Make a deal?" Neal asked.

"Sure. You give them the whole story, a little bit at a time, so they're convinced they're beating it out of you. You give it to them too early, they think it's a lie. So take a few lumps and then start to tell them everything. A little bit at a time."

Neal couldn't believe he was hearing this. "If we tell them everything they'll probably kill the boy."

"The boy is dead."

"I don't believe that."

If Graham could have reached Neal he would have grabbed him and shook him. Instead he looked at him long and hard and said, "Son, the boy is dead. You have to face that. We didn't get to him in time. Maybe there were things we did that we shouldn't have, or things we didn't do that we should have. I don't know. But the boy is dead, Neal."

"It's nothing we did. It was me."

"Who gives a shit?" Graham yelled. "Jesus, will you grow up? Cody McCall is dead, and we're probably going to join him real soon. The only chance we have is to try to drag this out long enough for Levine to look up from his account books and realize he hasn't heard from us in awhile and he'd better come looking. And when Ed comes, he'll arrive with a bad attitude and an army. And I want to live long enough to see that. So drop the it's-all-my-fault crybaby shit and start thinking about how you can make them torture you for as long as possible."

You're right, Dad. The only chance is to talk and drag it out. But you're wrong about the boy, Graham. I just goddamn know that Cody is alive. And that should be reason enough to hang on.

The door opened and Randy came in carrying two sawhorses. Cal Strekker came in behind him. He had a sledgehammer.

"See, what we did with Harley," Cal said, "was we laid him on his back on the floor, set one horse under his knees and the other under his ankles. Then we tied his ankles to the second sawhorse. That way Harley's legs was stretched out nice and tight. Then I swung this hammer down and . . . whoo."

Neal felt every nerve in his body jump out from his skin. It was Graham who had the balls to ask, "What did you have against Harley?"

"He wouldn't give up his boy," Cal answered. "That got the reverend questioning Harley's commitment to the cause, which got the reverend praying, and old Yahweh must have told him that Harley was a race traitor. Carter came in here himself to ask Harley the questions. Harley confessed."

"Before or after you broke his legs?" Graham asked.

Cal grinned. "Long time before that."

Neal was trying to work up enough voice to ask about Cody, but Graham shut him off with a look and said, "But you kept at him anyway, didn't you?"

"Yahweh said," answered Cal. "Or Carter said Yahweh said, which amounted to the same thing. See, Harley had been bonded in blood, so Carter said he was the worse kind of traitor. Said the devil was in him and that we had to make the devil howl. And we did."

Cal sat down on one of the sawhorses and told them all about it. He enjoyed telling the story, seeing the terror in their eyes, feeling them flinch and sicken, watching them as they came to the realization that the same things were going to happen to them.

So he told them how they'd left Harley chained in the bunker and gone out and got a billy goat and come back in and the reverend told Harley to have sex with Satan's animal. And how Harley refused, so they brought the boy in, held a gun to his head, and asked Harley again, and this time Harley just couldn't do it fast enough and Carter said that it proved he was in league with the devil. So they took the boy out, and then they wrapped a rope around the chain on Harley's cuffs, and ran that through the pulley on the ceiling, and hoisted Harley up and took turns on him with a knotted rope till Harley passed out, so they left him hanging there and the cuffs rubbed his wrists raw and his hands got all swollen because there was no circulation.

Cal told them how they came back later that night and the first thing Harley croaked out of his throat was to ask about his boy, and

Carter said that Yahweh would take care of the child and Harley started crying then, just blubbering—like to make you sick—and Carter told Harley to confess that ZOG had sent him and Harley did. They let him down then, cuffed him behind his back, and forced him on his knees, and Carter stuck a broom handle up him and then they left him there like that. And when they came back Harley was bleeding like you wouldn't believe, and moaning, and Carter said he was talking to Satan but they needed to hear Satan howl. So they broke Harley's fingers, then his arms. And that was when they did the trick with the sawhorses and the hammer and they thought he was going to die right there, and Randy here was such a pussy he said maybe they should just shoot him then. But Carter said that Satan would take him in his time and Carter went back to California. And Harley was a tough bird and just wouldn't give up the ghost and he was groaning all the time and letting off such a stench, and that's when they got to talking about how there really was more than one way to skin a cat. So Cal started taking a knife to him and peeling off big strips—you should have heard Satan howl then—but they didn't get too far and Harley just finally died.

"But it took what, Randy?" Cal asked. "Couple of weeks?"

"More like three, I think, start to finish."

"Whatever," Cal said. He got off the sawhorse, squatted in front of Neal, smiled, and said, "And guess what, Neal buddy? The reverend just finished praying about you. Guess what old Yahweh told him?"

Neal didn't answer. He wanted to ask about Cody. He tried to. But he was afraid to move as much as a muscle, he was so close to crying, or throwing up, or worse.

Cal saw it, and the psychotic gleam in his eyes flared more brightly, and he answered his own question. "He said you and the one-armed bandit here was both sent by ZOG. That you're both in league with Satan. That we need to make you howl."

Neal felt himself shaking. He tried to control it but he couldn't. His right leg just started jumping all on its own and he felt as if his head were drowning, and tears were just about to overflow from his eyes when he heard Joe Graham's blessed, blessed voice.

"When you pick out my goat," Graham said, "make sure you get a pretty one."

The door opened again and the Reverend C. Wesley Carter walked in.

Neal closed his eyes and took a deep breath. Now it starts, he thought.

Cal turned to Graham and grinned. "You're first, smart-ass."

Graham knew that. It's why he'd mouthed off.

Randy and Cal took the cuffs off Graham and stripped him. Then they laid him on his stomach across the sawhorses. They wrapped a heavy rope under his arms and tied it down. They did the same to his ankles so that Graham was stretched out across the sawhorses, his feet hanging off one side and his head off the other. They arranged it so that his face was a foot from Neal's.

While they were doing this, Carter was tying knots into another rope, saying, "We have to find out who you are and why you're here, and we have to find out quickly. I'm very puzzled that you helped us rob the armored car, and I'm concerned that the shipment of arms—in fact, our entire haven here—is in jeopardy."

He finished with the rope, raised it over his head, and asked Graham, "Who sent you?"

Graham struggled for breath. His back already felt as if it might snap from the strain of holding his weight.

"Satan sent me," he answered.

Neal made himself look at Graham as the rope came down on his back.

Graham sucked in some air. "Satan or Tom Landry, one of the two."

The rope lashed down on his shoulders.

Two, three, four, five more times before Carter spoke again.

"Who sent you?"

"Harley McCall's ex-wife. Alimony."

The rope came down again.

Graham's face was red with strain. Sweat dripped off his jaw. His back was already raw.

Neal tried to reach out and hold Graham's head, but the chains were too short.

"You're killing him!" Neal yelled.

"Shut up," Graham snapped at him. Then he asked Carter, "Hey, what about my goat?"

Five, six, seven times Carter's arm swung. Flecks of blood flew across the cell with each stroke.

Cal stepped around to the front of the sawhorses and lifted Graham's chin.

"You got anything funny to say now, smart-ass?" he asked Graham.

Graham swung his head back and forth. Sweat poured from his face.

Neal kicked Cal in the back of the leg to get his attention. "I'll kill you, you dirty bastard," Neal said.

"You're a hoot, Neal," Cal answered.

You're doing this for me, Dad, Neal thought. You're buying time for me. You mouthed off to Cal to make him mad, to make him start with you instead of me.

Carter raised his arm to start again.

Neal shouted to Carter, "Hey, Rev! Is it true what I heard about Yahweh and little boys?"

Graham craned his neck and shook his head at Neal.

Neal ignored him. "For that matter, is it true what I heard about you and little boys?"

Carter dropped his arm and stared at Neal.

"Shut up, Neal," Graham murmured.

"Yeah, Rev," Neal said, forcing himself to smile, "I'm not sure I heard it right, because your wife's mouth was full at the time, if you catch my drift, but I thought she said that you liked to—"

Carter stepped over Neal and raised the rope. "You piece of filth," he said.

Come on, come on, do it. Start on me for a while.

"But your time will come," Carter said. He turned back to Graham.

Sorry, Dad. I tried, I tried.

Graham lifted his real hand, smiled weakly, and slowly raised his middle finger at Neal.

"Did ZOG send you?" Carter asked.

"Zog who?" asked Graham.

Carter raised his arm and was about to bring the rope down again when the door opened and Bob Hansen walked in.

He looked worried and excited at the same time.

"The truck is here," he said. "The arms have arrived."

Carter dropped his arm. "We have to move quickly. These two can wait and tremble in the fear of Yahweh's wrath."

He dropped the rope and paced to the door. Carlisle and Strekker followed him.

"Untie him!" Neal yelled. "For God's sake, at least cover him up!"

Strekker turned around. "I'll be back," he said and shut the door behind him.

Graham craned his neck up. His face was pale with pain. His hair was matted with sweat, and blood was dripping off his back.

"We're winning," he rasped.

Cal stepped out into the compound and saw a rented moving van parked outside. The truck was bright yellow with black stenciled letters that read TROJAN TRUCKING on the side.

"People think I'm carrying rubbers," the driver said as he hopped down from the cab, "but actually I went to USC."

That's kind of funny, Cal thought. But neither Carter nor Hansen laughed, so he put on a scowl and gave the driver the cold eye.

The driver rubbed his hands together and blew on them. "It's a little colder here than it was in LA," he complained. He looked at the compound and asked, "You guys expecting company?"

"Would you be Mr. Mackinnon?" Carter asked him.

"I wouldn't be if I had a choice, but I don't, so I am."

"I'm Reverend Carter, this is Bob Hansen."

"Nice to put a face to the voice."

"I'm surprised you came alone," Carter said.

"I can take care of myself," Mackinnon answered.

Cal heard this as both a comment and a threat.

The Mackinnon guy looked around at all of the boys and smiled. He sure enough looked like he could take care of himself. He had a body like a bear, and anyone looking hard could see the form of a large pistol holstered at his belt.

Hansen asked, "What have you brought us?"

"I've brought you enough stuff to send a whole battalion of kikes and niggers back to their maker," Mackinnon said. "But unfortunately, I can't give it away."

"The money is in the safe," Hansen said.

Mackinnon smiled. "That's good enough for me. After all, we're all on the same team, right?"

Cal stepped forward. "I want to take a close look at this stuff before we pay," he said, trying to stare Mackinnon down.

Mackinnon didn't stare down easily. "And who are you?" he asked.

Hansen stepped in. "This is Cal Strekker. He has ranger training. He's our tactical instructor."

"Well, Cal," Mackinnon said, "I'm looking out here at all this flat ground and those hills back there and I'm thinking about what you're going to need to defend your perimeter. I brought some mines that can be tripped off by contact *or* blown by switches from your watchtowers. I brought some rocket launchers same as the Afghanis have been using to shoot down Soviet helicopters. You're familiar with them, I'm sure. Carry them right on your shoulder, pull the trigger, and whoosh. I brought five crates of M-16s, and they have the bugs worked out of them by now—they don't jam the way they used to during the southeast Asian war games. I even brought a .50 caliber air-cooled machine gun you can set right in that bunker over there and chop up any assault coming across that flat. *And* I even brought you some mortars, because that's going to be a problem for you if your enemy has any mortars of his own sitting back in those hills. He could turn this into another Dien Bien Phu unless you have some arty of your own to dig him out.''

Cal was impressed but didn't want to show it. He said, "Well, we plan on doing more than just defending ourselves.''

"Of course you do," Mackinnon replied, "so I also have two very nice sniper rifles—Swiss—some infrared scopes, and three superb .22 automatic pistols.''

"We ain't plinkin' cans here, mister," Cal said.

"Of course, it takes a real professional to use one, but a well-placed .22 in the brain will get the job done quickly, neatly, and quietly.''

"Silencers?" Cal asked.

Mackinnon spread his arms wide and said, "But of course.''

Cal grumped a little more then said, "Sounds okay, Mr. Hansen, but I think we better test a few of these things before we turn any money over.''

"Wouldn't have it any other way," Mackinnon answered. "I'll need to show you how some of this stuff works, anyway.''

He stepped around to the back of the truck and started to lift the door. Cal followed him and looked inside at the crates. He pulled a pack of cigarettes from his shirt pocket and held it out to Mackinnon.

"No thanks," Mackinnon said. "I'm trying to quit." He hopped into the truck and said, "Cal, you want to send some of your men over here to unload this stuff?''

Cal waved the gang over and set them to work. He asked Hansen, "What about the prisoners?''

Carter stepped in. "I'll deal with the prisoners.''

"Yes, sir." That was fine with Cal. He was far more interested in the weapons Mackinnon had brought, and there was plenty of time to have some fun with that one-armed wise guy and that smart-ass Carey. With any luck they might break Harley's three-week record. So let them wait.

*　　*　　*

"So far we're winning," Graham repeated to Neal. "We kept them talking for a half hour and now we've caught a break with this arms shipment arriving. With any luck they'll be busy playing with their new toys for a while, which means more time for Ed to wake up and come get us out of here."

"I wish he'd hurry," Neal answered. He didn't think Graham could survive much longer, not with the cold, the pain, and the shock. "You were great, Dad."

"Hell with these guys," answered Graham. "We're not dead yet." But we're going to be, son, he thought. And the only thing I can do for you now is to try to keep the terror out of your mind. Stop you from imagining what the pain is going to be like. "Have you started working on your story yet?" Graham asked.

"Not really."

"Get on it," Graham snapped. "Think up layers on top of layers."

"You got it." I know what you're trying to do, Dad, but I'll play along. It gives us something to do, and I think we're in for a long wait.

Then Carter and Randy came back in.

"Where's Dad?" Shelly asked her mother.

They were standing at the kitchen counter. Karen sat at the table, peeling potatoes.

"On the roof," Peggy answered.

"Again?" Shelly laughed. "Who does he think he is, Santa Claus?"

"Honey, your father has always thought he was Santa Claus, the Easter Bunny, and Peter Pan all rolled up into one. He's still working on this big surprise of his."

Karen asked, "When do we get to see it?"

"Tonight, he says."

Shelly rolled her eyes dramatically and said, "It's going to be a long afternoon."

Up on the roof, Steve held the last of the wires down with one hand and pounded the U-nail down with the other. He wanted to finish up before the storm came in and made him stop.

He looked up to check out the clouds again. Yep, he thought, looks like we're going to have a white Hanukkah.

Then he heard the far-off crackle of rifle fire coming from the Hansen place. Knock yourselves out, boys, he thought. Because I'm going to knock you out tonight.

Shoshoko heard the gunfire too. He looked up from the rabbit he was skinning and listened closely. The sound was coming from the valley, close to the base of the mountain. But what could they be shooting at, using so many bullets? Or was it just the white man's silly habit of constantly testing his aim? A wasteful, childish game, Shoshoko thought.

Yet from his dream, he knew that the white men would be coming up the mountain and that the bullets would be for him. He went back to skinning the rabbit. They needed the meat, and it was not his fate to die in the daylight. The white men would not come until the night.

Cal could tell that the constant popping sound of the boys trying out the sample M-16s was annoying Mackinnon. The man didn't like working with explosives anyway; his fingers looked numb with cold, and he was sweating profusely even though he was lying in the snow. But the arms dealer sure as hell knew what he was doing, Cal could tell that. He watched as Mackinnon finished arming the mine, then brushed some snow over the top of the metal disc that looked like a large dinner plate.

"Mark this down as 'AV, RC 3,' " he told Cal, who stood above him making sketches in a notepad.

You don't have to tell me, Cal thought. It was critical to record the location and type of the mines. This one was "antivehicle, radio-controlled number three," the last of the mines they'd planted on the road. They'd put one right on the turnoff from the main road, another one about halfway down, and this last one right under the compound gate itself; if anything ever managed to ram the gate in, they would blow the hell out of it right there.

They'd laid a dozen 'AP, CD'—antipersonnel, contact-detonated—mines in an irregular pattern around the outside of the compound. These were the sweet little puppies that exploded as you stepped *off* them, giving you the cheerful choice of standing perfectly still and getting shot or hitting the dirt with whatever was left of you after the mine blew up underneath you. They also planted twenty-four dummy mines. The only way you could tell they were duds was by stepping off them and seeing whether you were alive or a memory.

The idea was to force any attack into narrow unmined lanes that you had covered with presighted rifle fire. This would equalize the firepower of your small force against your enemy's larger one. With discipline and training, one good man with an M-16 could take care of his own lane while a centrally located heavy machine gun could sweep the entire field of fire. Your best marksmen stayed up in the towers with their sniper rifles and picked off the enemy's leaders. A good fire team could turn an enemy attack into a debacle in moments. It would take trust, of course. Every man was literally betting his life that every other man was doing his own job. And Cal was going to make goddamn sure that was the case.

"Let's go up the tower and label the switches," Mackinnon said. "Then let's call it a day. I'm beat."

They'd put in a full one. They'd unpacked the crates of rifles and test-fired half a dozen of them. Then Cal had set the men to assembling and cleaning the rest and they hiked down near the base of the mountain, set up some targets, and started sighting them in. Then Mackinnon took Cal and Randy and talked them through the intricacies of the Schmidt Rubin 31/55 sniper rifle, a Swiss beauty with a bipod stand, capable of delivering a 190-grain bullet with great accuracy at long range. Then he and Cal started the long, sweaty work of laying the mines.

Now they walked back into the compound. The late afternoon sky had turned a sullen, threatening gray.

"Why don't we put the switch box in the southeast tower?" Cal asked. "That gives us the best view of the terrain."

"We can put a box in each tower and one in the bunker, if you want. It's a simple matter of override switches. That way you don't have to worry about being in one particular place to detonate the mines."

"Sounds good to me," Cal said. He was impressed. Mackinnon had put some thought into this deal.

So Mackinnon charged four battery-run toggle-switch boxes and set the frequencies. They taped one into each guard tower and another one into the main bunker room. He showed Cal which switch detonated which mine. By the time he was finished it was dark out.

"Now you can blow the hell out of any ZOG bastard who tries to come in here," Mackinnon said.

"That's good," Cal answered. "We might be needing to any time now."

Mackinnon's eyes went flat and cold. "What do you mean?" he asked.

"Well, we have a couple of prisoners who . . ."

Cal saw Mackinnon's jaw drop in disbelief and his face flush with anger.

"Prisoners?" Mackinnon hissed.

"Yeah. Couple of prisoners, I—"

"You assholes let me bring these arms into an insecure area?"

"It's not insecure, it's—"

"ZOG would put me away for life if they caught me with this shipment! Are these guys cops? FBI? Secret Service? Customs?"

Jesus, the guy is flipping out, Cal thought. He said, "I don't know who they are. We haven't really started questioning them yet."

"Well, we're goddamn well going to start now!"

Cal saw Bob Hansen walking over with that sour look he got on his face when he didn't think things were going the way he wanted.

"What's happening here? What's the yelling about?"

"Where's Carter?" Mackinnon yelled.

Cal almost smiled, because he'd never heard anyone yell at Hansen before.

"He's back at my house, having a rest," Hansen answered.

"His ass is in the sack and he's got mine in a sling?"

Cal had to put his hand to his mouth and fake a cough.

"What's the trouble?" Hansen asked. Cal could tell the boss was starting to get pissed off.

"The trouble is," Mackinnon said with exaggerated patience, like he was talking to the slowest kid in the fifth grade, "that you guys have let me drive a truckload full of illegal arms into a place the law seems to have targeted. That's what the trouble is."

"We're taking care of the——" Hansen started to say.

"You're not taking care of shit!" Mackinnon yelled.

Cal saw Bob Hansen go positively pale.

"Where are they?" Mackinnon asked. He looked away, put his hands on his waist, and shook his head.

"They're locked up," Cal said. He pointed at the small bunker. "Right over there."

Mackinnon said to Cal, "Let's go."

Hansen butted in. "Now wait just a minute. This is none of your concern. Reverend Carter——"

"You did search them for transmitters, didn't you?" Mackinnon asked.

"We were about to do that when you came in," Cal lied. He was some kind of embarrassed, especially because about half of the boys were standing a few feet away watching the whole scene.

He was grateful when Mackinnon turned his rage toward Hansen. "I want my money right now. Then I'm out of here."

Hansen's face looked like stone. "Come to the house with me. You'll get every damn penny."

"You're damn right I'll get every damn penny. But bring it here, to the truck. I'm not walking into any house with you. Half the National Guard might be hiding in there," Mackinnon answered. He turned back to Cal. "You're about the only half-competent guy around this place. Will you go with him to get my money?"

Cal looked to Hansen and the boss nodded curtly.

"I want to see these prisoners of yours," Mackinnon said. "I've been dodging these asswipes my whole life. I can probably look at them and tell you what agency, which office, and how they like their coffee."

Cal yelled to the gaggle of men who were standing around pretending not to listen. "Jory! Dave! Take him to see the prisoners! Keep your eyes open!"

"I don't believe this," Mackinnon muttered as they walked over to the bunker. He reached under his coat, pulled his pistol, and laid it down in front of the bunker.

Dave and Jory stared at him.

"You don't go into a cell with your weapon," Mackinnon explained. "What if they grab you and take it from you?"

"They're chained to the wall," Dave said. "And Randy's in there."

"Then what do you need a gun for?" Mackinnon answered.

They laid their guns down and went inside. Randy closed the door behind them. He turned the light on and Mackinnon looked down at the one man shivering on the floor and the other one a bleeding lump stretched out over two sawhorses.

Then he lost his temper.

Ed's spinning back kick slammed into Dave's solar plexus and knocked all the air and most of the will to live right out of him. Dave crumpled to the floor gasping for air, his legs kicking spasmodically like a cockroach set on its back.

Randy pulled a combat knife from his belt and stabbed down at Ed's neck. Ed shifted to the left, brought both arms up, and crossed them to form an X. He blocked the knife, held Randy's wrist, turned around and under Randy's trapped armed, then slammed Randy's wrist down on his own collarbone. The knife dropped from Carlisle's hand as his elbow snapped with a dry crack. Carlisle screamed as Ed spun the broken arm around behind his back, held his neck down, and pulled the shoulder out of its socket. Ed kicked Randy in the face, breaking his nose and one cheekbone, and then let him fall to the floor.

All of this took maybe five seconds, and Jory stood watching in shock before he organized his legs to head for the door. Ed lunged and grabbed him by the back of the belt, heaved backward, and threw him over the top of his shoulder. The boy landed hard on the floor, his head snapping back and smacking on the concrete. He was out.

Ed quickly untied Graham and cradled him in his arms.

"You've been working out," Graham murmured to Ed.

Ed gently set Graham down. Then he took off his big coat and laid it out on the floor. A Velcro strap under the left arm held a large automatic pistol. Another strap fastened what looked like a small, flat black box. Ed set these things down, then wrapped Graham up in the coat. He looked at Graham's swollen eyes, which were now more like slits. "Who did this to you?"

Graham pointed his chin at Randy. "He's one of them, but I think you already broke every bone in his arm."

Ed nodded, saw that Dave was struggling to make it to his hands and knees, pivoted on his right foot, and drove a side kick into the man's jaw. Dave's head banged into the wall and he slumped to the floor again.

"Neither of you smoke, huh?" Ed asked. "I need a cig."

He bent over Dave's unconscious body and found a pack of Marlboros and some matches in his top shirt pocket. He took a cigarette and lit it, then took a drag and exhaled with a contented sigh. "It's been a long day," he said.

"Uh, Ed?" Neal asked. "Maybe you could let me loose?"

"Sorry, I got carried away."

He took the key ring off Randy, found the right keys, and unlocked the handcuffs.

Neal rubbed his wrists to work the circulation back into them. "It's nice to see you, Ed," he said.

"It's nice to be seen," Ed answered. His back to Graham, he mouthed the words *can he walk?*

Neal shook his head.

"You asshole," Graham muttered. "Why didn't you tell us what you were planning?"

Ed handcuffed Dave to the wall as he said, "What if you got captured, which you did . . . and tortured, which you did . . . and you broke? Which you didn't, but it's early. This way you had nothing to tell them."

"Thanks a lot. So, you have an army out there?" Graham asked.

"I came alone," Ed answered. He pointed at the bodies slumped on the floor. "I *am* an army."

Which is a pisser, Ed thought. He had a hit squad standing by in Reno. This was supposed to have been a recon trip. Find out what the hell was going on with Carey and Graham and also set SOS up on a federal arms charge as well as the robbery rap. Not to mention get the Bank's money back. He hadn't planned to find Neal and Joe chained in a bunker. And when he'd seen Graham trussed up, bleeding and in pain, he knew there wasn't going to be time to get to Reno and back. Not unless he just wanted to recover their bodies.

Jory was crawling over to the wall.

Ed gestured with the handcuffs, "Come here, kid."

Jory stuck his hand out and Ed chained him to the wall.

"So do you also have a secret plan to get us out of here?" Graham asked.

Well, I did, Ed thought. "That depends on how many of us there are," Ed answered. "Cody?"

"He's dead," Graham answered.

Neal started to say, "He isn't—"

"Neal doesn't think so," Graham said.

Neal kicked Randy in the stomach. "What happened to the boy?" he asked.

"I dunno."

The hell you don't, Neal thought. He grabbed Randy by his broken arm and yanked him up.

Randy howled. "I don't knooooow!"

Neal cranked the broken arm around in a complete circle. "You tell me, you little Nazi piece of shit," Neal said. He threw Randy face-first into the wall, straightened the fractured arm out along the concrete, and slammed his hand into Randy's broken elbow.

Randy pointed frantically with his good arm—pointed down at Jory. *"He* killed him, *he* killed him,'' Randy panted. "Carter said the boy had to die . . . the seed of a traitor . . . none of us wanted to do it . . . he volunteered. Took him out into the rabbit brush and shot him.''

Neal let Randy go, looked down, and saw the guilt on Jory's face. He grabbed the knife off the floor and slid to his knees in front of Jory. "You filthy . . .'' Neal pressed the knife point against the soft part of Jory's throat.

Neal felt the heavy whack of Graham's artificial hand hit his wrist and knock the knife out of his hand. He grabbed his arm and looked to see Graham kneeling beside him.

"What?'' Graham asked. "Did they turn you into one of them?''

Neal let go and sat staring at the floor. He couldn't meet Graham's eyes. I've just tortured a wounded man and tried to kill a sick boy, Neal thought. Maybe they have turned me into one of them.

Then he heard Jory whimper, "I didn't kill Cody.''

What? "Who did?'' asked Neal.

"Nobody. I was supposed to, but I didn't. I took him away and hid him.''

"Where?'' Neal demanded.

Jory's eyes had a glassy stare. "To the Place of the Beginning and the End.''

"What the hell are you talking about?''

Jory smiled a shy, secretive smile. "I'll take you there,'' he offered. "I'll take you to see the Son of God.''

Then Neal heard Strekker's voice outside the door yell, "Mackinnon, we have the money!'' The door opened and Cal stood at the top of the stairs.

Strekker was just too goddamn quick. He took in the scene, made his evaluation, and kicked the door shut.

Neal could hear him outside, yelling to the rest of the men. Then came the sounds of boots pounding in the snow, the clickity-clack of rifle bolts, and the clang of the compound gate swinging shut.

Great, Neal thought, we're locked in the bunker, locked in the compound, and surrounded by a couple of dozen well-armed, well-trained fanatic killers.

"So," Ed said, "you guys ready to blow this joint?"

Steve Mills adjusted the small cap on the back of his head and stood up at the end of the table.

He cleared his throat, looked at Peggy, Shelly, and Karen, and said, "As you know all too well, I'm not usually at a loss for words. But tonight, for the first time in my life, I'm celebrating a holiday in honor of my father and my grandparents. I never knew . . . never really cared . . . what made them give up their identities as Jews. I always supposed it was just to fit in a little easier in America. And I guess it worked, because I've always felt just a hundred percent at home in this country. But until recently I guess I never realized that there was a price to pay for that comfort, and that my grandfather and my father paid that price. That price was their heritage, and their identities, and I'm afraid some of their pride. And so tonight I'm honoring a holiday I don't know much about to try to give a little back. Maybe to reclaim a piece of myself that got lost. And to give something back to you, Shelly, that you were cheated out of."

He saw tears well up in his wife's and daughter's eyes and had to stop and clear his throat again.

"It wasn't that we were ever ashamed of being Jewish . . . and we're damn well not ashamed of it now. It just wasn't something we thought a lot about, just like we don't think a lot about being Christians too, I guess. It just wasn't a big deal.

"But then I saw my daughter"—he paused to smile at Shelly—"being abused because her father is half Jewish, and it sure started being a big deal then. I figure my grandparents suffered for being Jews in Russia. That's probably why they came here. And they had that fear in them, so they laid low about being Jews because they didn't want their kids to suffer the way they did.

"And God bless them, but I think they got it wrong, because this country . . . if it means anything it means that you don't have to hide who you are and you don't have to bow down to idiots who hate you for it. And I love this country.

"Karen, thank you for being our honored guest tonight and sharing this new tradition with us. And Peggy, I hope all your Irish Catholic family forgives you for sitting in here . . ."

"I wouldn't have missed this for the world," Peggy said.

"So, Shelly," Steve said, "in honor of your grandparents and great-grandparents and the whole bunch of them who came before, would you light that candle now?"

As Steve watched and Peggy cried softly into her dinner napkin and Karen Hawley beamed, Shelly Mills in her white dress, her hair hanging long and straight and shining in the soft light, stood and lit the candles in the menorah.

When she finished, Steve poured the traditional wine into everyone's glass and gave the traditional toast, "L'chaim—to life."

"You know I'll kill him!" Neal shouted out the firing slit. He had Jory in front of him, Ed's pistol pointed at his head.

"I know!" Hansen shouted back.

"We're coming out now!" Neal yelled back. "We're getting in that truck and we're driving to Austin! We'll let him go when we get there! If I see, hear, or even smell anything I don't like, I'll blow the shit out of him! Do you understand me?"

"I understand!" Hansen yelled.

Neal turned to Ed, who had Graham over his shoulder in a fireman's carry. In his other hand he held the little black box.

"You ready?" Neal asked.

"Let's do it."

Neal took his hostage by the collar and pushed him to the door.

"Are you sure you can make this shot?" Hansen asked. He was worried. They'd done everything Neal had demanded. They'd unlocked the bunker door, opened the compound gate, and put the keys back in the truck's ignition. They'd shut off the searchlights and taken the men out of the guard towers.

But a lot could go wrong, especially if Cal missed the shot.

"I'm sure," Cal answered.

He was lying beside Hansen just inside the fence on the other side of the compound. Cal had the sniper rifle, its bipod planted in the snow, trained on the bunker door. The infrared scope gave him a perfect view in the darkness.

He had a man crouched in each tower and more men in the main bunker. Each one had his new M-16 locked, cocked, and ready to rock. One of Carter's bodyguards was behind the machine gun in the main bunker, ready to sweep the forty yards of open ground that lay between the prisoners and their truck.

The gate was open now, but Cal had Craig lying out in the sagebrush ready to swing it shut just as soon as the firing started, just in case any of the intruders did make it into the truck.

But none of them are going to make it, Cal thought. Not carrying a wounded man. That'll slow them all down, and Neal buddy will make an easy target, no matter how hard he tries to hide behind Jory. I'll just have to shoot young Hansen first and then take out Neal.

And on the odd chance that the big son of a buck gets to the truck, we'll just blow him to hell with the mines.

So come on out, boys. We're ready for you.

"How many do you think are out there?" Ed asked.

"Twenty or so," answered Neal. "Each of them with one of the rifles you brought them."

"Life's a bitch, isn't it?"

"It's about to be," Neal answered.

He grabbed his hostage tighter and pushed the door open.

Cal watched through the night scope as Neal came out, holding his hostage in front of him. Ed followed, holding the one-armed little bastard over his shoulder like a grain sack.

"Is that Jory?" Hansen whispered. It was hard making him out in just the moonlight.

"Yep," Cal answered. He recognized Jory's cowboy hat. Too bad for Jory. He'd give it maybe another ten yards to try to get a clean shot at Neal's head, but after that . . . well, so long Jory.

That bastard Carey was doing a good job staying covered. Five yards, six yards . . . Cal trained the cross hairs on Jory's head.

"Don't shoot, don't shoot," Hansen whispered.

Seven yards, eight . . . Cal started to put pressure on the trigger.

Okay, he thought, you have to get two shots off quick. First Jory, then Neal.

Nine yards . . . ten. At least it will be quick, Jory. Cal squeezed the trigger.

The bullet blew the cowboy hat off Randy's head and splattered blood, bones, and brains over Neal. Neal let go and dashed for the truck. He heard the footsteps as Jory broke out from the bunker and came running behind him. The searchlights came on and bathed the compound in harsh white light.

Cal saw what was left of Randy's face as his body spun and hit the ground. In the half second it took him to see his friend die, he lost Neal in the scope.

"Shit!" he yelled.

He stood up to signal Carter in the southeast watchtower.

The brownshirt bodyguard behind the machine gun waited until the lights came on, then aimed the gun a few feet ahead of the big man who was staggering forward, carrying the wounded man. He'd give him a little lead and then snake his fire backward. It was going to be almost too easy.

He got his aim and pressed the double trigger. His world exploded in an orange blaze as the gunpowder flashed up from the breach and seared his eyes.

*   *   *

The Reverend C. Wesley Carter heard the shot and then the scream, so he stood up in the watchtower. He put his hand to the detonator box and waited for the signal.

Cal could hear the screaming coming from the main bunker. "Don't shoot any of the new guns!" Cal hollered. That son of a bitch Mackinnon had probably booby-trapped every one that he hadn't demonstrated.

One of the men in the tower heard Cal yelling but couldn't make out the words. He had a perfect bead on Neal, though. He pulled the trigger and the gun blew up in his hands.

"Hold your fire, everybody!" Cal yelled. "Get your own weapons out of the bunker!"

He looked to the gate and saw Vetter swing it shut.

"I've got you trapped, you son of a bitch!" he yelled at the truck. I hope I can still take you alive, he thought. I'll take months to kill you.

Neal dove into the back of the truck, pulled Jory up behind him, and shut the doors. A window slid open at the front.

"You all right?" Ed shouted.

"We both made it! How's Graham?"

"He's okay, but the bastards closed the gate on us!"

Ed turned the ignition, hit the gas, and started for the gate.

Cal watched as the truck lurched forward. It was still all right. There was plenty of time to get the old weapons. That truck wasn't going to ram through that gate.

Ed pointed his black box out the window and hit the button. The mine went off and the gate blew off its hinges. He hit the gas harder and rumbled down the road.

* * *

Carter watched the truck go through the gate. He was almost happy it had made it. Now, he thought, I will blow you back to hell. He checked the diagram Strekker had given him. He started to count down from five.

Cal picked himself up after the blast went off. It was chaos in the compound—the wounded were screaming, men were running all over hell and back looking for guns. What the hell happened with the mine? he wondered. Did Carter push the button early?

He looked up to the tower and could just make out Carter with his finger on the detonator box. So either Carter had panicked and pushed the wrong button or . . .

He started running toward the tower.

Carter saw the truck get near the mine hidden under the snow on the road. He also saw Cal running toward him. Not to worry, Mr. Strekker, I'm on the ball.

Cal waved his arms wildly and yelled, *"Noooooo!"*

Carter saw Cal give the signal. He flipped the toggle switch marked AP, RC 2. And that, he thought, will blow them back to the devil.

The first bomb went off in the ammunition bunker. It blew the wooden door off and, as Ed had planned, set off at least fifty secondary explosions as mortar shells, rockets, and bullets blew up in the fire. The next blast crumbled a watchtower. The next set off the tear gas Ed had placed in the detonator battery in the main bunker.

Cal hit the dirt and kept his head down as debris flew and the secondary explosions from ammunition belts, grenades, and mortar shells turned the compound into a junkyard. So the bombs were in the batteries of the detonator boxes. And now that lunatic preacher had the override switches and was clicking them off one by one. Cal buried his head in his arm and waited it out.

Craig Vetter lay in the snow. He took aim at the truck's rear tires, said a quick prayer that his weapon wasn't one of the sabotaged ones, and shot.

---

* * *

Neal felt the truck sink on its flat tires. He grabbed Jory by the collar, opened the door, and rolled out. Bullets smacked into the truck above him.

Ed jumped out, crouched behind the front of the truck, and scrambled over to the passenger side. He pulled Graham out and slung him back over his shoulder.

"Neal! Get ready to move!" he yelled.

Carter watched the world turn into a whirling chaos. Flames were everywhere, sulphur burned his eyes and his nose, screams filled his ears as the truck full of devils drove away even though he was madly flipping the switches. Another watchtower buckled and crumpled to the ground. Yahweh's haven was falling apart around him. He ripped the detonator box off the post and gripped it next to his chest. He shook it angrily.

Then he flipped the last switch.

A second later, all of the mines around the compound perimeter went off, sending up blasts of earth, snow, and smoke.

Craig dove for the ground and covered up.

Neal crawled over to Ed. "There's a ranch two miles north of here. It's the only house. I'll meet you there."

Ed nodded, hefted Graham, and started toward the main road at a trot. Neal crawled back to Jory.

"How can we get to this place?"

"I usually ride there."

Neal thought about it for a second. The corral was a good hundred yards south. They could make it if they started now, while the explosions were still keeping heads down.

"Let's go!"

They sprang to their feet and sprinted toward the corral.

A few minutes later Cal Strekker got up and went to inspect what was left of the compound. There wasn't much—three towers were down, the ammunition bunker was destroyed with its $200,000 of new weapons, the main bunker was intact but inundated with tear gas. His troops weren't in such good shape either. Most of Carter's brownshirt bodyguards were on their hands and knees, coughing, choking, or vomiting. He had two badly wounded—the machine gunner with his seared eyes and the man in the tower who was missing three fingers.

Worse yet, he knew he wasn't going to get the time to rebuild the compound or the company. ZOG had infiltrated the organization and laid a heavy hit on it. Next would come the official police with warrants and all the legalities. And there were three men running around out there who could testify.

He yelled around the compound until he had his own men assembled. Carter could take care of those useless LA neo-Nazis by himself.

Hansen came up beside him.

"Have you seen my son?" he yelled. "Have you seen Jory?"

Cal looked around the compound. He didn't see the boy. He looked out across the sagebrush flats and saw a horse with two riders in the moonlight.

"I don't know," he said to Hansen. He pointed at the horse and riders galloping toward the mountains. "Is that him?"

Hansen peered into the night and recognized his son. But who the hell was with him?

Dave Bekke limped up to Hansen. "There's something you ought to know, sir."

"Right now I think there's a whole lot I ought to know."

"I heard Jory tell Neal that he didn't kill that little boy," Bekke said. "Now maybe he just said that because Neal had a knife to his throat, but . . ."

"But *what?*" Hansen yelled.

"Jory also said something about the boy being the Savior, the Son of God. Said that he took him and hid him in 'the Place of the Beginning.' "

Carter pushed into the center of the circle and asked, "He used those words? The Place of the Beginning?"

"Yeah, he said he hid him in the Place of the Beginning and the End."

"That's ridiculous," Hansen said. "How do you expect a two-year-old child to survive out in the wilderness on its own?"

"I don't, sir. That's just what Jory said."

Cal said, "I'll bet that's where he's headed and I'll bet that's Neal Carey with him."

Vetter added, "Jory spends a lot of time around those caves up the mountain."

"We have to find that child!" Carter commanded.

Hansen took over. "Cal, we'll take some men with us and track Jory up to those caves. Dave, you take a squad and track down that Mackinnon, or whoever the hell he is. You might start by heading toward that Jew's house. I wouldn't be surprised if he set this whole thing up. Go on now, get moving!"

Carter pulled Hansen aside.

"This is very exciting, Robert," he said.

Hansen shook his head. "It's *over* here, Reverend. ZOG will be swarming all over this place by tomorrow. Our only chance is to find these people, kill them, and go into hiding ourselves."

Hansen felt the full bitterness of his own words. His dreams for this valley, this haven, this white bastion were shattered.

"You don't understand, Robert!" urged Carter. "This may be it! Maybe Jory was inspired to take the child! Maybe he has found the Place of the Beginning and the End, the sacred home of the lost tribe!"

"I *don't* understand, Reverend."

"I don't think Jory took the boy, I think the boy took Jory. The boy led him to the sacred place. This may be the child. You remember Revelation 12:5: 'And she brought forth a man child, who was to rule all nations with a rod of iron: and her child was caught up in God, and to his throne.' But the dragon fought for the man child, Robert. And the man child was hidden while the battle raged. And the dragon was slain by the angels. ZOG is the dragon, we are the angels! The battle is on! It's here, Robert! It's here!"

Hansen looked around at the wreckage of his dream.

"What's here?" he asked.

Carter's eyes gleamed. "The End Time!"

Shoshoko crawled to the mouth of the cave when he heard the wind come up. Clouds rolled across the moon and suddenly it started to snow as the sky changed from shimmering black to dull gray to shining white.

Shoshoko knew that the snow had been sent to ease his spirit, to soften his walk to the other side. The child would go down from the mountain just as the snow came down from the sky.

He was sad to leave the earth, but all men did. He was sad to leave the boy, but that was their fate. He sat down at the edge of the cave and started to sing his death song.

It was the End Time.

12

*N*eal held on tightly as Midnight picked his way up the narrow path. Cedar boughs swung back and threw snow across his arms as the horse pushed through. More snow was falling on his head and back, blowing in his face.

He felt the horse stagger up to level ground and then heard what sounded like a chant coming from somewhere up above. It was a sad but oddly tranquil song in the voice of an old angel floating on a cloud.

I wonder if this is what it's like to die, Neal thought. A slow ride in a tunnel of whiteness with an angel singing you home.

Midnight found his way between two rock walls and they descended down a draw. Then the horse turned sharply right and then left, and suddenly Neal could see.

They were in a box canyon of red rock cliffs with sparse cedars clinging to narrow shelves. The north cliff face blocked the wind and most of the snow. They were isolated from the rest of the mountains and the valley below. They might as well have been in another world.

Now Neal realized that the chanting came from the cliff on the north side. He looked up and saw a small circle of light about fifty feet up on the rocks, and the voice seemed to come from that glowing orb. This is getting really spooky, he thought.

"What am I hearing?" he asked Jory. He pointed to the circle of light that seemed to float on the sheer cliff. "What the hell is that?"

"That's the angel," Jory said calmly. "The guardian."

"Is he guarding Cody?" Neal asked.

"Always." Jory stopped the horse. "I usually walk from here, but we might need your horse this time. I think we can walk him most of the way up there."

Neal swung down as Jory hopped off. Jory took the reins and led Midnight as they hiked to the base of the cliff. They jagged west for a few hundred feet and then Neal saw that there was a narrow shelf of rock that led like a ramp up to the light. He got scared as they made their way up the shelf. It seemed like one slip would send him plunging down the sheer rock cliff.

One foot at a time, he told himself. Just think about placing one foot at a time.

Even Midnight seemed edgy, carefully placing his hooves down on the slippery rock. Only Jory didn't seem concerned. He had his head down and just plodded up the ramp toward the light.

As they got closer Neal saw that the light wasn't mysterious at all. It came from the mouth of a cave. As they got closer still he recognized the flicker of a small fire.

Jory stopped and listened to the chanting. When he heard a pause he made a sound like a bird.

The singing stopped and a similar birdcall came back.

Jory pressed on until they came to a large fissure that split the rock diagonally. "This is far as we can go with the horse," he said.

Neal watched as Jory led Midnight about twenty feet into the fissure and tied the reins to a scraggly cedar bow. He came back out and led Neal another thirty yards up the shelf until they came to the cave mouth.

It was a shallow indentation in the rock, maybe four feet high, ten feet wide, and a couple of feet deep.

Neal saw a tiny man sitting perfectly still, backlit by the fire that seemed to be burning from inside the rock. But there was no smoke. The man certainly could be no more than five feet tall, if that, and he looked ancient. He was wrapped in what looked like rabbit skins. His silver hair was long and matted.

Jory pointed behind the old man and then pointed to himself.

The small man shook his head. Then he pointed at Neal.

Then the man got up into a crouch and Neal saw the light burning behind him. The man crawled into the light. Jory followed, and both men suddenly disappeared. Neal got on all fours and crawled into the biggest part of the light.

It was a hole, a small, round tunnel entrance. Neal crawled for about ten feet in total darkness and then he saw the cave.

A fire was burning. Lying beside the small fire, wrapped in wild sheepskin, looking dirty and thin but peacefully asleep, was a small child. His face was turned to the warmth of the fire and his eyes were closed. His thin lips were open slightly and Neal could see them purse as he breathed.

Neal could stand up now—easily, for the chamber was twelve feet high in the center. The air was clear because the smoke from the small, efficient fire was drafting out the back of the cave.

Neal walked to where the child was lying and gently pulled the sheepskin blanket from the boy's head. He looked at the dirty blond hair and whispered, "Hello, Cody. It's nice to meet you."

He pulled the cover back over the boy and looked to Jory for an explanation. Jory just pointed at the cave walls.

Neal looked around him then and suddenly understood.

There was no telling how old the paintings were, but even in the faint, flickering firelight Neal could see that they were beyond ancient. They told stories of a time when men hunted giant animals on foot, and women gathered seeds and roots, and thunder and lightning were the music of God. They spoke of an age when men battled lions, and women hid their children in the safety of the cave, and when God sometimes took the children anyway, took them to the heavens.

And seeing them, Neal understood. Understood how poor, sick Jory, who had been taught what he had been taught and who had seen the horrors he had seen, could come to this prehistoric spot and think he had found the place where the lost tribe of Israel, the Aryan ancestors, had settled in the promised land.

For on those figures where some color survived and faces could be clearly discerned, the color on those faces was immutably, unmistakably, white. Especially on the smallest figure, clearly a child, who was depicted reaching his arms up to the sky toward a large figure that was not quite human but had a head formed by three concentric ovals. The child's hair was yellow.

"White people," Jory said. "The sons of Seth, the sons of Jacob. This proves that we were here long before the Indians. The old man here even says so."

The old man nodded and pointed to the cave paintings. In a combination of his own tongue and sign language he tried to tell Neal his people's legend about the race of white giants who once walked the earth. They were men of strength and courage, men who had knowledge. And the Sun loved them, so he gave them hair the color of dawn and dusk and eyes the color of the sky. For he meant them to join him in the heavens, and indeed, one day the white giants disappeared. But the legends said they would come again at the end of time, come again to rule the earth, to save it from the new whites, the ones who were everywhere but not quite men. For the new whites had come with their machines and guns and diseases and ruined the earth and most of the people died. The rest ran away and hid in the mountains, found the canyons and the caves, and waited for the white giants to return, waited for the foretold child of the Sun to come back to the sacred place. And the ones who were everywhere but not quite men would try to kill the child, and there would be a terrible battle between the good spirits and the bad, and many would die. But the child of the Sun would live, and the people would be reborn and rise from the earth, which would be clean again. And the child of the Sun would rule and all would be peaceful, as in the days when the white giants strode the earth.

Neal looked at Cody McCall sleeping by the fire and tried to figure out how to get him to safety. He could make a sling from his jacket, perhaps, and tie it in front of him like one of those baby carriers he had seen women wear. It might work.

"The Book of Revelation talks about the same thing, Neal," Jory said. "It talks about the infant who comes again, and the serpent tries to kill it, and the angels battle the serpent, and . . ."

"And the child lives and rules the earth with a rod of iron," Neal interrupted. He'd read Revelation while studying the white suprema-cist movement.

"And *this is the child,*" Jory said. "So when they were going to kill him, I knew it was a terrible mistake. So I took him here, to the sacred place, the Place of the Beginning and the End."

Neal debated what to do. He could wait the storm out in the cave and go in the morning, but that would mean moving in daylight, and who knew where the SOS boys would be. Or he could move now under cover of darkness, but that would mean exposing the child to a dangerous trip at night through a snowstorm.

Just then the old man cocked his head toward the cave mouth. Then he mimed the trotting of horses.

Neal couldn't hear a thing.

The old man scrambled to the cave mouth and came back moments later. He counted to six on his fingers. Then he stepped over to the fire, wafted his hands through the smoke, and pointed to the ceiling.

Great, Neal thought. They're coming with guns and this guy's going to do magic tricks.

The old man reached into the pile of blankets and pulled out a contraption made of sticks, rabbit skin, and strips of hide. He mo-tioned for Neal to turn around and tied it onto his shoulders. Neal realized that it was a backpack for the boy.

The old man picked up Cody and held him to his chest, whispering soft cooing sounds in the boy's ear. Then he lifted him up and set him into the sack formed by the rabbit skins.

Cody woke up and started to cry.

The old man made shooshing sounds, but Cody kept crying and lifted his arms to the old man. The child was terrified to be on the shoulders of this stranger, and the words he was crying out in his fear were in a language Neal didn't recognize.

The old man spoke back to him, quietly but firmly, and Cody settled into a miserable whimpering but sat back in his seat. The old man covered him with a sheepskin and tucked it into the seat. Then he picked up his small bow and quiver of arrows and motioned for Neal to follow him.

"I'll stay here and hold them off," Jory said.

"Don't be an idiot, Jory," Neal answered. "Come on."

Jory leaned over, pulled the sheepskin aside, and kissed Cody on the cheek. Then he turned his back and crawled into the tunnel toward the cave mouth.

The old man turned around and waved his hand forward impatiently, as if to say, "Come on." He pointed to his nose and made a show of sniffing the air.

Neal followed the old man deeper into the cave. The old man disappeared into the rocks and Neal found the crack that led into another chamber. It was pitch-black.

Now what? Neal asked himself. I can't see a damn thing. Ahead of him he could just make out the sound of the old man sniffing the air.

Of course, Neal thought. The smoke must be ventilating out a draft. There was another way out. He reached behind him and put his hands under the backpack to lift it higher on his shoulders. Cody seemed calmer, as if he sensed they were following the old man.

Neal listened to the man's footsteps and sniffed the air for the scent of smoke.

Ed Levine leaned forward and adjusted Graham's weight on his shoulders. He was carrying him piggyback now, and Graham had enough strength to hold on with his one good hand.

It was the frigging cold that was the problem. That and the snow that was blowing in their faces and blinding them.

But Ed figured that wasn't all bad. It was also blinding the guys who were looking for them, and as long as he had his nose pointed into the freezing wind, he knew he was headed north. So the wind was like a sadistic compass, keeping them pointed toward the Mills place. Ed only hoped he could see the house when he got near.

He pointed his face toward the wind until he felt its maximum force, then put his head down and started slogging through the snow.

* * *

Strekker skittered back down the shelf of rock.

"The cave's just up there," he told Hansen. "There's only room for one man at a time to get in. They could pick us off one by one."

"I have to get into that cave!" Carter said.

Hansen ignored him. He was sorry Carter had insisted on coming—the reverend had just slowed them down. He looked to Cal for instructions.

"Billy, watch the horses," Cal answered. "Mr. Hansen, why don't you take the reverend and see if you can talk your way in? Craig and John, back him up."

"Where are you going?" Hansen asked him.

"I'm going to poke around a little more," Cal answered. Just in case there's a back way in. He slung his rifle over his shoulder, found a crack in the rock, and began to pull himself up the rocks.

Steve Mills looked out the window at the heavy snow, then pulled on his boots.

"You're not going out there!" Peggy said. It was more of a question than a statement.

"I just have a couple of things to check," he answered.

"On the big surprise?" Shelly asked. She and Karen were on the floor by the fireplace, putting in the last few pieces of the chocolate chip cookie puzzle.

"Yep," he said. He had that smug, quizzical look on his face that Peggy found simultaneously annoying and endearing. "Have that brandy warmed by the time I come in, woman."

"I'll warm you," Peggy answered.

Steve stepped out into the storm and walked over to the corner of the house. He checked a few wires, pulled the pack of cigarettes from his coat pocket, and lit up.

He smoked contentedly, thinking about his big surprise.

"Jory, it's your father! I'm coming in!"

Hansen lay on his stomach in the mouth of the cave.

No answer came back.

"Jory?"

Nothing.

Hansen shrugged at Carter, who was squatting beside him. The other two men stood just below the cave, waiting with rifles ready.

Carter yelled into the cave, "Jory! Is the boy with you?"

No answer.

"Is the boy alive?"

Silence.

Carter continued, "Jory! You've done a great thing! You've done Yahweh's will! Now do it again! Bring us the child!"

"Carey must be holding him," Hansen said. "I'm going in."

He pulled his revolver from his belt and slithered into the cave opening.

Jory crouched inside the tunnel. Coiled like a spring, he held Shoshoko's pointed stick in front of him and waited. As soon as Carter got in range he would finish him.

Hansen saw the stick just as it came stabbing toward his face. He dropped his head behind his arm and pulled the trigger four times. Then he waited for a few seconds and pushed the dead weight of the body in front of him until he felt it drop into the cave chamber.

"Come on in!" he yelled behind him. "I got him!"

He jumped down, shined his flashlight, and saw his son's body lying on the cave floor.

Cal Strekker reached the top of the cliff. He stood still for a moment to catch his breath and get his bearings. Then he caught a faint whiff of smoke. He followed it to the flat top of a small table of rock. A stream of smoke was rising from the hole and he thought he heard footsteps.

He backed off a few feet from the hole, unslung his rifle, and sat down.

Neal heard the shots and the yelling. Then he felt a sharp blast of cold and the scent of fresh air directly above him. The old man stopped just in front of him and pulled him ahead. He pointed up again, and

Neal could feel a blast of cold air and a few snowflakes falling on his head.

Cody started to cry again.

The old man pointed urgently.

It was dark and Neal couldn't see the cave walls. All he could see—ten, maybe fifteen feet up—were white flecks of snow. "I can't see," he whispered to the old man.

The old man started to push Neal toward the rock wall.

But I can't do it, Neal thought. He felt the rock. It was icy and slick. He couldn't see to get handholds or footing. He would certainly fall and hurt the boy beneath him. He could hear more yelling and footsteps behind them in the first chamber.

Neal planted a foot on the slick rock and tried to find a grip on the rock.

Cody tried to turn around and grab the old man. The old man held him for a brief moment and then turned to go back. Cody screamed in the pain of abandonment, cried his heartbreak out in a repeated shriek of a single word. For the second time in his young life, he had lost his father.

Neal dug his hands into the ice and started to climb.

"My God, my God, my God," Carter murmured as he looked at the cave paintings. "Yahweh be thanked that I have lived to see this."

Vetter called from the back of the chamber, "They've gone this way, Reverend! The smoke is drafting out the back!"

Carter stood in the center of the cave chamber, twirling around with his arms open.

"This is the place of our ancestors! This is our home!"

Craig yelled, "Reverend! Come on! We're going to lose them!"

Then Carter saw the painting of the blond child holding his hand up to a god. "Look! Look! It's the Son of God! It's the expected child! He's holding his arms up to Yahweh!"

Cody's shrieks echoed back through the cave.

Carter ran to Hansen. "Let's go! We have to rescue him from the dragon! We must save him from the Jew!"

But Bob Hansen was absorbed in wrapping the body of his dead son up in his coat.

Carter ran to the back of the chamber, pushed Vetter aside, and jammed himself into the fissure that led to the next chamber.

Craig could hear him yelling up ahead.

"The child of God! The child of God! The child of—"

Then the yelling stopped.

Craig eased himself into the crack.

Cal heard the crying right below him.

I'll be damned, he thought, the little bastard is alive. Crazy little Jory had it tucked away. But who the hell has been taking care of it?

He listened carefully and heard what sounded like feet kicking at the icy wall. He heard someone panting with exertion.

I could just fire down this hole, he thought. But if I hit the kid my ass will really be grass. He slung the rifle over his back and pulled his combat knife.

It might be Jory or it might be Neal, he thought. Dear God above, let it be Neal.

Neal was spread-eagled on the rock wall. He took three more gasps of air and then gingerly reached up with his right hand. His fingers felt along the smooth rock. Nothing . . . nothing . . . then a tiny outcrop. He gripped it with sore fingers and pulled himself up. His right foot slipped off the rock and he kicked with it desperately until he felt a small crack in the rock surface. He planted his toe, held on for another second, and then reached up with his left hand. He ran it along the rock until he felt a root. He grabbed it and pulled himself up again. He looked up and snow fell on his face.

Thank God, he thought.

Ed pitched forward face-first into the snow.

The impact sent a bolt of agony searing through Joe Graham's legs. He bit down on his artificial arm to stifle the scream as the headlights of the truck slowly passed them.

Flashlight beams swept the ground around them, and Graham heard the truck engine and voices yelling, "See anything?" "No!"

Graham could feel Ed's labored breathing underneath him. As the snow froze on the back of his neck and his lungs burned with the cold, he tried to remember a prayer from his childhood. He remembered the nuns telling him about a "sincere act of contrition," and from somewhere the first words came to him. He said them to himself: Oh my God, I am heartily sorry for having offended Thee, and I do detest all my sins . . .

The flashlight shone right on him.

Craig held the flashlight out in front of him as he trotted through the cave. Finally he saw Carter's form. The reverend was on his knees, bent in prayer. Craig ran up to him and took him by the shoulder.

"Reverend Carter, what—"

Carter fell backward into his arms. Dave shined his light into Carter's face. His eyes were wide open and his mouth agape. He was panting for air in small, rapid gulps. A tiny arrow was lodged inside his mouth, its point just sticking out the back of his neck.

Craig flicked off the flashlight, pulled Carter down, and laid his rifle barrel on the reverend's body. He ducked as another arrow whistled over his head. Then he shouldered the rifle, fired three rounds into the darkness, and started to crawl backward, using the reverend's body as a shield. Two more arrows thunked into Carter's chest.

As he shimmied out of the long, narrow passage he yelled, "Get out! Get out! It's an ambush!"

He pulled Carter back until they were back in the fissure. As Craig worked his way out the other side, he jammed Carter's body into the crack, then left it there.

Neal's muscles trembled with strain. He could see the sky now and the top of the hole, but it was a long reach to the next handhold. His legs were quivering too, and he didn't think he could summon the strength to make the final haul.

He clenched the root with his left hand, dug his feet in again, and reached his right hand up, trying to find something, anything, to hold on to. His hand grabbed at the air, found nothing, and grabbed again. Then his left leg gave out and slipped off the icy rock. The weight of the child on his shoulders pulled him backward and he started to fall. His right hand flailed in the air, the momentum took his left foot off the rock, and he slipped.

Desperately, he threw his right hand up. He stopped falling. It was a human arm, pulling him up from the hole, pulling him up into the cold, open air.

"Okay, everybody, get into your warm clothes. We're going outside," Steve Mills announced.

The three women looked at him as if he were crazy.

"What for?" Shelly asked.

"The surprise!" he said. "It's an outdoor surprise!"

Only my husband, thought Peggy, would plan an outdoor surprise in the middle of winter in the middle of the night. *"Now?"* she asked.

Steve looked at his watch. "You have fifteen minutes," he said.

"Do you have this confused with New Year's Eve?" she asked. Her watch said it was a quarter to twelve.

Karen finished her brandy and got up. It had been a wonderful evening, and a midnight surprise would be just the thing to top it off. She took Shelly by the hand. "Come on, kid! Let's see what your old man has up his sleeve."

"Sounds good to me."

Karen pulled Shelly up and they went off to get their coats.

Ed waited until the truck's taillights disappeared into the snow and then pushed himself up. "Are you okay?" he asked Graham.

"You think they have any booze at this house?"

Ed hefted Graham up a little higher and looked around. The wind had stopped blowing, the snow was falling straight down now, and he still couldn't see a damn thing.

"Which way is north?" he asked.

"On a map it's usually up," Graham answered.

"Which way is up?"

"You sound like Neal."

Ed turned left and staggered on.

Neal and Cal stood facing each other on the small table of rock.

"I couldn't just let you fall, Neal buddy," Cal said. "We've had this date for a long time."

Cal pulled his knife and held it out in front of him.

"I just want the boy," Neal answered. He shifted his weight to his back foot and let his shoe dig into the crusty snow.

"That's the problem. I would just shoot you, but the bullet might go right through you and hit the Son of God there. Besides, I want the pleasure of gutting you, Neal buddy."

"It's over, Cal. Get away while you have the chance."

"Oh, I'll get away, Neal buddy. And it ain't over. It ain't over until we win."

"You've lost! Don't you understand that?"

There's no time for this, Neal thought. He kept his eyes on Cal's face but used his peripheral vision to see the twelve-foot drop off to his left. Then it was a steep slope down into the draw where Jory had left the horse.

Cal inched forward. "You'll never beat us," he said. "You're weak. That's why you've let the niggers run wild in the cities and the Jews take over the government. They know you're weak. That's why we'll win. It's like tonight, Neal, you just can't pull the trigger."

Neal's left arm slowly moved upward and outward, hand open in the knife position. Obliquely Tame Tiger. Three years of practice on his Chinese knoll and he had never really mastered it.

It's time I did, he thought.

He slowly raised his right leg and pivoted on his left foot. He spun just as Cal sprang forward, giving him only the boy as a target. Cal pulled up for a split second.

Neal finished a complete revolution and shifted his weight forward as he brought his right foot down, his left hand raised in front of his face, his right hand open behind his head.

He struck like a viper, putting all of the momentum from the spin, all of his weight, and all of his concentration into his right hand as its edge smashed into Cal's neck.

The blow snapped Cal's head to the left and took him off his feet just enough to slip on the snow. He kept his balance for half a second and then slipped off the rock.

"Okay, Cody, hold on," Neal said. He sat down, looked for the flattest spot, and jumped for it. He landed hard but kept his feet, and then skidded, fell, and slid down the slope. He grabbed cedars on the way down to keep his balance and finally landed in the draw. A couple of minutes of scrambling got him to where Midnight was haltered. He untied the reins and the horse started to rear and buck. Cody started to scream again as Neal managed to get a foot in the spinning stirrup and haul himself into the saddle. Midnight reared on his hind legs and Neal almost pitched off backward, but his right foot caught the stirrup and he dug his knees into the horse's flank.

"Go, you son of a bitch!" Neal yelled. He turned the horse's head and spurred him down the draw. Right toward the edge of the cliff.

Hansen was carrying Jory's body and working his way down the diagonal shelf of rock when he heard the hooves coming. He turned to his right and saw a black horse coming straight at him out of the darkness.

"*Stop,* you son of a bitch!" Neal yelled. He pulled up on the reins and the horse reared again, kicking out his front hooves and slashing them at the man who blocked his path. Neal and Hansen exchanged startled looks, then Neal flipped over the reins and started the horse down the slick rock ramp toward the canyon.

Craig raised his rifle and sighted it on Neal's back.

Hansen screamed, "Don't shoot! He has the boy!"

Craig lowered his rifle. Hansen set Jory's body down in the draw. Then the three men raced down the rock shelf for their horses.

* * *

Bill McCurdy heard the yelling. He grabbed his rifle from the back of his horse and positioned himself at the bottom of the shelf.

Neal knew they were going to die. Midnight was galloping full stride down the narrow shelf of rock. The only reason he didn't slip and plunge off the side was that his hooves never seemed to touch the slick ground. Neal leaned low over the horse's neck. He gripped the reins in one hand and the saddle horn in the other. Behind him, Cody McCall was screaming. With laughter.

Then Neal saw a human form rise up just below them and raise his rifle

"Stop or I'll shoot!" Billy yelled.

"I can't stop, you asshole!" Neal yelled back.

Billy took aim.

Midnight saw Billy, turned, and without breaking stride, jumped off the cliff.

They seemed to be in the air for the longest damn time as Neal plunged forward with the horse. His nose was even with Midnight's shoulder and he felt as if he were looking straight down at the ground. Cody's weight was about to somersault him over the horse's neck.

They landed with a heavy thud that knocked Neal back in the saddle. Cody giggled with delight as the horse slowed to a canter and headed down the canyon.

Neal heard the sound of hoofbeats coming after him. He kicked Midnight back into a gallop.

Karen laughed as Steve made a big show of lining them up in the yard.

"Okay," he yelled. "Ready?"

"Ready!" they all yelled back.

"Are you *really* ready?"

"Yes!"

Steve paused dramatically, then said, "Close your eyes!"

Karen groaned in rhythm with her two friends. She was having a great time. She closed her eyes, stuck her tongue out, and felt the snowflakes melt.

"I'm going to start the countdown!" Steve yelled.

They all groaned again.

Ed had to rest but knew he couldn't. Graham was unconscious, maybe in shock. Any delay might kill him. But where the hell were they? Had they passed by the house and not known it? Were they headed in the wrong direction? Walking in circles?

His legs felt like concrete pillars and his arms felt like wood, if wood could ache the way his arms did. His feet were freezing and he was starting to worry about frostbite now.

Where in hell were they?

Lost. Lost in the middle of the middle of nowhere.

Neal reined Midnight to a stop at the western crest of the ridge. The valley below looked like a bowl of steam, all white and swirling and indistinct. He couldn't figure out where he was and the gang was gaining on him. He could pick out the sound of individual horses now and voices and he had to make the plunge down into the valley. But where? It wouldn't do a hell of a lot of good to go galloping back to the Hansen ranch.

The Mills place should be northeast somewhere, but something that small wouldn't be easy to find on the vast sagebrush plain below, at night, in the snow.

He couldn't wait any longer, he had to go. They were right behind him now. A couple more seconds to let Midnight get his breath . . .

"Five, four, three, two, one," Steve counted and threw the electric switch.

Karen Hawley looked up and saw the most amazing damn thing . . .

. . . A Star of David shining through the snow! Neal blinked in disbelief. Way out there, way down on The High Lonely, a Star of David pierced through the night sky like a beacon. A six-pointed star made up of dozens of lights, a star as big as a house . . . the Mills house.

Neal jigged the reins and Midnight dove over the crest.

Hansen about fell off his horse when he saw it. It had come out of nowhere. Just all of a sudden a Jewish star appeared in the sky and hung there like one of them UFOs. The three other riders clumped behind him, all of them looking at the damn thing.

Then it hit Hansen. "It's Mills' place. He strung them lights on his roof!"

"That Jew bastard," Bill McCurdy spat.

"Carey's headed *there!*" Hansen yelled. "Let's go!"

They pointed their horses at the star and crashed down the slope.

To Ed Levine it was like Hanukkah, New Year's Eve on Times Square, Mardi Gras, and—what the hell—Christmas all at once. It was a goddamn miracle, that's what it was, a sign sent from God. And the best thing about it was that it couldn't have been more than a hundred yards away.

He lifted Graham a little higher and broke into a trot.

"You like it?" Steve asked proudly.

"It's . . . big," Peggy answered.

"I love it, Dad."

Peggy said, "I'm surprised it didn't blow every light in the house."

"I rigged it to the generator."

Karen put her arm around Steve and said, "I notice you pointed it right at Hansen's place."

Steve nodded happily. "That oughta fry his *cajones,* I'd expect."

"You're asking for trouble," Karen added.

Steve grinned. "Mmm."

Bob Hansen watched the star as he rode, Jory's body bouncing behind him with the rocking of the horse.

It was that goddamn Jew Mills, contaminating the whole valley.

Mills was laughing at him, laughing at his defeat, laughing at the destruction of his dream, lording it over him. Mills had been behind it all. Mills knew about the sabotage . . . Mills knew that Carey was a ZOG agent . . . Mills knew the robbery was a fake, the arms shipment a setup. It was Mills' daughter who filled Jory's head with lies, Mills who sent Neal Carey, Mills who caused the death of his son.

My dreams are over, he thought. But I won't stop until Mills is dead.

Back up on the mountain slope Cal Strekker licked his wounds and watched the kike star pollute the sky. He cut a sleeve off his shirt, cut that into strips, and wrapped it tightly around his ankle. He didn't think it was busted, just sprained, but it hurt like all get out. It hurt worse when he pulled his boot back on, but the tight leather helped to keep the ankle from folding.

The side of his neck bore a deep purple splotch where Carey had tried to decapitate him with that sneaky gook shit, and the shoulder he had landed on was bruised up pretty good.

And now that friggin' star was blinking on and off like some kind of all-night kosher diner for Jewboys.

Well, Steve Mills might just as well wave a red flag in Hansen's nose, he thought. There's going to be one hell of a fight over by that star.

He grabbed a cedar limb, lifted himself up, and started working his way down the mountain.

For Neal it had all come down to a horse race.

It was flat out across the sagebrush, his black horse galloping, kicking plumes of snow behind him, cutting through the crisp air like a sleek, sharp ebony knife.

Neal bent low over his neck like he'd seen the jockeys do to cut down on the resistance, his knees high behind the horse's shoulders, his calves gripping Midnight's flanks.

It was desperate, terrifying, and lovely. The sounds of the hooves crashing on the snow, and the horse snorting, and his own heart pounding, all in rhythm, all in sync. And the musty horse smell in his nostrils, and the sweet sagebrush, and the snow. And the heat of the horse against the chill air, and his own sweaty skin beneath his clothes, and the damp warmth of the little body clinging to his back, and *goddamn, he was alive!*

He risked a glance over his shoulder and could see them coming. Bill McCurdy ahead of the rest. The best rider, the most reckless on the fastest horse, and Neal knew, just knew, that Bill was smiling. Then the three others clumped behind, Hansen on that big bay, coming fast but not too fast, steady so his horse would not get blown. And John's little gelding chopping away with its clipped gait on its short legs, but still coming, coming. And then Craig on that tall roan that cut the cows so well and never let one get around the corner. And they were all coming on, coming on, flying. Wild men on wild horses.

Neal kicked Midnight and leaned farther over his neck. He felt the horse surge a little more, and he would need that little more, because McCurdy was gaining. Heedless of the gopher holes that could snap a horse's foreleg in an agonizing instant, heedless of the sudden gullies that could pitch him over the horse's head and break his own neck, heedless of the patches of icy grass that could send the horse rolling over him, crushing his legs and rib cage and bursting his lungs, the cowboy was racing up, just winging on the tops of the rabbit brush, and he was only six, now five, now four horse lengths behind.

And Neal was just trying to hold on, just trying to stay in the saddle on the plunging, surging horse, and he knew that McCurdy was cowboy enough to ride beside him, reach out one arm, and take him off the saddle as if he were a rodeo rider and the buzzer had sounded. And that's all it would take, because the other three would be on them and Vetter's strong arms would take Cody from him and that would be the end.

He dug his feet into the stirrups and gripped the reins and kicked again, asking for a little more, please horse, just a little more. I know you don't have it, but find it. Please, you have to beat this other horse, because it's all come down to a horse race now and you're my horse. And Midnight found it somewhere and reached a little farther and pushed a little more, and Neal heard him grunt with pain as flecks of foam flew back from his mouth and Neal felt Midnight's heart pound at a literally heartbreaking pace.

I know I'm killing you, horse. I know I'm killing you and I'm sorry, but we have this child with us, you see, and you and I don't matter, and he felt Midnight surge again. Unbelievably to him, the horse took it up another notch, stretched it out, and they were flying. Flying like wild, sweating, heaving, gasping, living angels through the night sky.

Then Neal could see the lights in front of them, the silver lights of a star. He'd never loved an animal before and he'd never loved a child, and now he loved both and they weren't going to make it. Not any of them, because Bill McCurdy was right behind them now. Right behind them and angling to come up alongside.

Neal kicked Midnight to see if there was anything left, but the horse was smarter. The horse simply shifted to the right and got in front of his pursuer. Billy was a hell of a horseman. Without breaking stride he leaned left and took his pony with him and then started to pull even again. Midnight pulled left on his next stride and blocked that lane too, but this game couldn't go on forever, because the other horse was younger and faster and had by far the better rider. So when Billy jerked his horse out to the right again he came up so fast that suddenly they were riding side by side, saddle to saddle, boots almost touching, horses in stride.

Neal felt Billy's hand grab at his sleeve and he flipped the right rein over and tried to pull his horse away, but Midnight leaned *in,* laying his bulk against the other horse's shoulder and pushing him away and damn near bouncing Billy off his saddle.

It damn near lost Neal, too, but he managed to hold on with his left hand and keep riding. Then Billy was back again, right at Neal's side, his right foot out of the stirrup and poised on the saddle. Neal saw he was getting ready to jump, for God's sake. Jump and pull Neal and the boy off the galloping horse, and the Mills place was so close . . . *so close* . . . he could see the house now, and the wire fence. Then Billy swung his left foot out of the stirrup, staying on his horse just by the reins, that crazy cowboy look in his eye and his muscles coiled to spring and—

Midnight jumped to clear the fence and Billy slid off his rump and landed hard on the barbed wire. He ripped himself out, though, when the bullets started kicking the ground up around him.

Midnight seemed to sense he had done his job and slowed to a canter as he came into the yard, where Steve Mills stood with his rifle. The horse took two more strides then his heart finally gave out. Neal swung off the saddle a second before Midnight dropped and rolled onto his side. Neal got down on his knees and cradled the horse's head. Midnight's eyes rolled back, his mouth heaved streams of foam, his legs jerked.

For the first time in the whole damn ordeal, Neal started to cry. He felt Steve standing over his shoulder.

"Steve, I—"

"Your friends told me all about it. I'll take care of your horse. You better get that boy inside."

Neal staggered through the door into the kitchen. Karen took the pack from his shoulders and cradled Cody in her arms. The last thing Neal heard before he collapsed was a single shot from Steve's rifle.

13

*T*he boy's a survivor, that's the understatement of the year,"
Karen Hawley said. "He needs hospitalization, a ton of vitamins,
long-term psychiatric care, and his mother. I intend to start with the
hospital. Right away."

"What do you mean?" Neal asked. They were standing in Shelly's
bedroom, where Karen had Cody wrapped up in blankets on the
floor.

"I mean I'm taking him to Austin right now and calling a helicopter to take him to the hospital in Fallon."

"You can't do that," Neal answered.

Karen got her back up and stared at Neal. "You're forgetting that
I'm the child abuse officer for South Lander County, and this child
has most certainly been abused. I'm taking him into my custody. Do
I need to arrest you? Fine. Neal Carey, or whatever your name is,
you're under arrest."

"I mean you can't do that because the house is surrounded by
armed men."

It had taken three hours of intermittent sniping and return fire to
get a rough idea of how many men and where they were. Four, at
least, in the big hay barn, two more around the road, probably three
scattered in the sagebrush around the house.

And they have all night, Neal thought. All night and a good part
of the morning before we have a chance of getting any help.

"I'm not afraid of those dickheads," Karen said.

"You should be," Neal answered. Right now they're trying to

work out a way to rush this place. They know they have us outnumbered and outgunned. If Strekker were out there he'd have already put it in motion. Coordinate fire on all sides at the same time to keep us pinned down, then rush a few men with Molotov cocktails and set the house on fire. Hell, they're sitting right next to a tractor barn filled with gas tanks and plenty of empty bottles. Hansen's taking a little longer to work it out, but he will. Then it will be all over.

We have to make a deal.

"You can go in a couple of hours," Neal said, "when it's light."

"Do you think they'll let us through?" Karen asked.

"Yeah, I do."

If they're all lying dead on the ground.

Just then he heard a crash of glass downstairs and then the terrifying crackle of flame. He ran down to see Steve stamping the flame out in the kitchen while Ed fired a shotgun out into the night.

I guess Hansen figured it out, Neal thought.

They all dropped to the floor when bullets whined through the window.

"You want to burn, Jew?" Neal heard Hansen yell. "We got lots of gas here! Enough for our own little crematorium!"

Neal heard men laughing in the barn.

"Come out, Jew! Unless you want to burn! I want you, Jew! Stop hiding behind women and children and come out here!"

Steve said, "I'm going."

He started to get up. Neal grabbed him and pulled him back down. "The hell you are."

Ed crawled back to the window and fired a couple of rounds in the general direction of Hansen's voice.

"Out, Jew! Out, Jew!" came more shouting.

Then some comedian in the barn yelled, *"Juden raus, Juden raus!"* and the rest of the gang picked up the chant.

"Juden raus! Juden raus! Juden raus!"

Neal heard three shots crack through an upstairs window. Steve dashed up the stairs to find Peggy clutching Shelly on the floor behind the bed.

"Oh, God," he moaned. "Are you all right?"

"We're fine," Peggy answered. Shelly nodded. She had tears in her eyes but she made a point of smiling at her father.

"Get in the bathroom," Steve said.

"Let me have a gun," said Peggy.

Steve shouted out the window, "There are women and children in here!"

The answer came back, *"Juden raus! Juden raus! Juden raus!"*

Peggy saw the look in her husband's eyes and stated, "You are not going out there."

"Yeah, I am, Peg."

"Don't you give me any of that a-man's-gotta-do-what-a-man's-gotta-do bullshit, Steve."

Steve crouched beside his wife and stroked her hair. "But sometimes it's true. Sometimes a man does have to do what a man has to do."

"Daddy, they'll kill you!" Shelly cried.

Steve put his arms around them both and hugged them hard, then he got up and started down the stairs.

Neal grabbed him by the front of the shirt.

"Get out of my way, Neal," Steve said.

"I'm going out with you."

"This isn't your fight."

"I started it."

Steve shook his head. "They started it. Now, Neal, don't make me kick your ass before I go out and kick theirs. I might get worn out."

The chant got louder and wilder. *"Juden raus! Juden raus! Juden raus!"* The men outside were working themselves into a frenzy of hatred.

"Get out of my way, Neal," Steve repeated. His voice had the same edge it had had just before he slung that punch at Cal Strekker that night that now seemed years ago. He grabbed Neal's shoulders and started to push.

Neal tightened his grip on Steve's shirt. "I'm going with you," Neal whispered, "but let's make sure that we get done what we want to get done. You want to trade yourself for Peggy and Shelly. I want Karen, the boy, and my friends. There's no point in going out there unless we can make that deal."

Neal watched the man think about it for a few seconds.

"All right," Steve said. "See what you can do."

They went back downstairs. Neal sidled along the wall to the kitchen window and shouted, "Mr. Hansen! Tell your baboons to shut up for a few seconds! I want to talk!"

There was a pause and the chanting died down.

"What are you doing, Neal?" Ed asked.

"Shut up and reload the guns," Neal answered.

"What do you want, Carey?" Hansen yelled.

"I want to know what you want!"

A few seconds of silence went by before Hansen answered, "I want that Jew!"

"Which Jew, Hansen? There are three of us in here!"

Ed looked at Neal and raised his eyebrows.

Neal whispered back, "Well, I could be, couldn't I?"

It took Hansen a minute or so to digest the information, then he shouted, "Which three?"

Neal yelled, "Hansen, I'm not playing these games with you! Here's the deal: you give the women and the child safe passage out of here! And we have a wounded man—he goes too! When we see them safely gone, we come out!"

"Your wounded! Is he that one-armed man?"

"He is!"

"Is he a Jew too?"

"He's as Irish as a hangover!"

"Let me think on it a minute!"

"Don't take too long! It's my last offer!"

Neal waited and enjoyed the sweet silence. When you're trying to bargain your life away, he thought, the small pleasures are enough.

Then he heard Hansen yell, "Why do you want the boy?"

"I'm sending him back to his mother!"

"Why is that so damn important?"

"It's what I came here to do!"

There was a long silence and Neal felt the deal slipping away.

"Hey, Hansen!" Neal yelled. "It's what Jory wanted! It's why he took me to the cave!"

One long moment.

"All right!" Hansen yelled. "You have a deal! But know I mean to kill you!"

No shit. "I mean to kill you too, Bob!" Neal shouted. "But are we going to have a fair fight?"

"What do you mean?" Hansen yelled.

"I mean you have a dozen or so guys out there! There are three of us! Why don't you have a few of your boys sit this one out?"

"Why should I?"

Good question. "Because this is personal, Hansen!" Neal yelled. "You're not afraid of three Jews, are you, Bob?" Come on, Bob. Put your prejudice ahead of your brains. It's our only chance.

Neal, Steve, and Ed exchanged looks as they waited.

It seemed like a long time before Hansen shouted, "Okay! Three of us against three of you!"

"Four."

Joe Graham was standing on the stairway, gripping the rail to keep himself on his feet.

"Four," Graham repeated. "You screw-ups will need an extra hand, which is just what I have."

"Dad, you can barely walk."

"That's only because I keep tripping over my dick."

"You're leaving," Ed said. "That's an order."

Graham grabbed his own crotch. "Order this."

Ed looked at Neal and shrugged.

Neal shouted out the window, "Make that four, Hansen! Four of you against four of us!"

"None of your Jew tricks, either!" Hansen answered. "Out here in the open! In the corral!"

"None of your Jew tricks, Ed," Neal said. Then he shouted. "Okay!"

"Send out the women!"

Ed shook his head and pointed to his watch.

"No!" Neal shouted. "I don't trust you that much! We'll wait until daybreak when we can see the road!"

Hansen hollered, "Okay! But that's it! When the sun comes up!"

Neal turned to Steve. "You haven't heard a weather report, have you?"

Cal Strekker heard it all and couldn't believe his ears. Couldn't believe that Hansen would fall for this "fair fight" bullshit.

But it might work out, he thought. Might work out so all the witnesses to what had happened might end up dead. And if it didn't work out that way, well . . . he'd have to see that it worked out. There were other groups out there looking to fight. The battle would go on.

He rested his sore ankle for a few minutes and then moved on. He'd wanted to get a position with a good view of the corral and be in place before dawn.

It came in a hurry.

The storm passed and a bright orange sun rose over the Toiyabes.

Ed and Graham kept guard as Steve opened the sliding glass door and Peggy and Shelly stepped out onto the porch.

Karen, with Cody in her arms, turned at the door and started to argue with Neal again. "I'm a better shot than you and—"

"You have a job to do. Do it."

"This 'women and children first' stuff—"

Neal took her by the elbow. "I need you to do this. I don't know that they're going to honor the deal. You may have to fight your way through. Can you do that?"

Neal watched those incredible eyes flash in anger. "We'll get through," she said.

"I know you will."

They walked out onto the porch.

Neal hollered into the air, "Hansen, we're taking them to the car! Step out in the open!"

Hansen walked out of the barn.

"I have a rifle aimed right at your heart!" Ed yelled. "If anything—"

"Don't worry!"

Steve put his arms around his wife and daughter and they walked toward Karen's Jeep. Neal and Karen followed.

As they came around the house into the driveway Neal could see Bob Hansen standing near the corral and the barrel of Ed's rifle sticking out the window. He glanced up and saw men in the hay barn, high up behind stacks of bales, looking down. He could feel eyes on him, feel the hatred.

Steve held Shelly in his arms and kissed her cheek.

"See you in a little while, tiger," he said. "I love you."

"I love you too."

Steve felt her tears on his cheek. "Don't cry, sweetheart. Nothing bad's going to happen."

"I know."

She hugged him hard and then climbed into the backseat of the Jeep.

Steve and Peggy looked at each other.

"Gunfight at the OK Corral, huh?" Peggy said.

"I guess."

"I'll bring help," she said.

"I know you will. Oh, and beer and cigarettes, too, okay?"

She came into his arms.

"Damn, how I've loved you," he said. "And all I've given you is twenty years of crazy."

"Wouldn't have missed it for the world."

They kissed and he helped her into the passenger seat.

Neal and Karen stared at each other. They wanted to embrace, but something stopped them.

Too many lies between us, Neal thought.

Karen held the sleeping Cody out to him.

"You want to say good-bye?" she asked.

Neal kissed the boy on the cheek. "See you, kid. Tell your mom I said hello."

Neal and Karen avoided each other's eyes.

"You'd better get going," Neal said. "Be careful, huh?"

"Oh, yeah."

She got behind the wheel, shut the door, and started the car. She put it into four-wheel drive to deal with the snow.

Neal tapped on the window and she rolled it down.

"You have Anne Kelley's phone number?" he asked.

"In my pocket."

"Okay."

Their eyes met for a second. Then Karen rolled the window up, put the car in gear, and headed for the road.

Neal and Steve watched them go.

"I'll bet that coffee's ready," Steve said.

"Good."

They walked back inside the house.

Bob Hansen stepped back inside the barn. He knew the women wouldn't get far. Finley and the Johnson brothers would intercept them on the road once the car got out of view of the house.

Then he'd take the boy and go. Maybe up to northern Idaho or Washington State, where he could hide out. Maybe overseas to South Africa, where there were white men who wanted to stay in the fight. He'd leave the valley and raise this child right, this time. Raise him to love his race and not be ashamed of it.

But there was business to finish here first.

"You boys about ready?" he asked.

Craig Vetter nodded. He was carefully cleaning his gun, checking his loads.

Bill McCurdy grinned and giggled.

Dave Bekke looked scared, but Hansen knew he'd go through with it.

Hansen looked up into the hayloft where the men were hiding behind the bales.

"Are you men ready?" he asked.

One of them gave him a thumbs-up signal.

"Remember," Hansen said. "These are the dirty Jews who killed Reverend Carter."

Then Hansen looked back east, toward the mountains where Carter had died. Carter and his own son. Hansen saw the sun clear the mountain.

Strekker was glad for the light. He crept closer to the clump of sagebrush he'd selected, laid down, and peered through the telescopic sight.

Beautiful. The corral came into soft focus. An easy two hundred–yard shot. He adjusted the bipod so that it was firmly planted and waited for the show to begin.

Shoshoko felt the sun on his back. He felt honored and grateful that the Creator would be there to see his death. Also it made the tracking so much easier.

Neal sipped his coffee and watched the sky grow brighter.

I'm glad I'm exhausted, he thought. Otherwise I'd be completely terrified instead of just scared out of my skin.

The coffee was exquisite. Maybe this is the way condemned men feel, eating their last meal, savoring every little smell and taste. But I wished I had touched Karen one last time. I wish . . .

He looked over at Graham, who sat with a pistol at his side and a glass of whiskey in his hand. And Steve, who had a revolver strapped to his hip, a shotgun by his hand, and was lighting a cigarette.

He looked at Ed, who had a rifle in his lap, his own pistol tucked into his belt, and his shotgun strapped over his shoulder.

"Don't think about it," Ed said to Neal.

"Think about what?"

"Dying. None of us are going to die."

Neal thought about the men in the barn with their guns trained on the corral. He thought about Hansen and Craig Vetter and the other gunmen he'd be facing any minute. He thought about dying.

Then Neal heard Hansen's voice. "Come on out, Jews! It's sunrise!"

Neal stood up. He grabbed the old Marlin 336 and cocked a round into the chamber. Then he helped Graham to his feet.

"Good luck, Dad."

"Take care of yourself, son."

Neal felt his legs start to quiver and the fear rise in his stomach. He looked out the window and saw four men approaching the far end of the corral. Bekke, McCurdy, Vetter, and Hansen.

Ed got to his feet. "Everybody remember what to do?"

They all nodded. Ed noticed Neal's shaking hands.

"Hey, Neal," Ed said. "I ever tell you about my days in the Marines?"

What the hell? "No," Neal said. "I didn't even know you were in the Marines."

"Yeah," Ed answered. "I was a sniper."

He grinned at Neal and cocked his head to the door.

Neal propped up Graham and followed Ed out the door toward the corral.

The Jeep was cutting through the snow pretty well when Karen saw something move in a little dip ahead.

"Get down!" she yelled.

As they came over the dip, three men stood up in the road. John Finley raised a pistol in one hand and stuck his hand out for her to stop with the other. He had an idiotic grin on his face. The other two men lifted their rifles.

"Why, you arrogant bastards," Karen muttered.

She ducked her head behind the steering wheel and stepped on the gas.

She heard a thunk as the Jeep ran over the man. It was a few more seconds before she heard the rifle shots crackling behind her.

We must make a pathetic sight, Neal thought, as they slowly advanced in a row toward the corral. He was holding Graham under the arm and leading him along. He could feel the rifle barrels pointed at him from the hayloft to his left. Ed was on the right of him, Steve to the right of Ed.

In front of him, at the other end of the corral, Hansen and his men climbed through the metal bars and then stood in the corral waiting for them. McCurdy directly in front of him, then Bekke, Vetter, and Hansen on the far right, across from Steve Mills.

"Who's the best shot?" Ed asked Neal as they walked.

"Definitely Vetter, the tall one across from you. Then McCurdy, the runty one straight ahead. Then I would guess Hansen, then Bekke, the guy with the beard."

"Okay. You remember what to do?"

"I remember, I remember."

"Just checking."

Then they were at the corral.

Cal Strekker snuggled in behind the rifle and watched.

Let's see who's left standing, he thought. No sense in wasting precious time and bullets. Just for fun, though, he trained the cross hairs on Neal Carey.

Neal stood just inside the metal piping of the corral. He took a long, deep breath to try to steady his shaking hand.

McCurdy, Bekke, Vetter, and Hansen stood facing them on the other side.

"Are you ready?" Hansen called.

Neal heard some fear in his voice.

"We're ready!" Ed answered.

Hansen nodded and went for his gun.

"Now!" Ed yelled.

Neal remembered what to do. He grabbed Graham, dropped, and flattened to the ground.

Karen Hawley raced another half mile before the adrenaline let her stop the car.

"Are you all okay?" she asked.

"We're fine!" Shelly answered. But she remained lying in the backseat over Cody, who was crying to beat the band.

Peggy looked ashen but she nodded her head. "I think you killed that man," she said.

"Good," Karen answered. Then she punched the accelerator and headed for town.

The noise of the engine masked the blast of gunfire that came crackling over the valley.

It's all happening so quickly, Neal thought. Not like in the movies, where it goes in slow motion and the bodies twist and fall in a graceful ballet.

He'd hit the ground and the volley of bullets passed harmlessly over his head. He did what Ed told him. He kept his head flattened and just pointed his rifle up toward the barn and fired. Beside him he heard Graham doing the same thing with his pistol.

Bullets smacked around them, but the men in the barn were having a tough time shooting around the metal pipes.

Then he heard the steady pop of Ed's rifle beside him. Crack, crack, crack, crack. He inched his eye up and saw Bekke on the ground, McCurdy standing but bent over, clutching his stomach, and Vetter backing up, firing his rifle with one hand, blood streaming from the other.

Neal aimed at Vetter, fired, and missed. But Graham's two shots didn't, and Vetter crumpled to the ground.

Ed rolled, placed himself behind a vertical post, and fired up into the hayloft.

"Go!" he yelled.

Neal sprang to his feet and sprinted toward the bottom of the hay barn.

Bullets from Hansen's rifle stitched behind him as he ran. From the corner of his eye he saw Steve Mills get up and head toward Hansen, who was lying behind a post at the other end of the corral.

Neal ran for the bottom of the barn as Ed kept pumping rounds into the loft. Come on, come on, he told himself. Get it done. He grabbed a gas can, spilled its contents on the floor, lit a match, and threw it. Then he took three long strides and dove for the ground.

The fire rose quickly as it burned through the gasoline and dry hay. The barn was ablaze in an instant.

Neal heard Ed yell, *"Juden raus! Juden raus!"*

There was a moment's hesitation and then the three men in the loft stood with their hands up.

Suddenly it was strangely quiet, except for the ringing in his ears. Neal slowly stood up. He looked down at Graham, who in turn was looking at the two bullet holes in his artificial arm.

Ed had gotten to his feet also and was covering his prisoner with the shotgun.

Then Neal turned and saw Hansen and Steve facing each other at the far side of the corral. Each man had a pistol at his side.

"It's over, Bob," Steve said.

Hansen stood for a second, looked around, and raised his gun.

Steve raised his own and shot three times.

Hansen dropped.

Steve lowered his gun and walked slowly toward his old neighbor.

On the little rise of ground two hundred yards away, Cal Strekker watched through the telescope. He was glad he had decided not to join the battle. The big guy on the other side was damn good, and it was better to live to fight another day.

But there was time for one shot before he got away.

He would like to have shot Neal, but he didn't have the angle. Mills, however, made a pretty target as he walked across the corral, and there was a score to settle. He centered the cross hairs on Mills' head.

Steve stood over Bob Hansen and damn near cried. He had never killed anybody in his life and it looked like there was a slim chance he still hadn't. Only one of his bullets had hit. It had hit in the chest, but Hansen was still breathing. He looked at Steve with panicked, pleading eyes.

Well, thank you, Strekker thought as Mills came to a full stop and stood stock-still like a deer in the headlights. He centered his aim again and squeezed the trigger.

Steve Mills looked down at Bob Hansen and a hundred contradictory feelings ran through him. Hatred, anger, disgust . . . sorrow.
     He shook his head, then got down to try to save the sick man's life.
     He didn't hear the bullet whiz past his head.

Neal Carey did. He heard the shot and saw the glint of the scope a couple of hundred yards away in the sagebrush.
     He knew who it was, who it had to be.
     He grabbed his rifle and ran to find Cal Strekker.

A consolation prize, Cal thought. He saw Carey headed right toward him. He fixed his sights on Carey's chest and had him dead to rights when Shoshoko's arrow pierced his shooting hand. He rolled over and saw the little Indian notching up another arrow. Cal switched the rifle to his good hand and fired wildly, using every round to blast the old man to the ground.
     Cal staggered to his feet. He clenched his teeth and pulled the arrow out of his hand. He took a moment to look at the dead Indian and then started to limp away toward the safety of the mountains.

Karen leaned on her horn as she pulled into town. She rolled down her window and yelled, "Call the sheriff! Call the hospital! Call goddamn everybody and then grab your guns and get out to Mills'!"
     She rolled up to her house and ran inside. Peggy lifted Cody into her arms and she and Shelly followed Karen into the house. She was on the phone before they even got inside.

                    *   *   *

Anne Kelley answered the phone sleepily. "Hello?"

The woman's voice on the other end was breathless but strong.

"Ms. Kelley, you don't know me, but I have your little boy and he's safe. I'm going to take him to a hospital now, but he's all right. He's going to be fine. Let me tell you where to come."

Anne Kelley took down the information, hung up the phone, put her head in her hands, and cried.

Neal took a moment to say a few words over the body of the old man who had saved his life at least twice that he knew about. Then he started to track Cal Strekker.

It wasn't hard in the snow, especially with Strekker dripping blood.

Ed Levine stood in the corral and looked down at the bodies of the men he had killed. Dave Bekke lay flat on his back, his arms flung out and his legs spread in a grotesque parody of death. Bill McCurdy lay in a fetal ball, his face twisted with fear and pain. A few feet away Craig Vetter's long body was stretched out face-down, his hand still on the gun stock.

It was cold satisfaction for Ed that he had been right, that these thugs were shooters but had never been shot at. The feeling of bullets coming at them—the incredible noise—had rattled them, made them hesitate for those few fatal seconds.

He looked over to where Steve Mills was trying to stanch Hansen's bleeding, but he could tell by the sounds of Hansen's gasps that the effort would be futile.

Ed stood as the cold daylight paled the glare of the fire beside him. The acrid smell of gunpowder and the smoke streaming from the blazing barn burned Ed's eyes until tears ran down through the soot on his face like tiny rivers through a scorched land.

Joe Graham knelt against the corral's metal piping and watched the figure of Neal Carey get smaller as it trotted away across the flat sagebrush.

Graham turned his eyes for a moment to look at the scene of death and destruction behind him, then turned back to watch Neal running.

Run, son, Graham thought. Run long and hard and far away.

Neal found Strekker about an hour later. He was a hundred yards away, headed for the creek. He was dragging one foot behind him and clutching one hand in the other.

A wounded animal going for water.

Neal thought about Harley and Cody, about Anne Kelley, about Doreen. He thought about Shelly Mills and Steve. He thought about that horse.

Neal brought the rifle stock to his cheek and centered the V on Strekker's back. He started to squeeze the trigger when he remembered Joe Graham's face and heard his words: *What, have they turned you into one of them?* He lowered the rifle and watched as Strekker limped away.

Neal raised the rifle again and pulled the trigger.

He looked through his sights as the bullet took Strekker square in the back. Blood burst out the front of his chest and blossomed onto the ground like a rose in the snow.

Neal didn't go to check if Strekker were still alive or to give him a burial. He didn't walk back to the ranch. He just wiped his fingerprints off the rifle, threw it down, and started walking across the empty miles of The High Lonely.

Epilogue

Brogan poured another glass of whiskey as the stranger listened in rapt attention. Brogan had sold a lot of booze telling the story of the battle of Reese River valley.

The stranger, a salesman from Bishop, laid another five down and looked around the grungy, colorful saloon. A mammoth dog lay sleeping behind the bar. The only other customer was a bearded, long-haired man who sat at the last bar stool drinking coffee and reading a dog-eared paperback book.

"So then what happened?" the salesman asked Brogan.

Brogan went on to tell him how Milkowski had found the money somewhere to buy the Hansen place and so now owned the whole valley, and how the daughter had gone off to college at Brown, which he thought was in Rhode Island or one of them little East Coast states. The boy got back to his momma, who sent a postcard a few weeks ago saying he was coming along well, was going to be just fine. The one-armed man and the big bear of a guy just disappeared, and for a while the feds were all over town, asking a lot of questions. Then there was a whole herd of types from the state museum who went poking around the cave measuring shit and stuff, and they were just puzzled as hell about that Indian's body, because he came from a tribe that was supposed to have been extinct for about a hundred years. And Karen Hawley . . . well, she found herself a new man.

Brogan leaned over the bar, smiled, shook his head at the wonder of his own story, and waited for the question that always came so he could give the kicker.

Sure enough, the stranger asked, "And what happened to Neal Carey?"

Brogan shrugged dramatically, leaned over a little more, and said, "Nobody knows. Some say he froze to death out there. Others say he's still alive somewhere up in them caves. But no one ever saw him again."

Brogan left the man shaking his head and sidled down the bar. He poured more coffee into the bearded man's cup and smiled at him.

Neal finished the cup, climbed off the stool, nodded to the salesman, and headed out. Brezhnev lifted his head, and if Neal hadn't known better he'd have sworn the dog winked.

Neal would like to have had another cup, read a few more pages of *Roderick Random*, and maybe chewed the shit with Brogan for a while, but there wasn't time.

He pushed open the door, stepped out into the cool air, and walked up the hill to meet Karen for dinner. It was chili night at Wong's.